Nation of Dragons: Book One

The Dragon Sphere

Abel Gallardo

Printed in the United States of America
First Printing: 2016
Published by Sojourn Publishing, LLC

ISBN: 978-1-62747-230-2
Ebook ISBN: 978-1-62747-231-9

Dedication

For my parents, who always let my imagination run wild.
I can never thank you enough for your love and support.
Also, to my beautiful wife Michelle and our amazing kids,
Elijah and Zoé.
Thank you for always making me smile.

Chapter One
The Calling

The deadly tsunami wave raced towards me. With only a few seconds to think, I braced for impact. The salty breeze burned the open wounds on my bloodied body. The end was so close, yet I had to face it head on. Standing on the sea cliff I took notice of the sight above me. The moon, full and glowing, shot its bright white light through the openings of the dark, unrestrained clouds. A beautiful rage unleashed as the roar of thunder boomed and the surge of electricity zipped towards the tidal wave.

The power of the sea was overwhelming. Its destructive forces were in full display as it shredded apart the abandoned boats, leaving only debris in its wake. There was no escape. There was no saving me. Terror seized my mind. My muscles rebelled against my commands. The last thing I would feel was the whip of the wind and the battering rain pounding my already broken body. And as the wall of water slammed against me, my last thought before my end was of him... my father.

I open my eyes. The thought of taking my last breath is intense. My fists are clenched and beads of sweat form on my forehead. It's the same flash-forward, or premonition, or whatever you want to call it every time. I don't know whether it bears any special significance to what's going to happen now. It may not mean anything. But by the way things have been unfolding lately, though, I'd say it's too important to ignore.

My name is Landon Brown. I'm fifteen years old and a sophomore at Deacon High School in Albuquerque, New Mexico. I'm sure you've heard of me. I'm the star running back for the Deacon High Rams, and a pretty hot topic in the world of sports since I put on the pads in seventh grade. I've been a top prospect for many colleges because I'm fast, I'm strong and I have great vision. I know what you're thinking—*This guy's full of himself,* right? But I'm only telling it like I hear it. My mom never wanted me to be in football because she was afraid I'd get hurt—at least that's what she told me. But I'm invincible on the field. I mean, it literally takes an entire defense to bring me down. They have to *gang-tackle* me to get me to stop. Even then, many times I power myself out and score a touchdown anyway.

Sorry... sometimes I get carried away with myself. It's easier to talk about normal things—like running through entire defenses—than the other, not-so-normal parts of my crazy, twisted life. But if you were in my shoes and you knew the end of the world was coming, would you keep it to yourself?

My story goes like this—

On a boiling summer Saturday, I was outside passing the ball with my best friend, Xavier Rodriguez. Xavier reminds me of a hulked-up version of Shaggy from Scooby-Doo—at least that's the best way for me to describe him. The guy's six foot two, over two hundred pounds, with scraggly brown hair and only a few whiskers under his chin. He's the quarterback for our team. He's also a perfectionist. Coach might not let him throw the ball very much, but Xavier always makes sure everyone is on the same page and does their jobs right. He's like a second coach on the field with us, whether it's in practice or in games. Even off the field he coaches me—and that's the honest truth. You see, I've had to rely on Xavier to help me through many tough situations. He tutors me, which can't be easy for anyone to do. He also gives me advice that his dad has given him. That last one is really important to me, since I never knew my own dad.

On this particular day, Mom called us in to get some lunch, which she typically does on her days off. We walked over to my house from the park across the street. It's small because it's only Mom and me living there, but it's cozy. Mom loves the small, wrap-around porch. There are steps leading to the front door and big glass windows to the right and left of it, showing off the kitchen and living room when the curtains are up. Xavier and I walked in and leaned against the kitchen table.

"Thanks, Mrs. Brown," Xavier said, before stuffing his mouth with the amazingly thick peanut butter sandwich Mom had prepared for him.

I'm telling you, Mom is like the peanut butter queen. I guess it's something that she passed along to me, because I love peanut butter too. Both of us can eat it with anything—cookies, sandwiches, broccoli—and peanut butter shakes are the best!

The phone rang. Mom walked over to pick it up. She smiled as she stood by the kitchen sink, speaking quietly. But in an instant, her smile faded, the phone slipped out of her hand and a stunned expression came over her face. She looked out the kitchen window.

"You okay?" I asked.

Xavier didn't notice anything. He was finishing the last piece of his peanut butter sandwich with his back towards Mom.

"Hello, Hello? Anna?" a man's voice said on the other end of the line. Quickly, Mom walked over to the entrance of the house and opened the glass door.

"Why are you here?" she shouted. "You need to leave now! Stay away from us—you shouldn't be here!"

I walked up behind her to see what was going on. Standing on our porch was a man in a black suit. His hair was jet black and combed back. He was tan and had dark-brown eyes. He was wearing a white dress shirt underneath his black coat and bronze tie.

Okay, first of all, why would anyone in his right mind want to wear a black suit during July in Albuquerque? No, it isn't Arizona or Florida, but it still gets hot here. Second of all, what did this man want with my mom? I was worried about her; it seemed like she knew this man and definitely didn't want anything to do with him.

"Look, sir…" I said, trying to sound calm.

"Mr. Jensen," he corrected.

"Okay, Mr. Jensen. You're upsetting my mom and she doesn't want you here, so I think you'd better leave."

"Anna," he said, with a desperate tone in his voice. "We need to talk about… things."

Xavier came into the room just then and asked if everything was all right. "We can force this guy off the property if you need, Mrs. Brown," Xavier said.

"No, it's okay," Mom responded quickly. "I overreacted."

There was a slight quiver in her voice.

"Actually, I do need to speak with Mr. Jensen," she continued. "Boys, can you give us a few minutes?"

I hesitated, but Mom urged me to leave them. As I walked away, I could see that Mr. Jensen had a miserable expression on his face, as though I had brought him some sort of grief.

Mom's reaction was so weird. I'd never heard her mention a Mr. Jensen before. I sat down in the living room and looked out the window, keeping a close eye on Mom and Mr. Jensen. I could tell Mom was furious. I've been on the receiving end of her icy gaze, folded arms, and clenched fists more times than I wish to remember. Xavier asked me what all this was about, but I was as clueless as he was. I had this strong suspicion that whatever they were talking about had something to do with me.

Of course, Mom looking back at me from time to time through the living room window didn't make me think otherwise.

I could tell she was giving Mr. Jensen a piece of her mind, but Mr. Jensen stood there calmly, taking the verbal lashing. Why was Mom acting like this towards him? I juggled through my memory, trying to pinpoint a time when she may have mentioned something about Mr. Jensen. My mind was racing. Xavier was quiet, and Mom was doing her best to keep her shouting to a minimum.

Then what happened next really threw me off. The shouting stopped, and Mom rushed up to Mr. Jensen and wrapped her arms around him. Then she burst into tears. I jumped off the couch quickly. This definitely set off my weird-radar.

"Umm bro, your mom is crying all over that guy," Xavier pointed out.

"Yeah, I know. I'm not blind," I lashed back.

I was just about to go outside and demand some information when Mom broke away from Mr. Jensen and came inside.

"Mom, what's wrong?" I asked.

She took a deep breath before she spoke

"Landon, you need to go out and speak with Mr. Jensen," she said… Xavier stood up to go with me, but Mom asked him nicely to head home. He hesitated for a moment, and then respected Mom's wishes.

"I'll call you later, Landon," he said, closing the door behind him.

Xavier was protective when it came to Mom; we were both very protective of her.

Walking out the door, my mind became cluttered with so many questions. I felt small, as if I was on a stage and everyone was watching me, but it was only Mr. Jensen and I standing outside.

"Hello, Landon," the man began. "You look confused. I am sure that you have many questions on your mind, but unfortunately I am very limited on time...."

"Who are you?" I butted in.

Mr. Jensen locked onto my eyes. Then he took a deep breath and said, "I am your uncle—your father's brother."

I took a step back. I couldn't accept what he said. A whirlwind of emotions stirred in me—hate, rage, excitement. Panic, too. It was as if my mind had shut down, and my heart started performing double-time. I stared blankly at him. I must have had a stupid look on my face.

Mr. Jensen smiled.

"I felt it was time you knew your father's side of the family. It's for your own good, you know—and ours."

His words made my blood boil. *Time?* I had wondered my whole life about my dad's side of the family, and now this man was telling me that *he* felt this was a good time for him to introduce himself? *I'M FIFTEEN YEARS OLD!* I screamed inside. I was surprised that I was able to hold it all in. A short-fused hothead like me tends to react brashly in situations like these.

"So where is he then?" I asked. I tried to keep my composure, but I ended up following this with more attacking questions. "Where's my dad? Why didn't he come? Is he a coward? He couldn't face me so he sent you instead?"

"Be careful how you speak to me, boy," Mr. Jensen ordered. "You have no idea what sacrifices I have made in order to inform you about your father."

My muscles tensed. Now my mind was racing a hundred miles an hour. At the same time, and for some reason unknown to me at the time, I also began to fear Mr. Jensen.

"I understand this must be taking you by surprise, but I am sure you have wondered about the other side of your family before?"

He struck that nerve again. MR. JENSEN'S INSENSITIVITY = ME WANTING TO PUNCH HIM IN THE FACE. *Of course I wondered. Did he really think it didn't matter that no one on my father's side ever tried looking for me?*

"Okay then, uncle," I said sarcastically. "What do you want? Why are you here now?"

"Straight to the point, huh? Okay. The truth, Landon, is that your father is missing. He has been for some time now. It is not unusual that he would stay away from his... umm... family for years, but he has never stayed away as long as *this*. I have not seen my brother in thirteen years."

"I've never seen him," I blurted out. Mr. Jensen kept talking as if he didn't hear me.

"So what does all this have to do with you? I need your help!" he continued.

"My help?"

"Yes, Landon. You are at an age now where you could be quite useful to the family. Your father would have wanted you to know at around this time, anyway. And perhaps, if you decide to help me, you might be able to find your father."

I was shocked. Now he was asking me for help?

"Do you work for the mob or something?" I asked.

It was a stupid question, I know. But it was the only thing that came to mind at the time. I envisioned myself wearing a pin-striped suit and a fedora, holding a Tommy Gun and blasting away at some corner store, helping my uncle get back at some poor dude who owed him money.

Mr. Jensen grinned. "Landon, do you believe I'm a mobster?"

I shook my head but said nothing. My mob moment died there.

He looked down at his gold watch. Then he asked me to look into his eyes. A shiver went down my spine and my entire body turned cold. He stared straight at me and, as I gazed back, suddenly I saw a man with dark-brown hair that reached his shoulders. A few strands hung over his face. He looked similar to Mr. Jensen, with the same type of muscular build and tan. His goatee had a white patch near the bottom right corner of his chin. A scar in the shape of three claw marks came down under his right eye. He was wearing a black suit and white dress shirt like Mr. Jensen as well, but his tie had a picture of the Grand Canyon on it. I don't know how I knew it, but at that moment I realized I was looking at my father.

"His name is Drayden," said my uncle. "And I know you saw him. It was my purpose to show him to you. You belong to a very special family, Landon. Have you sensed a power within you that you cannot explain? We have taken notice of you—and for good reason. You have become something of a phenomenon in the sports world. You have no equal on the field because of your raw power and speed. Humans cannot explain your athleticism. But this ability is garnering too much attention, and it will lead to exposing a secret we have kept for centuries. You are jeopardizing our safety, but it is not entirely your fault. Your father has been lost—and he was supposed to be keeping an eye on you. You did not understand, so I do not blame you."

"Whose safety am I jeopardizing?" I asked.

"Listen, nephew," said my uncle. "I do not expect you to believe me when I tell you that the blood that courses through your veins is special—so I will show you instead. But before I do, I have something for you."

My uncle dug into his pocket and pulled out a dark-red object, the size and shape of a large marble. He handed it to me. "It is a bloodlust berry. It was your father's. He has had this one since before you were born. His intentions were to give it to you on your fifteenth birthday."

He paused for a moment before continuing.

"If you choose to find out who you are and how to unleash your potential, you must go to the Infernal Caverns in California. It is in the county of Modoc in an area called Crooks Canyon. There you will find a man named Alpha who will explain more. Show him the bloodlust berry—he will direct you further."

"How am I supposed to get there? It's not like I can afford to buy an airplane ticket whenever I feel like it."

My uncle flashed a sly grin, undoubtedly expecting me to ask him that.

"I will send a driver to pick you up tomorrow at 2:00 p.m. exactly. If you decide to go, you will enter the car before 2:05 p.m. Otherwise, he will leave without you. You do not need to take anything but the clothes on your back and the bloodlust berry. All your needs will be taken care of. I must go now, nephew. Time never stands still."

He gave me a warm smile and turned away.

"I thought you were going to show me something," I shouted.

He kept walking, ignoring what I said. Suddenly, a strong wind swirled around him and my uncle jumped into the air. It was impossibly high for any human to jump. Then he transformed. Crazy doesn't even begin to describe what I saw. He was no longer the strong-built uncle that I had just come to know. Right before my eyes, an immense light glowed all around him like a halo. Then the light spread, revealing a long, bronze serpent about twenty-five feet long, with four muscular legs protruding from its long body and two gigantic wings on its back. Its bronze scales gleamed in the light, almost blinding me. I couldn't turn away. On the top of the creature's head, two jagged horns that looked like deer antlers protruded. His snout was long, and it ended with a sharp, pointed beak. The face reminded me of a Tyrannosaurus rex, with beak and horns added. A powerful tail with a sharp end swung from side to side. Then the creature flew off into the clouds, leaving me stunned. Mr. Jensen, my uncle, had turned into a giant bronze dragon.

And he had said that I had this special blood in me.

Chapter Two
Son of War

I felt my heart jump out of my chest after watching my uncle incredibly transform. Immediately, I went inside to tell Mom everything.

She didn't even look shocked. She knew the day would come when I would have to leave her.

"I just thought there would be more time before you went away," she said. I could hear the upset in her voice.

I won't lie—I felt betrayed by Mom. She should have told me. Why did I have to find out like this? Without saying another word to her, I left her and went up to my room.

My room was the best place in the world. There, I could relax and leave all my worries outside the door. I had my fifty-inch big-screen TV mounted on the wall, and my bed on the opposite side. The walls were painted blue and silver after my favorite NFL football team. Posters and cut-out magazine pictures of my all-time favorite athletes were scattered across the walls. My iPod was on the nightstand next to the bed. I picked it up, put on my headphones and pushed "play." Then, I fell on the bed and thought about what my uncle had told me. Could I really be the son of a *dragon*? What's that berry for? What else does Mom know that she hasn't told me? So many questions flooded my mind that soon I wasn't even paying attention to the music. It didn't really matter; my brain was overloaded. I closed my eyes and soon fell asleep.

A few hours later, Mom woke me up and told me to get ready for dinner. I woke up groggy. My vision was blurry and my head hurt. I went to the bathroom and washed my hands and face, then went to the dinner table. Mom had prepared steak and potatoes for dinner. She was trying to cheer me up, I know, because this was my favorite meal. She usually makes me steak when I've had a rough day.

"Landon," she said softly, "You need to know that I'm not really sure what all this dragon stuff means—for you or for anyone. When I met your father, he never showed me who…" she paused briefly then corrected herself, "…I mean *what* he was until you were about six months old. I never got an explanation on how this would affect you as you grew up. All he ever said was that you wouldn't change like him, but that you would be powerful. I'm really sorry, Landon. *This* is the reason why I didn't want you to play football. It wasn't really for your safety—it was for the safety of the other kids."

Mom's emotions started getting the best of her again, and tears slid down her face. I didn't want to overwhelm her with questions, but I needed to know more. Gently, I asked her if Dad had mentioned anything about going to the Infernal Caverns in California. She nodded her head.

"You are the spitting image of him, you know," she said.

I had lighter skin than the man I saw in my uncle's eyes, but my dark, wavy hair and brown eyes did resemble his. She also told me that Dad was a very loving father, and that he was happy when I was born. I guess that made me feel good for the moment. Still, I wasn't sure how I felt about him as a person. Then Mom grabbed my hand.

"You need to find your father, Landon," she said. "I know you can do it."

Something was different about Mom. For years I'd assumed she was trying to hold me back. We always had arguments about my playing football. Anytime I roughhoused with any friends, she freaked. But now she was letting me go. I felt the confidence she had in me.

I promised her that I would try my best, but that I wouldn't do it at the risk of abandoning her. She didn't argue with me.

After dinner, Mom said that Dad had mentioned something once about a "Great Awakening." She didn't know what it was, but she did remember that Dad had been nervous about it.

"It was probably nothing," she said, with a wave of her hand. "Your father worried a lot, but not in a scared way. He was a wise man and he always had a lot on his mind."

I wondered why Mom didn't appear angry with how things turned out. My dad had left her alone with me since I was a baby, and yet, as we talked, it seemed as if she still thought he was the greatest thing ever. The way she spoke about him did make me mad, though. But I didn't want to fight with her, so I stood up and gave her a kiss. I told her that I loved her, and went to my room.

Time zipped by, and before I knew it, it was two o'clock the next day. My ride was outside waiting for me, just as my uncle had said it would be. Mom was tearing up and squeezing me half to death as I stood by the front door. I checked my pockets to make sure the bloodlust berry was there, and also to give Mom the hint that I needed to go. It was time for me to say good-bye, and it was harder than I thought. I really didn't know how long it would be before I could see her again. Eventually, Mom loosened her grip around me and I stepped away, feeling very unsure of what was about to happen.

One thing I learned right away was that my uncle owned his own limousine company. *Jensen Co.* was written on the side of the black stretch Hummer that was waiting right outside my house.

The driver stepped outside the car and ran to open the door.

"Mr. Brown," the man acknowledged with a nod, as I entered into the very spacious and luxurious vehicle. The door shut behind me. I waved goodbye to Mom, but forgot that the windows were tinted and she couldn't see me. The vehicle started up and I was on my way.

It took about a half hour for the driver to navigate his way to a remote area near Los Lunas, a city just south of Albuquerque. In a clear, flat area, I could see a private jet plane with the *Jensen Co.* logo on its side, preparing to take off. The vehicle pulled onto a dirt road and parked about fifty feet away from the plane. The driver ran around and opened my door. He pointed to the plane and said that it would take me to my destination.

The first hour of flying wasn't so bad. We hit a little turbulence, but nothing really scary. The second hour was pretty rough, though. There was something in the clouds that I couldn't make out, and that made me very nervous. I asked the pilot if he had noticed anything strange, but he just smiled and said, "Don't fly much, huh, kid?"

It was true. I had only flown a couple of times, and I'd been a nervous flyer on both of them. Still, as I looked out the side window of the small plane, I was pretty sure that something was out there. It didn't take long to find out that I was right.

The plane hopped, as if something had bumped it from underneath. I didn't say anything because the pilot didn't say anything. Then it happened again, and again after a few seconds. The pilot's confident expression began to fade. For a moment, the hopping stopped. I looked down and realized that I was holding on to the seat belt buckle so tight that I had dented it.

"I haven't felt turbulence like that in a while," the pilot said.

I was glad he said "in a while" because I was getting ready to think the worst. This pilot was a professional, right? He obviously would have known the difference between mere turbulence and what it felt like if the plane was actually being bumped by something.

TTTHHHUUMMPPP! Suddenly, something crashed into the right wing of the plane and flipped us onto our side. The pilot was panicked now. The color drained from his face. His body stiffened. I shot out a yelp that sounded like a mix between a bark and howl.

The pilot gathered himself and steadied the plane.

"What was that?" I managed to squeak out.

The pilot looked in his mirrors to catch whatever it was that had just hit us. Then he shook his head.

"That was not turbulence," he said. "We were hit by something."

I was quiet the rest of the trip. The pilot didn't say much, either.

A few hours later, we landed in a clearing near a valley. I had never been happier to be on the ground. I felt as though I was in the middle of nowhere, although I knew a city was only a few miles away. I had seen it on the way down. We were at the bottom of a rocky slope, looking up at a system of caverns located near the top.

"I was told to get you close to the caverns, but you have to make your way inside them from here," said the pilot.

In reality, it didn't matter. I could hike up the slope in no time, plus I was glad to be out of the sky. I thanked the pilot for his help and wished him luck on his way back.

Before I began my trek, I took in the scenery around me. There was something majestic about the area. Rocks and dry grass made up most of the terrain, and as I hiked farther up the slope, the more the river at the bottom shimmered in the sunlight. A nice breeze swept by and cooled my skin. The sound of tiny feet shuffling through the dirt and dry grass filled my ear, probably a small lizard running to a bush so it could avoid me. Another noise caught my attention. Was it music? As I got closer to the top, I could hear it clearly. Someone had cranked up the volume to some '80s heavy metal in one of the caverns, as if trying to announce to the world—*This is Where the Party's At.*

I climbed up a massive boulder in order to reach the entrance to the cave that the music was blaring from. When I pulled myself over the rock, I stood facing the entrance of the cave. There I saw a guy. He was dancing around a large fire with his hands and fingers positioned as if he was playing the guitar. I tried to hold it in, but I laughed so hard I even overpowered the music. Then the music stopped—and so, it seemed, did time. I looked up to see everyone watching me. I didn't notice the others before. There was a group of people off to the side, staring directly at me, along with the crazy air-guitar guy.

"Can I help you?" he asked.

"I'm looking for Alpha," I said, my voice shaky.

"You're in the right place, brah," air-guitar guy said, with his best surfer-dude impression. "I'm Alpha!"

I had pictured Alpha differently in my head. This guy was in shorts that looked like swimming trunks, a Metallica T-shirt and the typical surfer-dude shark-tooth necklace around his neck, although his looked like *real* great white shark teeth. He had dirty blonde hair that came down past a little below his shoulders. He looked like he was in his late twenties, and still in his prime. His eyes were blue, he had a pointy nose, and he was built like a tank.

"Are you here for orientation?" Alpha asked.

"Orientation?" I said awkwardly.

"Yeah, brah," he said. "Before you rudely interrupted, I was getting into my rhythm. I was just about to present this fine group of half-lings with how I'm going to run their training. So, if you don't mind, you should take a seat with the rest of the group and let me finish the righteous riff that was about to go down."

I sat down next to a punk rock-looking guy with three piercings on his lower lip, and watched as Alpha put his arms in position to play his air guitar again.

"Play!" he shouted directly at the fire that was burning in the middle of the cave. The music blasted again. I had never seen anyone pretend to play an instrument so passionately. He was making weird faces, and jumping around the fire, while his hair swung around him. Was my uncle serious about sending me to this place? How was it possible that this guy could guide me in the right direction?

After the song finished, Alpha welcomed us to the caverns.

"Congrats on making it before sundown. It looks like we have a bigger crowd than usual," he said, even though there were only five others beside me, sitting by the fire.

"For the last few centuries," he continued, "I have been assigned to train you half-lings in combat. The first thing you dudes and chicks should know is that I don't mess around. I also get righteously upset if someone interrupts me when I'm in the middle of a wicked guitar riff."

Everyone stared at me.

"So, what is the first order of business?" He muttered to himself. "Oh, right, let's start here. Does everyone know why I call you half-lings?"

We all looked around, hoping that someone else would answer.

"Because we are half-dragon and half-human," said a girl, sitting at the far edge, on the opposite side of me.

"Correcto!" said Alpha enthusiastically. "Good job, Green Eyes. Sometimes dragonoids aren't really that informed before they get here, so it's usually a good question to ask. And just so you know, everybody, I didn't come up with that term, dragonoid. That is what *you all* are technically called."

I glanced at the girl who had just answered the question. She did have captivating green eyes and long lashes. The color of her eyes reminded me of emeralds. She was pretty, with light skin and long, auburn-colored hair tied back into a ponytail. Her perfect pink lips widened into a soft smile, revealing a cute dimple on the left side of her face.

"Snap out of it, Romeo," Alpha ordered me. "You were checking out Miss Green Eyes and blanked out. You need to focus!"

The others laughed their heads off, and Miss Green Eyes, as Alpha called her, blushed. I'm pretty sure my face turned as red as a tomato. I just sat back and looked straight ahead, trying not to think about how Alpha had just called me out in front of everyone.

"Anyway," he continued, "we will start training tomorrow by finding out what you already know—and then we will move on from there. My job is to make sure that you all know your strengths and can use them to the best of your ability. I can't make orange juice out of lemons, though. For those of you who don't know anything about your dragon-parent, I will give you the rundown on who they are and what abilities you will need to try to master. We will start at 6:00 a.m. sharp, and lights out will be at 9:00 p.m. And don't complain to me about my training regimen or I will take away your eating privileges. Trust me—you do not want to lose those."

Alpha sounded more and more like a drill sergeant as he explained the activities, and how his way is "the only way." He was definitely passionate about training, and if he'd really been doing this for centuries, I figured it probably wasn't a good idea to get on his bad side. Alpha assigned us sleeping bags and spots to sleep. My spot was the farthest away from the fire, but I didn't mind.

"Before there are any questions on anything I've said, I'm going to introduce my staff. Some of you have met one of my helpers already—some of you haven't yet," Alpha said, as his bright blue eyes settled in my direction.

A girl with long, curly black hair walked up beside Alpha. I made sure to not make it as obvious as before that I was looking at her; still, she was stunning. I mean, I must have said *Wow* in my head about twenty times. She was wearing a white blouse, blue shorts and white sandals. She had a beautiful smile, her dark brown eyes glowed by the fire, and the light shimmered on her olive skin.

"This is Purity," said Alpha. "She is second in command and will help in some of our training activities."

Purity waved to us and examined all of us with a serious look on her face.

"The fire beside us is Travis. He doesn't talk, but he provides us with a lot. He lights up the cave, heats it for us, provides my rockin' music and makes crazy green-chili cheese burritos. Our last staff member isn't here right now and usually stays in his own cave. His name is Primus. We'll visit that dude eventually. Now, does anyone have any questions?"

Immediately, the guy sitting next to me asked, "How are you qualified to train us?"

Alpha turned to him with a wicked gaze, as if he were about to show us all what he was capable of. Slowly, his expression changed to a grin.

"Brah," Alpha said calmly, "I understand that you don't know who I really am. But never question a man who lives in a cave whether he is qualified to train you in survival tactics."

"Maybe it's worth your while to understand who I am. I'm not going to go into too much detail, but I will just say that I have been training dudes like you since way back—and I mean *waayyy* back. My mission is to ensure quality destruction in any war, so I've never turned anyone away who wanted to train under me. The only thing that's changed over the last couple of centuries is that I mainly train half-lings now. Nevertheless, my mission is still the same. I am skilled in all styles of combat. And, of course, I am fully capable of shredding rock guitar riffs with the best."

Alpha seemed tense as he looked around the room. I couldn't tell what he was focusing on, though. Silence invaded the cave, making us all feel uneasy. The only noise that we heard was the crackle that Travis the fire was making. For a moment, Alpha seemed lost, as if he knew he had made a wrong turn twenty miles back. But just as quickly his eyes lit up, he shook off whatever daze he was in, and with a proud look on his face he hit us with information that made me so uneasy it felt like boiling oil was churning in my stomach.

"My father," he said, "is one of the four horsemen of the apocalypse. I am the Son of War."

Chapter Three
How to Catch the Wind

The first night in the cave, I didn't sleep well at all. I was actually happy when Alpha quietly sneaked towards Travis the fire and said, "Play," waking everyone up with the loud boom of heavy-metal music.

When you want people to wake up, that is definitely a good way to do it. Of course, you will have a lot of grumpy individuals on your hands—but what do you expect when you wake teenagers up at 5:30 in the morning? I was expecting Alpha to yell "Rise and shine, dudes!" or something else to encourage us to get up even faster. But our combat expert was too deep in his trance, unleashing his imaginary guitar skills. After a few minutes of shredding air and head banging, he was ready to go—and he expected us to be ready too.

Cleaning up was easy because of the "cleansers" further down the cave. The cleansers looked like what I imagined a time machine would look like. They were big, silver metal tubes that a person entered for showering. Toothbrushes, toothpaste, soap, shampoo and razors were all provided inside. The cleanser even dried you off once you were finished. Clothes and sneakers were also provided in the tube, so you could change in there before you headed out on your merry way. If anyone were hoping for a selection of clothes, they'd be disappointed. We all wore white mesh jogging pants, plain white T-shirts, and white sneakers. By 6:00 a.m., everyone was ready to start the day.

Alpha's first order of business was to have us introduce ourselves to each other.

He pointed to me first and said, "Why don't we start with you, Romeo? Just give us your full name, where you're from, and something cool about you."

The other five trainees had their eyes fixed on me. I told them my name, that I came from New Mexico, and that I was considered the best high school football player in the country.

"Gnarly!" Alpha chimed in. "We have a celebrity."

The next guy had a blond crew cut, blue eyes, and a serious demeanor. His name was James Braddock. James was from Orlando, and in training to be a professional boxer. The guy reminded me of a pit bull. He gave off an intimidating vibe with his cold, hard stare. After that, Shade Gambino introduced himself. He was from New Orleans and an artist. Shade reminded me of a rock star. He had a mop of smoke-black, scraggly hair with long bangs that dropped in front of his face, which he'd push away from his eyes every minute or so. Three shiny silver rings pierced his bottom lip, and a tiny but easily detectable scar marked his left cheek.

Alpha asked Travis for a sheet of paper and a pen. Then he put his hands in the fire and pulled them out without getting burned. He started jotting something down on the paper.

"You all don't have to stop," he said. "Let's continue with Miss Green Eyes."

The girl moved up towards the fire and said, "My name is Aurora Meadows. I'm from Alexandria, Virginia, but we move around a lot because my father's in the military. I play volleyball for my high school team."

This time I limited myself to just hearing her speak, and didn't stare at her.

"Next," Alpha demanded.

A girl with fiery red hair and extremely rosy cheeks introduced herself as Amy Jane Watkins. She was from Lansing, Michigan, and she could hold her breath underwater for five minutes. Finally, Derek Foster, the last guy, introduced himself. He was from Denver, Colorado. He built cars with his dad. Derek's dark brown skin made the rest of us look extra pale by comparison. His hair was neatly corn-rowed, and he was the only guy among us who had any facial hair, although it was a very light mustache. But he was the shortest, too, around five foot four.

After the introductions, Alpha wanted to find out who our dragon-parent was. With a syringe in his hand, he explained how he was able to discover this. Alpha would take blood from our dragon vein and then Travis would decode our dragon genes. He explained that, as dragonoids, the dragon vein was the single most important vessel in our bodies. It's found on the left side of the neck. Two things can be determined from the blood in our dragon veins: who sired us, and our chance of growing wings.

Everyone's eyes widened when he mentioned the part about the wings. He blew it off, though, as if it were no big deal, and explained that the genetic makeup on our human side almost always rejected the wing gene from our dragon side.

"Who's first?" Alpha asked, holding the syringe in the air while grinning menacingly. He was doing his best impression of an evil doctor.

"I'll go," James Braddock said.

Alpha stepped beside James. Then he cocked his head to the side and stuck the syringe in his neck. He drew the blood, transferred it to a small vial, then threw the vial into the fire. Once Alpha finished drawing everyone's blood, he sent us running outside, asking us to sprint up and down the rocky slope six times before coming back. Once outside, we all ran at a steady pace, except for Aurora. She ran like a horse on fire and pretty much left us in the dust. When we had all made it back to the cave, a sheet of paper hung on the rocky wall closest to Travis. All of us huddled around it the way we did in football, to see whether we'd made the team or not. But this information was about our parents. The sheet of paper read:

DNA Results

Landon Brown—Father is Drayden, 35%, Meet me in my office at 9:00 am.
James Braddock—Mother is Jada, 55%
Shade Gambino—Father is Shadow, 70%
Aurora Meadows—Mother is Shea, 80%, Meet me in my office at 10:00 am.
Amy Jane Watkins—Father is Maelstrom, 0%
Derek Foster—Father is Primus, 30%, Meet me in my office at 11:00 am.

Just then, Alpha popped up and said that those who needed to see him in his office would find it past the cleansers near the dungeon room. I had no idea there was a dungeon room, but then again, I didn't know Alpha had his own office. The cavern was long, from what I could see, and the passageways looked very complex.

Purity had joined us, and Alpha explained that our first lesson, sword fighting, would begin after breakfast. He had us gather around Travis; then he ordered eight breakfast burritos. Plates immediately stacked up inside the fire and, as Alpha pulled one out, a burrito appeared on it. I had to admit it was probably the best breakfast burrito I'd ever had in my life. It was stuffed with eggs, ham, sausage and green chili—and the tortilla tasted homemade. There was another ingredient in there that gave the burrito that extra *ZING!* I couldn't tell what it was—but I figured it was magic.

Afterwards, it was time to get down to business. Purity was in charge of the sword- training exercise. She was amazingly graceful with her sword as she showed us how to defend against many types of attacks.

"It is important to practice these defense tactics over and over so that they can become second nature. The best offense is a good defense," said Purity.

After some intense practice with a sword, in which I almost cut my leg off, it was time for me to visit with Alpha in his office. As I walked through the cave, I imagined how lonely it must be when there wasn't a group of people like us newbies around. Travis's crackle echoed through the cave as I advanced beyond the cleansers. I noticed a wooden door to the left with a sign that read *DUNGEON ROOM* on it. A red glow showed through the cracks of an old wooden door, and heat radiated from inside. A little further down was another wooden door, this one without a sign.

I opened the second door and saw Alpha sitting behind a desk, looking as though he was working on something.

"Hey Romeo," Alpha began. "Have a seat."

As I walked in, I noticed weapons neatly placed all around the space. They were beautifully crafted from the shiniest metals and most precious stones that a person could use to create an instrument of death.

"Look, dude," Alpha said. "I'm not going to keep you from your training very long, but I just wanted to speak with you personally about your father Drayden. I knew he had been missing for some time now, but to tell you the truth, I'm surprised that he had another kid. He claimed that his previous kid was going to be his last."

"Why would he say that?" I asked.

"Brah, your dad is an *Earth Mover*. Like him, his kids can bend the terrain to their will, depending on how powerful they become. That's a problem in itself, but imagine one who's powerful but can't control it? Well, that was the problem with the son he had before you. He couldn't control it, and he caused a lot of damage. It got so bad that some of the other dragons put a bounty out on him. That was twenty years ago, but still, no one knows what happened to him. He was fifteen when his powers went haywire. Then he disappeared."

Alpha shrugged and leaned in a bit closer to me from across the desk.

"Your dad was pretty hurt with the whole thing, so he took an oath to never have any more kids."

"What was the name of my dad's other son?" I asked, regretting that I'd never had a chance to meet this person who would have been my brother.

"It's hard to forget his name because of all the drama that unfolded. His name was Brandon... Brandon Phoenix."

"Well, it didn't take my dad very long to break his promise about not having kids. Just five years later, he had me," I said angrily. I clenched my fist and wanted to punch something. I thought dad's major flaw was leaving Mom and me behind, but from what I was now being told, it seemed his kids were his mistakes.

Alpha shot me a look of concern about my tantrum. He went on to explain the importance of learning to control my power because of what had previously happened to Brandon. He said that someone might already know that I exist, and could be plotting to kill me because of the threat I posed. That wasn't a very encouraging thought.

Just then, I remembered being attacked on the plane ride over here. I told Alpha that I had noticed something following us before we were hit, but I couldn't make it out. I asked if he knew who it might have been. He looked dumbfounded.

"Dra... Dragons don't move that fast, brah," he looked at me in shock. "Well, I mean I only know of one dragon that was capable of flying at extreme speeds... but it couldn't have been him."

"Why not?" I asked.

"He's been locked away in the Dragon Sphere for more than a millennium."

I was getting ready to ask what the Dragon Sphere was, but just then Purity charged in to the office.

"SOLDIER IS ATTACKING US!" Purity shouted, her face pale with concern.

Alpha, Purity and I sprinted to the opening of the cave and looked down the rocky slopes of the Infernal Caverns. The others were swinging their swords wildly in the air, but I couldn't tell what they were trying to hit. Alpha ordered everyone to run back to the main cave. They retreated as if their lives depended on it. I noticed a powerful gust of air lifting one of the trainees fifteen feet in the air. It was James. In an instant, he slammed down on the ground with a hard thud. A couple of the others hurried back out and helped him into the cave.

"Are you okay?" Amy Jane asked worriedly.

James was out of it, and he looked as if he'd had a concussion. I was pretty sure that hits like the one he'd just taken could cause one. Alpha ordered all of us to give him some space as he examined the boy's eyes.

"Romeo! Miss Green Eyes!" Alpha barked at us. "I want you to go back out there and capture that wind demon!"

We both had puzzled looks on our faces. How would we be able to fight against a wind demon?

"Romeo, focus your mind on using the ground around you. Miss Green Eyes, take command of the winds and use them to bring the enemy down. You have to work together on this. I know you can do it."

After Alpha ordered us out, we started down the slope. We did not say anything to each other. I focused on trying to see the wind demon, but there were no disturbances in the air or ground. How could Alpha just send us out here like this? Then I heard some bushes rustling. I turned toward the noise and heard a boisterous laugh.

"HA! HA! HA!" a deep, hoarse, evil laugh echoed down the slope. "Why does Alpha insist on sending stupid kids to stop me? I AM SOLDIER!" The wind blew furiously. "I am the mightiest of warriors, yet he still dares to send children to stop me! His curse makes him more foolish by the day."

"Show yourself, wind demon!" I said, hoping that he would just leave instead.

"HA! Every year I come, the brood of half-lings gets more pathetic. I have no form, stupid. So how can I show myself?"

"Don't call me stupid!" I roared back.

I felt my temperature rising and my muscles tensing up. I couldn't see him, yet his voice seemed to echo all around me. Aurora, however, had her eyes fixed on something.

"What is it?" I asked her.

"I can see him," she said in disbelief. "I can make out his form. It's as if the air is bending around his body. He's about twenty yards straight ahead, and about ten feet off the ground. It looks like he's waiting for something."

Just then I heard a loud rush of wind swirling towards me. The force knocked me to the ground. I picked myself up right away.

"WATCH OUT!" yelled Aurora, as I felt the full force of a fist against the left side of my face.

The wind demon swirled towards Aurora. She rolled to the side, then put her hand up and blocked a blow from above. With a clenched fist and eyes closed, Aurora pounded the air, hoping to hit the demon. It was a powerful blow that summoned a strong gust of air with its force. I noticed dust and small fragments of rock blast off from the ground as the demon's invisible body landed on them. I ran to the spot where the demon had hit the ground, hoping to hit him while he was down. Before I could even swing, though, I was lifted ten feet in the air and dropped straight down.

As I was about to land, Aurora pushed a pocket of air towards me to break my fall. Unfortunately she missed, and I ended up hitting the ground. I landed hard on my back. Nothing was broken and my head didn't hurt; I took it as a good sign.

"Are you okay?" shouted Aurora.

I nodded and asked where the demon was. Before she could answer, she shot a powerful gust that blew me away.

"What the…?" I called to her as I rose angrily to my feet. Then I suddenly realized what she had done. The demon had been right above me and had smashed a crater into the ground where I was lying just seconds before. If she hadn't pushed me back, he would've tackled me deep into the earth.

"He's down!" she yelled.

Dust, pebbles and other debris slid into the deep crater created by the wind demon. I felt an intense rush of energy flow through my body as I willed the freshly made crater, where the demon had landed, to collapse onto itself. I compacted the rocks, dirt, and branches into a spherical shape and enclosed the wind demon within it.

"LET ME OUT!" called the demon. "I am Soldier the mighty. I will destroy you stupid kids!"

"We should let Alpha know that we trapped him," Aurora suggested.

I nodded in agreement but was speechless. I was astonished that the earth listened to me. The energy that ran through my body actually moved the ground. Aurora waved her hand in front of my face and snapped me out of my shock. She looked exhausted, even though we'd only been out here for a few minutes.

"Are you okay?" I asked.

"Those wind blasts drained me," she said, her warm smile assuring me she was okay.

We turned back to the cave to inform Alpha of our success.

"AAARRRGGGHHH!" screamed the wind demon, as he exploded the rocky sphere he was trapped in. The demon was furiously gasping for air. I could see him now; his body was covered in dirt and other debris. He was about six feet tall, with a muscular build, and he was wearing… was that a toga?

"Where did you get the dress?" I mocked.

The demon howled in anger and swirled towards us. Aurora and I evaded his attack by rolling away from each other. I got up quickly, sprinted towards him and punched him in his midsection. Before I could get another punch in, he blasted me with a gust of wind that knocked me on my back. But the dusty figure was holding his gut with his left hand and wincing in pain. Aurora shot a blast of wind at him that pushed him face first to the ground. Instinctively, I raised my right arm and willed a patch of earth below his face to rise up and strike him. The demon roared.

Then he pushed himself off the ground and took to the air.

"I thought you didn't have a form?" I teased, feeling more confident. "You can't hide now, you dirt bag!"

He looked more like a dirt statue. The demon jetted towards me and tackled me to the ground. We both got up quickly, but I met face first with his right hook. My body spun around but I stayed on my feet. I managed to block a kick aiming for my midsection, and an immediate right-handed jab after that. Aurora jumped behind the wind demon and evaded a roundhouse kick by barely ducking in time. I swung at his face, but the demon grabbed my arm and uppercut me, sending me into the air and then straight onto my back again. When Soldier turned around, though, his face met with Aurora's elbow. She struck his midsection, making him lean forward and setting him up with a devastating knee kick directly to his face.

Aurora kicked at Soldier several times while he was on the ground, but he managed to block them all. He pushed himself away from her by shooting air into the ground and catapulting into the sky. I couldn't see if the demon was bloody, but I knew I was. I could feel warm liquid dripping down from my own mouth. Then Soldier started spinning in the air, his body moving faster and faster with every full rotation. The air around him swirled and started forming what seemed like a mini-tornado. Aurora shot a blast of air towards him but it was swallowed up in the rotation. She ran towards me and told me that we needed to get back to the cave. She tugged at me to follow her but I didn't budge. It wasn't by choice. My feet were sunk into the ground, tucked under the earth as if the dirt was holding me down.

The demon tornado started moving towards us—lifting, tossing and destroying anything in its way. Aurora looked shocked that I wasn't as terrified as she was.

"Landon, we can't fight him anymore! We need to leave now!"

I wasn't ready to budge for two reasons—first, the ground wasn't letting me go and second, I knew that I could defeat him.

"I need your help," I said to Aurora. "We can beat him but we need for him to try and swallow us up in his tornado. I will hold us down—but once we get into the eye, you need to blast him from underneath. We can do it!"

Aurora looked at me as if I were crazy, but I sensed that she wanted to finish this fight just as much as I did—especially since she had done more damage to the wind demon than I had.

I concentrated on the ground below me, as I felt the earth attach itself to my feet and reinforce my position.

"I'm going to have to hold on to your waist while you aim at him, okay?" I warned.

She just nodded and closed her eyes, waiting for the high-powered winds to envelop us.

Soldier laughed. "You stupid kids! This will be your final stand."

Our clothes flapped hard as they were pulled by the powerful wind, and our skin turned ice cold.

"Here he comes," Aurora mouthed but I couldn't hear the actual words because the mighty gusts were too loud.

Dust and pebbles slammed against our skin, pegging us like paintballs. The tornado was slowly pulling me out of the ground. I could feel my body fighting the force, but I didn't know how much longer I could hold it or how long I could hold Aurora.

"HIT HIM NOW!" I yelled, with all my might.

Whether she heard me or not, I do not know. But the next instant, Aurora shot a blast of air right underneath the wind demon and sent him flying out of the tornado. The winds immediately stopped, and the demon slammed hard against the ground. Aurora ran towards him and pushed the air between them down hard on his chest, pressing him deep into the ground.

"Landon, trap him again like the last time," she ordered.

I didn't know whether I had enough strength, but I had to try. The ground around Soldier folded over him, and packed him within a square-shaped entrapment of earth. Aurora moved away and watched as I kept packing dirt and rocks into his tomb. The force felt as though I was holding the rocky entrapment in my hands and squeezing with all my might. Then all of my strength gave way, and I collapsed to the ground. The rocky square entrapment, the size of a basketball now, was placed within the crater.

"I'm pretty sure he won't break out of that one," Aurora said with a grin.

"I… hope not," I responded, still trying to catch my breath.

She came over to me and helped me off the ground. We picked up the rocky vault, with Soldier inside, and walked up towards the cave.

Chapter Four
Puppets

I had to admit that my first day was really exciting, even if I did take a decent beating. My left eye had swelled up and was almost completely closed. Alpha immediately switched my nickname from Romeo to Cyclops. I didn't mind, though; it was cool that he allowed Aurora and me to relax for the rest of the day. Purity would stop by periodically and tell me that she was going to bring me something to help me feel better. I told her that I was fine, even though I wasn't. I had never taken a beating like that before, but I only asked for some water.

Aurora and I had some time to talk while the others were training outside. I had complimented her on her fighting skills, and joked that she missed breaking my fall, during the fight, on purpose. I asked her why she had decided to come here and train with Alpha, and she told me that it was just the curiosity of finding out what she was capable of. She already knew that she was part dragon because her father had told her. She had met her mother several times throughout her life, but only in human form. Earlier, Alpha had spoken with her and told her that her mom was an Elder Dragon like my dad. Her mom's name was Shea, and she was known as the *Sky Queen*.

I was a little jealous that Aurora got to meet her dragon-parent and that I still hadn't met mine. I'm sure it was just as tough for her to have seen her mom only a few times throughout her life, though. Being raised by one parent was hard, and we both felt that little or no guidance from our dragon-parent left us with a big hole inside. Aurora explained that she needed to join a bunch of activities to help her cope with the long absences from her mother. Her favorite was kickboxing, which explained her good moves during the fight against Soldier.

The rest of the day went by quickly. At one point, Purity came by and forced some medicine down my throat that put me to sleep for a few hours. When I woke up, the swelling in my eye was completely gone, but it was still a nice black-purplish color. My body didn't ache anymore either, and I felt rejuvenated. It was about 5:00 in the afternoon, and training for the others had stopped.

"Hit the cleansers," Alpha ordered.

The other students, pouring sweat, didn't hesitate to get cleaned up.

After everyone finished at the cleansers, we all sat down by the cavern wall where Alpha had first given us his orientation speech.

"Play," Alpha ordered Travis the fire, and heavy-metal music penetrated throughout the cave and echoed off the cavern walls. Alpha got into his rhythm by pretending to play the wild guitar riffs on his air guitar. Once the music stopped, Alpha acknowledged Aurora and me on our fight against Soldier, the wind demon. He explained how every year for the past eleven years, on the first official day of training, Soldier would attack the trainees. Alpha always sent two students out to fight him, but none had ever been able to defeat him until today. He felt that the wind demon provided his students with a good lesson on why it was important to train, because we never knew what might attack us—or when.

"So you knew that we would get attacked by that thing, and you still allowed us to be out there?" Shade Gambino asked bitterly.

"Brah, I'm here to train you. The wind demon provided a good example of why you need that training. Other than learning to control your powers so that you won't be reckless, you half-lings are prone to getting attacked by everything. You all have a big, bright, neon-glowing bullseye on your back, and that's why your dragon-parents set up this training. There's more to it, but I'll have Primus explain that tomorrow."

As soon as Alpha mentioned Primus, Derek Foster put his head down shamefully. I remembered that Primus was Derek's dad, but I didn't understand why Derek looked so sad about that fact. None of our parents had been there for us either throughout our lives, but this was a golden opportunity for him to spend time with his. Then it hit me. In the morning, during our introductions to each other, Derek had said that *he enjoyed building cars with his dad*. He had just learned that the person he had known as his dad his whole life wasn't his real father. I knew that this had to sting.

After dinner, Alpha let us use the rest of the evening to get to know each other. Even Purity joined us. Everyone was cool, but we were all so different from one another, and some of us, like Shade, had some very radical ideas. I mean—who thinks about starting a war against the dragons, especially when we haven't really developed our powers yet? Other than that, though, we all had a good time, and I'm glad that I didn't look like a total loser in front of Purity. She told me that she had given me lamb's blood in liquid capsule form to help heal me. She had also told me that she had given it to James Braddock today, which killed any chance for me to think that she was giving me special treatment. Apparently, lamb's blood has special healing properties for dragons, and it's a major part of a dragon's diet. I really wanted to know more about the subject—and about her—but I was too nervous to ask her anything. I don't know why she made me so nervous; I'm actually really good when it comes to talking to girls.

The evening flew by, and all of us were exhausted and ready to call it a night. None of us knew what Alpha had in store for us the next day, so getting rest was crucial.

The next morning, we started the day by taking a field trip to the next cavern over. We were on our way to visit Primus. The cavern was extremely dark inside. Purity brought out a flashlight and guided us to a wooden door that had a *DO NOT ENTER* sign on it. Alpha opened it and we continued. A faint light shone in the distance, but it was still too dark to see anything else. I did notice that we were descending as we walked towards the faint glow, which got bigger as we progressed forward. It also started to feel like the temperature was rising.

CLANK... CLANK... CLANK! A noise echoed off the walls that sounded like metal pounding metal. We had reached another door that had red light seeping through the cracks.

When Alpha opened up the door, an extreme heat bombarded us. Red light lit up the cavern walls; boxes with *Blayne Crow Inc.* labeled on the side of them were scattered everywhere; and a giant portable heater stood in the center. A hammock was set up near the entrance to another room. The clanking noise was getting louder as we walked forward. My eyes widened in wonder when we walked into the next room. Piles of gold and precious stones filled an entire side. Diamonds, rubies, emeralds and other precious stones of different colors sparkled across the room.

A tall, bald, muscular man was hammering down on an object on top of an anvil. Sweat glistened on his dark skin. He wore protective goggles, a white tank top, and blue jeans. Burn marks stained his clothes and his brown work boots. With every strike of the hammer, sparks flew off. The man looked up and saw us all gathering around the room. Immediately, he stopped working and walked over to us. With a welcoming smile he received us.

"Greetings, young ones! My name is Primus. I welcome you to my home."

Primus took off his goggles and looked right at Derek Foster.

"This must be him. My boy is finally grown." Then he turned to Alpha. "He looks healthy, does he not?"

Primus waited for his boss's approval. Alpha nodded.

Derek Foster looked exactly like his father, only thirty years younger. Derek was shorter than his dad and had hair on his head. Other than that, they were identical.

"Primus is the best blacksmith in the world," said Alpha. "He has created some of the most beautiful—and most deadly—weapons around for the last five hundred years."

Looking proud, Primus asked us all to sit on the ground. Sweat trickled down his clean-shaven face.

"You do not understand how important it is to have you all training here under Alpha. Not one of you knows what it is like to have a normal life, and we understand that. If you have not yet been attacked, you are lucky. But if you have, then you understand that it is important to know how to protect yourself. I will not lie. You have all been bred for a purpose. It may seem harsh for me to say this, but there is almost a ninety-nine percent chance that love had nothing to do with your siring."

Just like myself, I could tell that the others didn't like hearing that. Mom had told me that my dad was a loving father; now I wondered if that was even true. I imagine dragons would have to be master manipulators. Otherwise, why would their human partners consent to having babies with them?

"Do not think of us as cold-hearted creatures," Primus continued. "In many instances, we do form strong bonds with our sons and daughters as they get older. The truth to your siring, though, is that you all ensure our protection. Dragons do not command the same power as you dragonoids do in human form. Some of us are skilled warriors in human form—but we cannot manipulate the elements, or vanish, or use our full strength."

"Why would you want to fight in human form to begin with?" James Braddock spoke up.

"Some time ago, dragons used to roam freely without fear and were left to themselves. Times have changed much. Knights sought us out to kill us, in order to prove their bravery. We were hunted for sport. Kings would seek our treasure and send armies to destroy us. Dragons have only become more vulnerable over time, as the humans' technology has become more advanced. When we transform into humans, we are in hiding. But just because we are hiding does not mean that we are helpless. We learn to do battle as a human would.

"And before anyone asks," he continued, "we cannot stay in human form for more than four hours at a time, nor do we feel we should have to. We are proud creatures. You all should be proud as well."

"So we were born to protect you all from humans? That's lame!" I blurted out. I know it was a rude thing to say, but I couldn't help myself.

"We have been able to remain hidden from the humans for many years," Primus explained, looking at me sternly. "The main reason for that is because dragonoids have been our… how do I say this…? ambassadors. You represent us in the human world, because you can be among the humans for an indefinite amount of time. You all are important in a political respect as well. Dragons are diverse in ideals. Some may want another's territory, or fight for a position of power, or wish to wage war against the humans and jeopardize our safety. I understand that some have also been careless with their powers and have caused quite a stir. But still, the last thing humans would ascribe their power to is to being half-dragon."

"What about dragonoids who grow wings?" Shade Gambino asked, rather forcefully.

"They are few in number, and many times they go into solitude or find a safe haven because they understand that they do not fit in the human world. The point of all of this is that being born a dragonoid comes with a purpose. Many search their entire lives for their purpose and do not find it. The Creator has blessed us with many things in life, and a purpose is the most satisfying of all."

"Wait a minute," I shouted angrily. "Let me get this straight. You're saying that our purpose in life is to serve the dragons' will? Are we supposed to just buy this garbage? What do we look like, puppets?"

Primus examined me as if he was staring at his next meal.

"I understand that this is not something you wish to hear, young one. You want to prove that you have free will and that the Creator has given you all that you need to carve out your own path. But such an idea is misguiding. Purpose is not a tool of confinement. In fact, many find it liberating to know that there was a reason for them to come into the world. Others find freedom in the idea that their steps have been ordered, and that the all-powerful Creator watches over them."

"I don't believe in that kind of freedom," I argued.

"Then share with me your take on it," Primus said sharply, folding his arms across his chest and glancing at me with amusement in his eyes.

"I don't believe in anything," I said.

"You must elaborate, my boy. Everyone believes in something."

"I just said I don't."

"Of course you do. If you believe that there is no supreme being, then that is a belief in itself."

"Okay, then that is my belief."

"The tone in your voice makes me speculate that you are angry at me for believing the way I do? Why?"

"Because I can't stand the fact that a person fools themselves into believing in a supreme being, and thinking they are ultimately good, when I see nothing but evil in this world. Why would a supreme creator allow so many bad things to happen? I can't accept that evil has any purpose in this world. And this idea that I was born to serve someone else doesn't sit well with me either."

Primus looked at Alpha, as if he knew what he should say but hesitated to say it.

"There is no easy answer to that," Primus responded. "In fact, an explanation may get you even more upset. All I can say to you, young one, is that having faith in your purpose will aid you in many hardships to come. None of us know how anything will turn out, and life can seem chaotic, but faith is an outstretched hand guiding us through the mayhem. You are privileged, do you know that? Billions of people put their faith in something, but most will never see the things that you have seen or will encounter in the future. A glimpse of our world, young one, would make any skeptical human a believer in the Creator."

"How can you say we are privileged? This is a curse!" I shouted.

"It is yours. You may see it as you wish. But know that it would not have been given to you without a purpose. We all have a role to fulfill!"

Before I could respond, Primus walked towards the treasure. A strong wind radiated from his body and an immense light blinded us all. When we opened our eyes, Primus was in dragon form, a twenty-foot, red-scaled serpent. His muscular forelegs were only a few feet away from us. Razor-sharp talons protruded from each toe. Massive wings stretched out from his back, each wing looking as if leather had been draped over an extra arm. His snout was long, and two deadly fangs showed. He had two long horns on his head that arched back. His tail swung up and down, slamming against the gold and precious stones and making the ground shake beneath us.

Alpha told us that it was time for us to go, and he thanked Primus.

"I think you got him angry," Aurora said with a mischievous smile.

"I'm just glad he didn't eat me," I responded. I could hear the others mumbling to one another, but I couldn't make out what they were saying.

Walking out of the cave felt good. It was sunny outside, and the breeze was just right. I couldn't wait to get started on our training. One thing that I had to agree with Primus on, even though I wasn't going to admit it to him, was that there were forces out there, like the wind demon Soldier, that were capable of powerful things. I knew I had to be ready for them.

I felt like an outcast the rest of the day. I couldn't understand why, I didn't think I'd acted like that much of a jerk back in the cave with Primus. In fact, I thought most of them would agree with me that being used to fight the dragons' battles was a harsh reality. During our sword-fighting exercises, Aurora told me that the others were worried about me. The reality was that most of them felt awkward being around someone who had just fought a demon, but still questioned the powerful forces at play. I don't think they liked the fact that I said we were cursed, either. I tried not to focus on any of it, and just concentrated on my training.

During the lunch break, Purity walked up to me and asked me how I was doing. I told her that I was okay, but she wasn't convinced.

"What did I do?" I asked.

"Nothing," said Purity. "Well… I guess we're just not used to someone talking back to a dragon the way you did earlier. Dragons are very wise and have seen many things. It was considered a blessing for Kings to receive counsel from them. They are not used to someone questioning what they say—and especially their beliefs."

So maybe I did disrespect Primus a little, but I couldn't also help but feel that I had some legitimate concerns. Maybe I just didn't like the way Primus put it, and that's why I reacted the way I did.

"Well… if you are not seeing things or hearing voices at this point, then you should be okay," she said.

"What?"

"Well, dragons have a tendency to instill madness or fear on those who upset them. They can't do it to other dragons, but they can do it to us just by looking into our eyes," Purity said calmly. "If Primus wanted to do that, he already would have."

"Has it ever happened to you?"

"Oh, no. I walk on eggshells at this place. I'm just happy that Alpha has given me a place to stay."

"What do you mean?"

"Well, technically, I shouldn't be here."

"Why is that? I thought Alpha said that he would not turn any dragonoid away from training?"

"Well that's the thing. I'm not a dragonoid. I'm fully human. Alpha has been taking care of me since I was three."

I wasn't sure how to react to the news. I knew Alpha would be willing to train anyone, but then I also thought he was supposed to uphold the dragons' wishes of their secrecy from humans. I asked her why she had been here at such a young age. She explained that she really doesn't remember, because she was so young, but that Alpha found her wandering around near the valley. No one had ever come back to claim her or look for her. She was abandoned. Alpha allowed her to stay, but was punished for it, because he took in someone he could not train. As she was telling me the story, I saw tears sliding down her cheek.

"I'm sorry, you don't have to keep telling me if you don't want to," I said, trying to comfort her.

"It's okay," she responded. "I don't mind remembering the past, especially because of how wonderfully things have turned out for me. I have a place to call home, and a great teacher in Alpha. I get to see things that many humans don't get a chance to see, I learn history from the Son of War, I can read in four different languages and I'm working on a fifth. I am in great shape and I can defend myself. I really love it here."

I couldn't believe how she had switched such a negative situation into a positive one. These last couple of days, I had been angry because I had yet to meet my father. Purity, on the other hand, was abandoned by her entire family and she was able to overcome it. Her story lifted my spirits. After that, there was only one question that I had on my mind.

"What was Alpha's punishment for letting you stay?"

She wiped the tears from her face, and said with a slight chuckle, "His father fused him with Ryan Cooper. That is the body that Alpha is currently in, and that is why he badly imitates a California surfer."

Before I could say anything else, she asked me to go back with the others and eat something before we continued our training. On my way to lunch, I thought to myself about how all of us here have come to the Infernal Caverns from different paths. None of us knew that this was something we were going to do; it was an option that was put before us and we happened to choose it. I decided at that moment that it shouldn't matter what someone else tells us what our purpose is—even if they're right, we still have to live our lives in our own unique ways.

Chapter Five
The Destroyer

"I want you to close your eyes. Okay, now visualize your target. Just relax your mind and let your body sense the distance. Let the ground tell you where everything is. Do you feel the burning sensation in your chest?" Alpha asked.

"Yes," I responded.

"Good—now push that energy towards your arms. You should feel them get tense. Good, it looks like you got it. Now when I say go, I want you to unleash that power right underneath the target. Ready… set… *go!*"

I felt energy pulse through my arms as I raised them in the air, willing the ground underneath a wooden dummy to rise and knock the target forty feet high.

"Now volley him!" Alpha ordered. Just before the wooden dummy hit the ground, I willed the earth to rise again at a forty-five-degree angle, knocking the target left. Then I did it again, but this time to the right. I continued to volley the wooden dummy, watching as wooden limbs started flying everywhere. When I stopped, the only thing remaining of the doll was its torso.

"Good job, Cyclops," Alpha said encouragingly. "You're getting better at controlling your power, brah! It will only be a matter of time before you have full control."

It was nice to hear Alpha's encouragement. I had been training with him and the other trainees for two weeks now. He had been drilling us so we could learn how to control our powers, especially after I caused a small earthquake in the cavern by accident. A nightmare had triggered it; I still don't think I could've controlled it.

"Okay, so you're progressing well on manipulating the earth, but we still need to work on the quakes," Alpha said. "Maybe one of these days you could set us up for some mud surfing!"

"What is that?" I asked.

"I'm just joking, brah. It includes you causing a mudslide and riding it like a righteous wave. Sounds amazing, right?" I nodded my head, pretending that the idea was a good one.

"Oh, I almost forgot," Alpha said, "you have a visitor coming in fifteen minutes, so you should get cleaned up. We're just about done for the day anyway."

I asked Alpha who it was, but he ignored me and went on to help one of the other trainees. As I walked up the rocky slopes, I noticed some of the other students working on their powers.

Aurora was showing off as usual. She had pockets of air swirling around her in the form of three funnels. The rotating air picked up loose rocks, dirt, and anything else that got in its way. Much closer to the main cavern entrance, I saw James Braddock crushing large boulders with his bare hands. He punched one boulder so hard that it exploded on contact. It didn't crumble or split into many pieces. It literally exploded! What was interesting about James was his ability to breathe poisonous gas. His mother Jada is a green dragon, and from what I hear, the poisonous gas that they breathe is among the most lethal in the world. Once Alpha and James went down near the valley, and Alpha showed him how dangerous it was. He had James blow out the poison gas onto a flower—and immediately, it withered.

After getting cleaned up, I saw someone standing at the entrance of the cave. I immediately recognized who it was.

"Landon. How is my nephew?" Mr. Jensen asked.

"I'm good, thanks. Do you know how my mom is doing?" I asked.

"She is fine, actually. I have checked up on her a couple of times since you left, and she is keeping herself busy to make the days go by faster. She does miss you, my boy, but all is well with her."

The other students came in and passed by us as they were heading to the cleansers. Aurora gave me a funny look as if she were trying to ask, *who's that?* Then she also headed for the cleansers.

"Let us speak outside, Landon," Mr. Jensen requested.

Uncle Jensen told me that he wanted to check and see how things were coming along for me here with Alpha. He was also worried because his pilot had told him about our incident on the way to the Infernal Caverns. He claimed that someone who had a grudge against my father must have tried to kill me, but he couldn't figure out who else would've known that I was Drayden's son. He encouraged me to train hard so that I could start looking for my dad as soon as possible. I didn't think it was a good idea to mention that I had decided I wasn't going to search for my dad—so I didn't.

I asked my uncle if he would let Mom know that I was safe, and that I was going to visit her as soon as possible. He smiled and said that he would.

"Did you show the bloodlust berry to Alpha?" he asked.

I had completely forgotten about it. Once I changed clothes, I had never thought to go through my pockets and get it out.

"Umm… no, not yet," I mumbled.

"It is important, my boy. These berries are very rare, and some will pay a very high price for them."

With that said, Mr. Jensen gave me a warm smile, wished me luck, and was on his way.

Alpha came up to me not too long after my uncle had left.

"You must be an important person if you have a dragon coming here specifically to see you," he said.

I told him that he was just checking to see how I was doing. I mentioned that Mr. Jensen was my uncle, and that he was the one who told me to come here.

"Bane is your uncle?" he said with a surprised look.

"Who is Bane?" I responded.

"The man that just left, his name is Bane. Let me see... Oh yeah, why didn't I think of that before? Drayden and Bane were both sons of Ithacus. That was your grandfather's name. Anyway, it doesn't matter. I just completely spaced out why Bane might want to see you."

"Well, I have something that I was supposed to show you when I first arrived, but I forgot. My uncle just reminded me of it. Let me go get it."

I hurried off and went through my pants pockets. When I took the berry out, I examined the small, blood-red orb. I hope it hasn't gone bad, I thought to myself. I ran back to Alpha and showed him the bloodlust berry.

"Whoa! I haven't seen one of these in centuries," Alpha said admiring the orb.

"My uncle said you would tell me what to do with it?"

"Well, it depends on what you want. Dragons will buy these babies off you for a really good price."

"Why? What is so special about them?"

"They cure *flashbacks!* Dragons get them all the time."

"What's so bad about that?"

"Brah, imagine living life for hundreds and hundreds of years. A lot of stuff can happen in that time span. Now, imagine getting a constant reminder of specific events in your life, whether good or bad, all the time for the rest of your life.

It can drive you crazy! Don't worry, you'll know what I'm talking about eventually."

"What? Am I going to start getting flashbacks too?"

"Yeah, but I hear that it's never as bad for dragonoids because their life is short compared to dragons. Being reminded of something for fifty years isn't as bad as for five hundred or a thousand—although some dragonoids have informed me of having flashbacks that weren't their own, but of their dragon-parent. I'm not sure why that happens to some and not others, but it does happen."

Maybe I should save the berry for myself, just in case that starts happening to me, I thought. But then Alpha told me that Primus would exchange his blacksmithing services for the bloodlust berry. Primus has been responsible for creating the most legendary weapons that have ever been wielded—powerful weapons that would put the mighty Excalibur, created by Primus's father Kreon, to shame. There was no convincing needed. Gold or precious stones would make me rich, but not even treasure could buy a weapon from the blacksmith dragon Primus. I told Alpha that I wanted to see Primus and have him craft a weapon for me.

"I'll take you first thing in the morning," said Alpha.

The next morning, Alpha sent the others for the regular morning "Death Jog." This was what we called the series of laps up and down the rocky slopes from the Infernal Caverns to the valley below. We were up to fifty laps now. While they went running, Alpha and I went down to visit Primus. We had seen Primus a few more times since my first encounter with him, and I made it a point to be very respectful. Once reached Primus's working quarters, Alpha told him about the bloodlust berry and how I wanted him to craft a weapon for me. Primus smiled and agreed.

Primus asked me a series of questions to get a feel for what type of weapon would suit me best. He had me swing steel rods, slash with iron bars and thrust with a bronze prototype sword. Then he had me alternate, using the same weapons made with different metals. I also had to defend myself from various weapons Primus threw at me—an act that he really seemed to enjoy. Primus and I even sparred, making me look totally inadequate. Then after all the questioning and testing, Primus gave me his assessment. He said that my defensive movements would better suit a short, straight sword, which would support my attack style as well. He thought my slashing and thrusting were average and that I needed a weapon that would support my horrible battle form, although Primus did agree that some of the best warriors were free-style fighters.

In terms of what type of metal to choose for my weapon, Primus did not like the bronze, steel or iron. And because he thought I was a sloppy fighter, he wanted to craft something for me that would make up for this flaw.

"Why I have not thought of this before, I do not know, but I know exactly what to create that would suit your needs perfectly," Primus said confidently. "I am going to fuse the Gladius Hispaniensis with the Macuahuitl. It will be my finest work." Then he turned to Alpha.

"Alpha, because of the material I will be working with, do you have any spirits I could use for the forging?"

"I actually do, brah. In fact, Cyclops caught one his first day here. Right, Cyclops?" Alpha looked at me. I just nodded my head. Alpha continued, "I have him locked up in the dungeon room. I'll go get him for you."

Right before going, Primus asked me to show him the bloodlust berry. When I showed it to him, his eyes widened with excitement. He told me that he would need a couple of days to complete the sword and he would summon me when it was finished.

After breakfast the next day, Alpha said that he wanted to give us the rest of the morning to recharge. Then he said that by lunchtime he wanted us to form two teams. We would be given a series of challenges to compete in. The winning team would get to choose whatever they wanted for dinner for a whole week, which was a pretty big deal since the only thing that we had eaten since we'd been there were burritos. It didn't take us long to figure out what the teams were going to be. James Braddock, Shade Gambino, and Amy Jane Watkins teamed up, which left Aurora, Derek Foster and me on the other squad. Each team kept to themselves until lunchtime to speculate about what challenges lay ahead.

After lunch, Alpha and Purity led us to a meadow just outside the area known as Crooks Canyon. Green grass and small white flowers swayed in the breeze. The rays of the sun reflected off the brilliant little blossoms, creating a blinding sparkle. Purity set the bag she was carrying down on the grass, and Alpha separated us into our teams. He positioned us roughly fifty feet away from each other.

"This is where today's challenges will be held. You all have trained very hard up to this point, but this friendly competition will allow you to see where you stand amongst the others. I expect the best from every one of you—and everyone knows what's at stake."

"There will be a total of five challenges; four individual and one team," Alpha explained. "Each team will choose a person to participate in an individual challenge, but everyone on the team will take part in at least one. The challenges are as follows: sparring with no powers, sword-fighting duel, foot race, sparring with powers and the team challenge. We will begin with the first sparring contest. No powers will be allowed this round. You have thirty seconds to choose your contestant."

As soon as we huddled up, Aurora and Derek picked me to fight in the first sparring match. My opponent was James Braddock. We walked up to each other and shook hands. I stared down at his knuckles and immediately wished I had passed on this challenge. James had been crushing boulders with his bare knuckles. One punch from him and I knew I'd be history. Right before we were about to start, Alpha chimed in with the rules.

"Whichever one of you dudes can knock the other one down three times or knock him out completely wins the match."

Alpha said "Go!" and James immediately ran after me. His hands were up by his face in a boxing stance, waiting in anticipation for what I was going to do. My game plan was to catch him off guard and bring him down with a defensive takedown. He lunged at me, thrusting his right hand towards my face. I barely blocked it with my left forearm. Before I had time to think, his left hand was coming in for an uppercut. I managed to slightly move my head in the nick of time, feeling the breeze of his fist passing right by my ear. My only reaction then was to push myself away from him. With open palms, I slammed my hands against his chest and gave myself some breathing room.

He charged at me again, swinging his fists but always snapping them back in place to defend. I dodged a few jabs, some uppercuts and barely inched away from a right hook. I was so busy defending and dodging that I couldn't attack him. I had to try and bring him down—and soon. He came at me with a right cross, but I was able to sidestep to my left. I caught his arm and rotated it down, back towards his body. Then I was able to flip him onto his back.

"One point for Cyclops!" yelled Alpha.

I could hear my teammates cheering for me.

Before the next round began, he stared me down with those deadly blue eyes. I was trying to use James's aggressiveness against him, since he didn't seem to let up. He was back to jabbing at me, and trying to set himself up for the knockout punch. The force of his punches was so hard, even blocking them hurt. And the focus in his eyes was unsettling. He was determined to take me down. He sent another right hook towards my ribs, but I jumped back to evade the swipe. Then he rushed in and jabbed me with his left hand, square on my chest. The force knocked me back, but I stayed on my feet. He rushed in again, launching his right fist towards my face. I ducked underneath it and stuck a knee into his gut. I immediately followed that with an elbow to the back of his head, which sent him towards the ground, face first.

"Two points for Cyclops," Alpha shouted.

All I had to do was knock him down one more time and I would have the match. James got up slowly, his expression making me feel very uneasy. He was holding the back of his head where I'd elbowed him, but then went back to his boxing stance. He launched himself at me, hurling punch after punch and trying to get through my defense. Punches slid off my arms and shoulders as I placed my hands in front of my head to defend my face. Each time a punch slid off my body, it left a burning sensation. He was making me angry because I couldn't attack without letting up on my defense. Frustration and anger started to boil up inside me. James was relentless with his flurry of punches. Finally, I just snapped. I charged him head first, hitting his chest with the crown of my head. He hesitated and winced in pain. I saw an opening and launched a right hook aimed directly at his jaw. I missed. James had ducked underneath it and began firing away at my abdomen. I couldn't catch my breath. When I looked up, a cold, bony fist crashed into my face. Then everything went blank.

Aurora, Derek and Purity were huddled around me when I woke up. The good thing was that I felt no pain. The bad thing was… well, I had lost the fight.

"How long have I been out?" I asked.

Alpha answered, "Dude, for like an hour!" Alpha answered, shaking his head. "Purity gave you some lamb's blood, but you're not going to like the new shiner on your face."

I couldn't believe that I'd been out for so long. The rest of the group was waiting for me to wake up. The team challenge was next.

Alpha gave me a few minutes to speak with my team before we started. Aurora told me that she had won the sword-fighting duel against Amy Jane, but it had cost her some hair, which she wasn't too happy about. James Braddock had beaten Derek Foster in the foot race challenge, which consisted of running past the valley and up the rocky slope, then picking up a three-hundred pound sack filled with green chili, provided by Travis, and bringing it back to the meadow. Derek had to do back-to-back challenges because I was still out. He barely beat Shade in an all-out fire brawl, and now we were tied at two challenges a piece.

None of us knew what the team challenge was going to be. Alpha pulled a glass jar from inside the bag that Purity brought with her. I couldn't make out what was in it.

"Okay guys, this is it," Alpha said. "In this last challenge, the first team to catch Apollyon wins."

Alpha opened the lid on top of the glass jar and released a small creature. It looked like a blue snake with black streaks running down its side. It had wings, and four horns stuck out the back of its head. A pink, fork-like tongue lashed in and out of its tiny mouth.

"Apollyon is an *Amphiptere*, which is a winged dragon with no limbs. Yeah, he's small, but don't let his size fool you. He is very dangerous and a wicked trickster," Alpha said, excitement in his voice.

We were each given a small jar to catch Apollyon with. Alpha whispered something to the small dragon, then sent it off. The challenge was on.

Everyone rushed the tiny blue creature, trying to be the first to capture it in the jar. It flew low and in circles, as if it was taunting us. James and I were the first to get to it. We closed in on it from each side. He and I dove at the creature, but crashed into each other as it flew up and over us. Shade Gambino hurled a ball of fire towards it but was unpleasantly surprised as the fireball deflected harmlessly off the creature and directly back at him. Aurora shot a gust of air at it, but her blast came back and knocked her to the ground. Everyone quickly noticed that trying to use our powers against the tiny dragon was useless.

Then Apollyon dove directly at us, as we huddled together on the ground below. Everyone swung their jars wildly in the air hoping to catch it, but all we caught was air and the head of the person closest to us.

"Ooowww! Ouch!" everyone said at once, as we held our aching heads.

Behind you, something whispered in my ear. I immediately turned around and swung my jar, barely missing Aurora's face but hitting Derek hard on his cheek. Without hesitation, Derek shot a fireball at my chest, knocking me back ten feet.

"Why did you do that?" Aurora scolded Derek.

"He hit me first," replied Derek.

The other team moved away from Derek and Aurora, and huddled together to come up with an idea on how to capture the creature. I ran towards my team and, even though I wanted to deck Derek, I told him I was sorry. We needed to come up with a plan or we would lose the challenge.

"Let's try blasting him with air and fire at the same time to see if we can catch him off guard," Aurora suggested. We ran towards the other group, who were already swinging relentlessly at the creature while it weaved between them effortlessly.

ZAAAPPP! The creature let out an electrical shock that paralyzed the other team. Our team stared in shock as the other team stood frozen.

"Oh, man, he shoots electricity too," Derek said, kicking the dirt with his foot disappointedly.

"Okay, new plan," I said. "We still might be able to catch him off guard. Let's run after him as if we're trying to catch him. Then, when he's in between us, we separate. I'll push grass and dirt into his face to distract him while Derek shoots a fire blast at him from above. Try to hit his back, Derek. Aurora, you push him against the ground with a wind gust and I'll catch him while he's down."

We ran after the winged serpent and surrounded him. I could tell that he was daring us to catch him because he did not fly away. According to plan, the three of us circled the creature then jumped back. I willed the ground below the tiny dragon to explode, sending grass and soil flying. Derek shot a fire blast on top of the serpent. The blast slammed the dragon against the ground, but it still was able to let off an electric shock that blew Derek away. Aurora blasted the ground with strong winds and pinned the dragon.

The creature squealed, "Let me go!"

Just as I was about to scoop Apollyon into the jar, I felt a sharp pain in the center of my back. Shade had shot me with a fire blast, and stunned me just enough for Amy Jane to run up beside me and deliver a roundhouse kick to the back of my head. She dove at the creature and securely placed him in her jar. We had lost the challenge.

Alpha praised us for all our efforts and declared James, Shade, and Amy the victors. We made our way back to the caverns. James and I had to carry the three-hundred-pound bags of green chili back. Even though we were disappointed, Aurora, Derek, and I felt good about how we'd performed. Our teamwork ultimately led to Apollyon's capture, but we just couldn't capitalize on it. Alpha allowed me to examine Apollyon when we got back to the cave. I wondered how something so small could be so powerful and destructive. It was really an amazing creature. The tiny, scaled serpent lay coiled on the bottom of the jar, sleeping. Its wings were folded in, showing it was done for the day.

"I didn't think any of us would've been able to catch it," I said out loud.

"Well, you all seemed pretty determined," Alpha offered. "Apollyon's a bad little dude. It's surprising that you all were able to use your powers to catch him. You must have really surprised him."

"Yeah, what's the deal with that?" Aurora asked. "He was deflecting everything we threw at him."

"That's just one of Apollyon's abilities. I think Landon caught him by surprise and he let his guard down. Everyone did a great job."

Training resumed as normal for the next three days. Dinner was a little better, as James, Shade and Amy picked their favorite dishes to change things up from the normal burrito-fest we were used to.

On the fourth morning following the challenges, Alpha and I went back to Primus's lair and he presented me with my sword. The craftsmanship was absolutely incredible. It was a twenty-seven inch, pure black, double-edged short straight sword. The hilt was made of ivory, designed with ridges for my fingers to grip it securely. The cross-guard and pommel of the hilt were made of ruby, and the blade was made from pure obsidian. The sword was forged with the spirit of the wind demon, Soldier, so that the obsidian and ruby couldn't break or become brittle. The spirit's essence was trapped forever in my sword.

After I gave Primus the bloodlust berry, he explained that his inspiration came from two weapons—the Gladius Hispaniensis, literally meaning Hispanic, or Spanish Sword, a short, straight sword used by the ancient Gladiators, and the Macuahuitl, a wooden sword with edges made from the volcanic glass obsidian, designed by the Aztecs. The Aztec sword was capable of chopping off a horse's head with one swing, and the obsidian material was so sharp that some claimed you wouldn't even feel it cut into your flesh. The Gladius Hispaniensis design was for both stabbing and slashing, which Primus said would suit me well. He even gave me a scabbard, which held the blade of the sword when I wasn't going to use it. It was made of black leather, with a shoulder strap, and it was decorated with a frame made of iron.

My sword was awesome. It felt perfect in my hands.

"What will you name it?" Primus asked.

I had never thought of naming it.

"I don't know," I replied.

"Perhaps something that has inspired you?" Primus suggested.

I remembered the small but powerful *Amphiptere* that we fought a few days back, and said its name out loud, *"Apollyon."*

"Destroyer," Primus said. "That is what that name means in Greek. That is a good name for a weapon."

I liked the sound of that.

I glanced at my weapon in admiration, and said, "This is the destroyer—*Apollyon!*"

Chapter Six
Flashbacks

Have you ever walked into a room with the latest gadget or wearing the latest trend and everyone stared at you, wishing they could have what you have? It had never happened to me before, until I showed up to sword training with *Apollyon* in hand and the scabbard strapped across my shoulder. Everyone huddled up to me, admiring the craftsmanship. I was so protective over my sword. I didn't let anyone hold it. Purity asked the others to get back to their training, then she pulled me to the side.

"Very nice sword, Landon," she said, admiring Primus's artistry. "Would you like to test it out?"

I couldn't say no. I was dying to try it.

Purity led me a little bit away from the others where no one could see us. She pointed her sword at me and asked me to disarm her. I moved first and lunged towards her, thrusting my sword directly at her and anticipating that she would block my attack by swiping it to the side. As soon as she did, I spun around in the direction that she pushed my sword and led with a backhanded slash. She evaded my attack by flipping backwards. Then she launched herself towards me, slashing down from above. I lifted my sword and blocked her attack. Again, she slashed down but I slammed my sword against the flat of her blade and pushed it away. Immediately I lifted my sword towards her neck. I had won.

As I lowered my sword, Purity slashed at me again. I fell back, barely evading the swipe but now on the ground.

"Hey wait!" I complained.

Purity waited for me to get up, but the seriousness in her eyes told me that she was ready for round two. Again, she stabbed at me. I twisted to my right to avoid it, but she still managed to slap me on the chest with the flat of her blade. She swung again, slashing down, but I rolled away to my right. When I got up, she stabbed at me, but I blocked it and pushed her sword away. She came back with a backhanded slash of her own. I ducked, but she kicked me in the face and knocked me on the ground.

She had her sword a few inches away from my chest. I swung hard out of frustration and hit her sword. We both looked shocked as I left her holding only half the blade. The other half was sent flying in the air. The match was over.

She apologized for being such a bad sport and for being so rough with me. She wasn't used to losing, so she had taken her anger out on me.

"You're training me well," I said, and meant it. She smiled. We started walking back to where the others were, when I began to feel dizzy. It was a new sensation for me. It felt as if everything around me was moving—and it was. Purity was talking about some move we needed to work on, but I couldn't focus on what she was saying. I had never been this disoriented before. All of a sudden, I blacked out.

"Who are you? Why are you here?" a deep, low voice echoed across a cavernous wall.

Fire was the only thing that lit up the inside of the cave, as its rays reflected off a mountainous pile of gold.

"I am here to rid you from this earth, monster," another voice replied from a distance.

Walking deeper into the cave, a knight covered in silver armor appeared. He had a sword in one hand and a shield in the other.

"Leave me, for I have no quarrel with you. I have done nothing to your kind," the deep voice said.

"Show yourself, monster! And fight me!" replied the knight.

Out of the darkness came an enormous bronze dragon. It was bigger than any others I had seen. It was at least forty feet long, and equipped with all the basics—long snout, sharp teeth, talons, and a powerful tail. It seemed as if its long neck could stretch to the roof of the cave. On its head rested two horns that curved forward like bull horns. Six spikes, each a foot long, protruded out of its tail, and jagged, bony horns came out from its spine, from the top of the neck to its spiked tail.

The knight gasped in fear, and clutched his long sword with a firmer grip.

"I have been hired by the King to stop the wickedness you spread among his land," he said to the dragon." You will no longer steal his cattle or murder his people. You must pay for these crimes—and your punishment is death."

"You foolish man," the dragon roared in anger. "How dare you accuse me of such thing? I have never taken human life, nor have I hunted in your King's fields."

The knight stepped back in fear. Could this be true?

"I do not care if it was you! I was sent to slay a dragon—and a dragon I will slay."

The soldier cocked his arm back and threw his sword at the dragon's vulnerable, exposed underbelly. The sword flipped in the air at a tremendous speed and hit...

Purity?

"Snap out of it, Landon," Purity said as she shook me. "You went blank for like five seconds. Did you even hear what disarming technique I want us to practice?"

What just happened? It felt like I had just been transported back in time or something. I told Purity what happened but she didn't find it weird at all.

"That happens all the time to you dragonoids," Purity said. "Most of the time it's about something that you have experienced, although I have heard some dragonoids say that they have seen their dragon-parents' flashbacks. Maybe that's who you saw—your dragon-parent?"

"What does it look like when we're having a flashback?" I asked Purity.

She laughed a little bit and said, "It just looks like you're focusing really hard on something, and your face is stuck there for a few seconds."

"It felt longer than a few seconds for me, though," I replied.

"I'm not sure how it works, but it usually lasts only a few seconds in real time. You know the saying, when someone's life 'flashes before their eyes?' It only takes a person a split second to see their whole life. I think this works the same way. At least, that's how Alpha explained it to me."

That night, after the best shrimp and lobster pasta dinner ever, ordered by Amy Jane, Alpha sat us all down. After his usual pre-speech air guitar session, he was ready to chat to us about a request from the Elder Dragons. We were instantly intrigued.

"This would be the thirteenth year this request has been made by the Elder Dragons," Alpha said. "A special holding cell called the Dragon Sphere was stolen thirteen years ago, and it still hasn't been found. Dudes and chicks have tried searching for it before. Some have never been heard from again. Even the Elder Dragon Drayden searched for the Dragon Sphere, and no one has seen him since. If anyone is interested in taking on this mission, I'm supposed to have you on your way to see Blayne Crow within the next couple of days."

Alpha looked around the room. His gaze rested on me for a few seconds until Shade broke in, "What is the Dragon Sphere holding?"

Alpha responded, "Well brah, it's holding a dragon. The dragon's name is Aremas and he's a pretty bad dude. He can affect the climate—and I mean *really* affect it. He's what caused the last ice age, which made a huge mess. He was getting out of hand, so the Elder Dragons at the time sealed him into the blue orb."

"Well, the last Ice Age was a long time ago, so he must be dead by now?" Amy Jane asked.

"Old age doesn't kill this dragon. In fact, he only gets stronger with age. It's in his genes. And that is just some background information on why the Elder Dragons want the Dragon Sphere back. If someone were to find a way to release him, we would have one very angry and powerful dragon on the loose," Alpha said, with a look of concern.

"How do we know he hasn't been released already?" Aurora chimed in.

"Because we're not freezing or dying of heat," Alpha exclaimed. "No more questions. I think I have given you enough information so far to decide whether you'll take on this task or not. So I need to know now, who will go?"

I had a conflict within myself. I thought, *why would I go on a mission that no one has come back from for these creatures that wanted nothing to do with me until now?* But the excitement of the challenge was overwhelming, and I was warming up to the idea of possibly being able to find my dad. Before I was able to say anything, Aurora stepped up and said that she would go. Then Shade rose to his feet and took up the task as well. After a few seconds passed and no one else rose to their feet, I stood up and declared that I would go too.

The next day was all about preparation for those who were planning to meet with Blayne Crow. We were to meet him in the town of Lakeview, Oregon. Blayne Crow was an Elder Dragon himself. He owned a chain of blood banks in many big cities, but Alpha said that he enjoyed the small-town atmosphere in Lakeview the most. He also owned many slaughterhouses. Alpha warned us that Blayne had the worst temper of all of the Elder Dragons, and was very arrogant.

"Tomorrow, the three of you will walk until you reach the town of Likely, which is not far from here. A driver will be sent to pick you up there and take you to Blayne's Blood Bank. You will receive further instructions from him. Tonight we will throw a party for you guys for taking on this quest—and because our chances of seeing you again are slim," Alpha said, as if it wasn't a big deal. He made up for it right afterwards, though, by saying that he was going to let the three of us call home. I looked forward to that. It had been about three weeks since I'd left Mom, and I hadn't spoken with her since.

Right before dinner, Alpha handed me a cell phone that he pulled out of Travis and asked me to keep my conversation short. I dialed the house number and waited.

"Hello?" The sound of Mom's voice sent a rush of emotion through me. She was the constant in my life. When I woke up she was there. When I needed something she provided it. When I was sad she comforted me.

"Hey Mom. It's me," I replied, with a soft, strained voice.

"Hi honey, it's good to hear your voice. How are you?"

"I'm good. I've been training a lot. I've missed you so much. Is everything okay with you?"

"Well, it's a bit lonely here, but I manage. Xavier comes every now and then and says hello. I miss you too, sweetheart. I'm just glad that you're safe. Your uncle has come over a couple of times to keep me company as well."

"Please let Xavier know I said hi. I don't have very much time to speak with you, but I wanted to let you know that I'm leaving tomorrow to try and find Dad. I mean, the trip isn't to necessarily find him, but I'm going to search for him anyway."

"Just be careful, Landon, please. I want to see you soon."

"I'm sure I'll be able to see you very soon," I said, hesitating slightly. "I'd better go now. I love you."

"Love you too, honey," she managed to finish, as if her throat had completely closed on her after that.

I wanted to tell Mom everything that I had experienced and learned so far, but there was too much to say in such a short time. Speaking with her started to give me doubts, though, about the quest. I didn't want to leave her alone much longer—or possibly forever. Was I doing the right thing? The good news was that I wasn't the only one feeling that way. Aurora had second thoughts as well after talking with her dad. But both of us were determined to follow through on the commitment we had made.

Everyone was having a good time during the party that night. Travis provided a karaoke machine, and Amy Jane showed off her singing skills. I was surprised. She was a really good vocalist and worked really well with Alpha air-guitaring in the background. The food was incredible. We had shrimp skewers, steaks, ribs, grilled chicken, potato salad, and mac-and-cheese. The steaks reminded me of home, and how Mom prepared them for me. I ate so much I started to feel dizzy.

A least that's what I initially thought was causing mc to feel dizzy.

The sword flipped furiously towards a giant bronze dragon, but with a powerful shift of the hips, the dragon swung his tail and slapped the sword in mid-air. The metal flew twenty feet and slammed against the cavern wall. Then the bronze dragon shifted his shoulders, took a deep breath and let out a powerful stream of fire. The knight raised his shield and knelt on one knee. The pressure of the dragon's fire almost knocked the warrior back, but instead he used all of his might to hold his ground. The dragon moved forward. He was fast, and gave the knight no time to collect his thoughts. He swung his powerful, spiked tail at the man, who rolled away just in time to avoid it.

The cavern shook as the dragon roared in frustration. Rocks fell from its roof and almost hit the knight. He darted for his sword, lying near the cave wall. He picked it up and charged at the dragon's tail. With a flick, the dragon knocked him onto his back and sent the nobleman's sword and shield flying out of his hands. Then the dragon slammed his powerful foreleg against the knight. The sound of metal being crushed echoed off the walls as the knight wailed in pain and fought to catch his breath. His screams were unforgettable and terrifying. Grief immediately replaced the anger that had filled the dragon's eyes, as he looked down and saw the man struggling to breathe.

"Forgive me," whispered the dragon in a low and somber tone. He inhaled deeply, only to exhale a burst of fire that engulfed the knight.

I couldn't tell if the knight screamed or struggled. The fire was too thick and brilliant to see through, and the crackling was too loud.

Everything was so real. It felt as if I were standing ten feet from where the whole scene was going down. The fire from the dragon's breath radiated an unbearable amount of heat, and the stench of burning flesh filled my nostrils. Muscles on the dragon's body flexed every time he took a deep breath and exhaled flames on the knight's body. Pretty soon, the only thing that remained was a pile of ash and liquid metal. Then the dragon walked over to the knight's sword and shield and picked them up. He threw the sword onto his pile of gold and was about to toss the shield until he noticed something. I couldn't tell what he was looking at, but his eyes were deeply fixed on something on the inside of the shield.

The dragon dropped the shield.

"No! This can't be! Why did no one tell me!" he uttered in horror.

I quickly glanced at the shield. Near the handle was an insignia:

The small symbol was carved deep into the metal. I had no idea what it meant, but one thing was clear—whatever the symbol represented was enough to devastate the mighty bronze dragon.

No one even noticed that I had just snapped back to reality. They were still eating and having a good time. What were these flashbacks trying to tell me? Were they intended to show me something for my benefit, or were they just there to haunt me? I wondered if any of the other dragonoids were having them. So many questions filled my head. But what really had me concerned was the feeling that the dragon that had killed the knight was my father.

"Hey Landon, let loose a little. You don't have to look so serious," Aurora said, walking up to me. I managed a smile.

"I just went into a daze," I said. 'This whole idea of finding the Dragon Sphere is throwing me off a bit."

"Well, we can focus on the serious stuff tomorrow, okay?" Aurora said gently.

I nodded my head in agreement. She grabbed my arm and pulled me toward the others, who were cheering as Amy Jane was finishing her song. It made me sad to think that I was going to be leaving the Infernal Caverns. At the same time, I was also happy that I'd been able to meet some really great people. I tried not to let the flashbacks of the past and the uncertainty of the future get to me that night. I was determined to have fun with my friends.

Chapter Seven
Blood Bank

The time to search for the Dragon Sphere was at hand. We finished saying our goodbyes to the rest of the group, and then Alpha sent them off to train. My head was in the clouds after Purity gave me a big hug. I don't even remember if I even said goodbye to her. I do remember that she said, "Come back in one piece," which my mind translated as *come back safely to me*. I noticed Alpha giving me a vicious stare as the rest of the group left. I stopped smiling instantly. Then he told us that we would need to go to a small café that was on Highway 395. We would get picked up there and be on our way. He went to Travis the fire and pulled out a cell phone, and told us that we could use it to call the cavern any time we wanted. All we had to do was hit send and we would be connected straight to here. The only bad thing about the phone was that we couldn't call anyone else.

Aurora, Shade and I left the Infernal Caverns and were on our way to the small town of Likely. Each of us carried a sleeping bag on our back, and I had my sword *Apollyon* safely secured in my shoulder strap. The sun was bright and the morning was cool as we headed southeast to catch our ride to Lakeview. Something was bothering me, though. I couldn't help but feel I had to watch Shade closely. I wasn't sure of his motives for wanting to join this quest, and quite frankly, I wasn't sure about him.

"I wonder how big this Dragon Sphere thing is?" Shade asked.

"I'm not sure," I said, "Hopefully not too big. It is holding a dragon, though."

"I'm sure we can ask Mr. Crow," Aurora answered.

As we continued walking, Aurora told us about a time when she was in elementary school and sneezed on her friend. She had sent the poor girl flying ten feet across the classroom. Her voice sounded sad as she was saying it, even though she was forcing a smile. Shade laughed his head off and I couldn't help but chuckle as well.

"It *is* funny," Aurora said. "We have been different ever since we were born. Yet when we're around others just like us, we can feel normal again."

"Who's to say they're not the different ones and we're the normal ones?" Shade responded. "I mean, why did we have to be laughed at and get called horrible names? Maybe we couldn't stand up for ourselves when we were smaller, because our powers weren't developed yet. But that has changed now. We don't have to take anything from them anymore. We don't have to feel inferior."

I sensed a rising hostility in Shade that made me even more nervous.

"Who are you talking about?" I asked him.

"Humans," he retorted.

"But you are half-human and your mom is fully human," I said. "You can't look at them as if they're an entirely different species."

Shade shot a fiery look at me.

"I am what I am. And to be honest with you, I don't even think my mom is human. She was cold and heartless, and didn't even want me. The fact that she was human makes me want to distance myself from them all the more."

"You shouldn't blame everyone else for one person's actions."

"I don't, but I'm just saying that I'm *not* human. Humans can't shoot fire out of their hands or jump fifteen feet in the air or run thirty miles an hour."

"That's true, but you're not a full dragon either. In fact, we don't look anything like dragons. We look like humans because we *are* human. We just have special qualities from our dragon-side."

Shade didn't respond. Aurora looked like she wanted to say something but decided against it. And I was thinking to myself how much of a hypocrite I was. Just a few weeks back, I had argued with Primus on how evil this world was, and now I was telling Shade Gambino not to blame everyone else for a single person's actions. I'm glad he didn't bring that up, because I wouldn't know what to say. I was starting to see things differently.

All of us were silent the rest of the way, until Aurora spotted a limousine parked on the side of the road.

"That must be the driver that was sent to pick us up," Aurora said happily.

She was right. The café was on one side of the highway, and the driver had parked on the opposite side of the road. As we approached the limo, the driver stepped out and asked if we were traveling to Lakeview, Oregon. We told him we were, and he opened the door for us. Just like that, we were on our way to see Blayne Crow.

The driver spoke through an intercom and told us that Lakeview was roughly seventy miles away. He mentioned that we were going to have breakfast with Mr. Crow, which sounded good because my stomach was starting to argue with me. He also advised that we only speak to Mr. Crow when spoken to. I remembered Alpha telling us that Blayne Crow had a horrible temper, so I didn't think the driver was a jerk for giving us that advice. The driver turned up the music for us and played some eighties heavy metal. We all laughed. We were instantly reminded of Alpha.

During our ride to Lakeview, Aurora asked me how my parents met. I felt bad saying that I didn't know, but that was the truth. I'd honestly never asked my mom. Aurora explained that her parents met while her dad was stationed in Alaska. While off base, her dad saw her mom Shea get attacked by two guys and he ran to help her. He was surprised to find, though, that she could easily take care of herself. She had broken one guy's nose and the other's arm. They both ran away in pain. Aurora's dad checked on Shea the next day to make sure she was okay, and the rest was history. They fell in love. Interestingly enough, Aurora's mom had shown Lieutenant Meadows her true form from the beginning, and still, he wanted to be with her. I thought that was kind of creepy. Of course, I didn't tell Aurora that.

We were all surprised when the limo came to a stop.

"We are here," said the driver through the intercom.

We couldn't believe how time had zipped by. We didn't even get to see the town of Lakeview. The driver opened our door and we stepped out in front of a building.

"How fitting," Shade said. "A big, red building for a blood bank."

The driver guided us to the main entrance, which had two red Greek-like columns holding up part of the roof. Once we pushed through the revolving doors, we were again astonished. I had never been inside a blood bank, but I had never pictured it like this. The walls in the reception area were two-tone, with silver on the top half and black on the bottom. Three long, black leather couches filled the waiting area. The floor was made of marble. Four black Greek-style columns stood in a single line, leading the way to the receptionist. The air was cool inside.

Our driver went up to the receptionist, a short woman with thick glasses and pointy ears, and asked her to take us to

Blayne Crow's office. She guided us through a long hallway to the elevator. Then she got in and hit the button to the lower level. A few seconds later, the elevator door opened and the receptionist told us that she couldn't go with us any further. She pointed to a door about twenty feet away. She said that we needed to press the button off to the right and the door would open for us. The hallway was lit by a few lights and the area was very dim. *So, was this the modern-day dragon's lair?* I thought. We walked up to the door and pressed the button, noticing the camera above the door that was aimed directly at us. A few seconds later, the door slid open.

Mr. Crow's underground office was huge. The left side of the room had an enormous shelf filled with thick, old books. On the opposite side, a large map of the world covered the entire wall. Four beautiful globes on elegant wooden stands were placed at each corner of the room, and straight ahead was a large desk with a rich cherry finish and a man sitting in a big, black leather chair. Stacks of paper were piled all over the desk. The man didn't even say hello; he just signaled for us to take a seat, pointing to the front of the desk where there were three black chairs. The man was searching for something on his desk.

"There it is," he said after lifting a stack of papers. He pulled out a debit card that was hiding under the pile and handed it to me. "Here you go. There are two thousand dollars in the account, so use it wisely. When you take money out of the ATM, remember the password is the year of my birth—1021."

"Wow, you're almost a thousand years old?" Aurora asked excitedly.

"You will be given a chance to speak soon," the man responded sternly. Aurora's excitement diminished.

He was wearing a black business suit with gray pin stripes. He had on a dark red tie, with **B.C. Inc** printed in black bold letters on the front. He had bright, piercing blue eyes and short, light-blonde hair. He reminded me of the world's oldest military recruit with his crewcut and serious demeanor.

"What is the money for?" I asked.

"Let me be clear, there will be a time for questions soon. For now, I will speak and you will listen. The money is my gift to you to help you on your quest. Use it for food or anything else that might aid you. Now, to real business," he said as he pressed a button on his desk. "We are counting on you to retrieve the Dragon Sphere. One of the Elders set out to look for it some time ago and has not returned. This leads me to two conclusions. The first is that a very powerful force must be holding the sphere. The second is that we are all in grave danger if someone is willing to fight an Elder Dragon for the Sphere. It seems, however, that the dragon Aremas has still not been awakened, or else we would have already felt his wrath. However, each day that passes is another opportunity for whoever has the Sphere to release him. None of us know where he might be, but I *will* tell you about my last encounter with the Elder Dragon Drayden."

Someone knocked on the door. Blayne pressed a button on his desk, the door slid open and a waiter came in with a cart of food. A few other employees entered and set up a small square table with chairs on each side. Blayne got up and walked over to the table and sat down. Then he asked us to join him. As soon as we sat, the waiter placed plates before us with a juicy, thick steak, fluffy eggs and seasoned potatoes. Then the waiter and the rest of the other employees left us alone.

Blayne told us that his last encounter with my dad was when he set off to find the Dragon Sphere, thirteen years ago. My dad had his suspicions that there had been more than just one person involved in taking the orb. A dragonoid would have been noticed wandering the temple of the Elder Dragons, so my dad assumed that a dragon was the thief. He also had his suspicions that a dragonoid must have been involved in keeping the Sphere hidden. Blayne explained that my dad had given the only clue he'd ever found to Zana, one of the other Elder Dragons, to hold for safekeeping.

"Even to this day, she has not revealed the clue to anyone," Blayne said. He paused a moment. I could see the anger rise in him and then dissipate. Then he continued.

"From here, you will want to make your way to Santa Monica, California," he said. "You must speak with Zana. When you get there, you will have to look up her address. Look for it under Zana Reed. I do not know where she lives and, quite frankly, I am too angry to speak with her to find it out! I don't understand why she just won't show the clue that Drayden found to those who are trying to help. Anyway, see what you can do to convince her to show it to you."

"How do we get to Santa Monica from here?" Shade asked.

Blayne flashed an irritated look at him, "I have already arranged for my driver to take you. The trip is roughly eleven to twelve hours—which should be plenty of time for you all to rest up, because you will need it. I will not provide any more money or transportation for you after this. It will be up to you to seek alternate transportation from that point on. I do, however, have a gift for each of you."

Blayne got up from the table and walked over to his desk. He pulled open the center drawer and picked up something inside it. Then he passed out silver chains to us. Each chain had a small silver fire charm dangling from it. When he put the chain in my hand, I felt my skin tingle.

"These are magical charms that should help you if you are ever caught in a bind. They only work if they are touching your skin, and the magic will wear out after two hours of use. Use them sparingly—you never know when you may need to draw on their power. Put them on now and move towards the office door. Let's try them out."

We had no clue how a silver chain and charm would aid us on our quest, but none of us were going to question the Elder Dragon.

A blinding flash lit up the room. Instantly, Blayne Crow had transformed into a monstrous dragon. His scales were a deep, dark red. He was terrifying. His long snout had one long, thick whisker on each side that hung down about two feet. He had two long horns that stretched away from the back side of his head. His wings were rubbing against the roof of the office, even though he was crouching down as far as he could. His belly was touching the ground and his massive legs were bent so that he wouldn't crash through the ceiling. His tail was thick and long, with a row of sharp plates that trailed from the tip of his tail to the top of his neck. A strong odor of sulfur and smoke filled the room. Without hesitation, Blayne shot out a stream of fire at us.

None of us could react in time. We were instantly engulfed in the flames. But for some reason, the pain of the flames centered solely on my foot. I stared down, expecting to find my foot completely charred, but then I realized that the fire was not burning me. I glanced through the flames and noticed that Aurora had stomped on my foot in an attempt to brush the fire off of her. Shade had stopped, dropped, and rolled because he didn't realize that he wasn't on fire. I settled Aurora down before she stomped on my foot again.

"None of us are burning!" I shouted to her through the loud crackle of fire. Shade Gambino noticed it as well, and lifted himself up off the floor. Blayne Crow had given us fire-repellent charms.

We were blinded by another flash. Blayne had transformed back into a human. Smoke sizzled off his clothes.

"You should take those off now," Blayne directed, as he pointed at the charm around my neck. "But before you go, let me offer you a drink."

He pulled out four wine glasses from under his desk, and a crystal jar with dark-red liquid in it. I was pretty sure that the dark-red liquid wasn't Kool-Aid. Blayne poured a small amount in each glass and asked us to take one.

"Lamb's blood is the tastiest, but human blood is a decent substitute," he said, admiring his wine glass. "Owning a blood bank has its perks for a blood connoisseur like myself. May you have a safe and speedy journey."

Blayne lifted his glass. Hesitantly, Shade, Aurora, and I did the same and drank along with Blayne.

"Awww!" the Elder Dragon said in delight. "Jeffrey Hammond, 1981!"

I was surprised. The blood actually tasted very sweet and gave me a lot of energy.

"Be careful how much blood you consume," Blayne warned. "If someone ever offers you more than what I offered, be alert—for they are trying to harm you. Dragons can consume however much they wish without any side effects, but not dragonoids. You will lose strength and get sick if you have more than what I have given you in a day. A small drink is meant to reenergize you, but that is all. Any final questions before I send you on your way?"

"Who is Jeffrey Hammond?" I asked.

"He was the human who donated the blood we were drinking. This was his blood, drawn in 1981. Good year. Blood does not taste better as it ages, the way wine does, but being in the freezer for years seems to make it that much more satisfying. At least to me it does. Any other questions?"

No one said anything.

Blayne wished us good luck and sent us on our way. Then we met with his driver outside the building. I expected the driver to look upset that he had to travel all the way to Santa Monica. Instead, he seemed very happy as he opened the door for us.

"Someone is getting a fat bonus for this trip," Shade commented, as he got into the car.

The driver didn't pay attention. He shut the door behind him, grinning widely. The limousine started and we took off.

Blayne Crow didn't seem to be as much of a grump as everyone made him seem to be. Sure he was bossy, but he was also very helpful. I mean, it was cool that he gave us money, fire charms, and a tip about healthy daily blood consumption. I wondered if he knew that I was Drayden's son. I wasn't sure whether that was information that I should hand out to just anyone. Either way, I had this strong sense that we were moving in the right direction. And I couldn't help but feel that the quest would be smooth sailing from here on.

Boy, was I wrong.

Chapter Eight
A Date with Destiny

One thing that we had to discuss before we came face to face with Zana was to come up with a way to convince her to give us the clue my dad had found. But even with so much time on our hands, we weren't able to come up with anything.

"We can tell her that you're Drayden's son, and maybe that'll be enough for her to give it to us," Shade said.

"I guess that's worth a try. It's not as if we've been able to come up with anything else," Aurora responded.

I didn't really think that walking up to Zana and saying that I should have the clue because I was Drayden's son would be very effective. We weren't making any progress with a plan, and we managed to change the subject every opportunity we had. We'd been riding all day, except for a few stops to use the restroom, eat, and pump gas. I noticed that at the last stop we made, the driver was stocking up on *Lightning* energy drinks. He seemed determined to get us to Santa Monica before the night was over.

"The last time I was in a car for this long I was five," Shade broke through a silent moment. His tone was somber as if remembering something painful. "It was one of my first memories. Mom told me that we were going to visit Dad somewhere on the west coast, but I don't remember where. She was actually nice to me for most of that trip. It was one of the few times that she made me feel loved."

Aurora and I exchanged glances at each other but dared not interrupt. Shade looked out the window and watched the blur of asphalt and trees speed by.

"I remember we stopped at a bakery, and I had this deliciously sweet cherry pie," he continued. "Even before we went into the bakery, the scent grabbed my attention. I didn't know it was cherry but I knew that I wanted it. She got it for me."

Shade paused and closed his eyes for a moment. The emotional pressure seemed to seep out of his ears. I felt a heaviness hit the cabin that made sucking in air a chore. He then continued his memory.

"Just because I wanted it, she got it for me," he repeated with a heightened voice. Then he cleared his throat. "After that, I remember playing on a beach, and then visiting Dad for a few hours. We didn't stay very long because Mom got upset over something. It was probably because he didn't really want us there. They argued some until she just picked me up and we left. I haven't seen him since. Mom would always say that I was his mini-clone. Maybe that's why she couldn't look at me in the end, because I reminded her of him too much."

Shade took a deep breath.

"Do you know why I like to paint?" he asked us, turning his attention away from the window.

"Because it takes your mind off of things?" Aurora offered.

"No, it's actually the opposite of that. It's because it reminds me of things. I paint pictures of the beach because it reminds me of that moment with mom. With each stroke of the brush, I can remember how mom's hair danced in the breeze—and capture her moment of kindness forever. Those moments can get stripped from you all too quickly as they happen in real time, but when you're painting they can last… last forever. I can reflect on that, and not always feel as abandoned as she made me feel."

"You don't have to feel like that. You have friends now," I said. "You have us."

"Thanks, but I'm not sure I'm the 'friend' type of person. I've gotten used to being a loner. Both of you are cool and so are the others back at the caverns, but I'm better off by myself. It's safer that way."

"Safer?" Aurora questioned nervously. I wondered if Aurora was thinking the same thing I was: *Safer for whom, him or us?*

Shade didn't answer. He just looked out the window and ignored us. Aurora and I gave him his space. It's easy to push away from people when the dysfunction in the family is at an all-time high. *But everyone needs friends*, I thought to myself, *especially when we're going through a tough situation.* I remembered how Xavier helped me through my grandmother's death. I was extremely close with her, and when she passed, it felt as though someone had snatched my heart out of my chest and stomped on it. Even Mom appreciated Xavier's being there to help light up our dinners and distract us from the pain. Xavier would always say, "Laughter is the best medicine." There was a lot of truth to that.

Shade and Aurora had both fallen asleep. I stayed up remembering highlights of the football games I'd played in, back in my "normal life" in high school. I wondered to myself if I would've joined football if I knew then that I was a dragonoid. I'm pretty sure I still would have. I love the sport so much. It wasn't fair to the rest of the players for me to be on the team, but to me it was all about having fun.

When night came, it seemed as if we were the only ones on the road. I couldn't see any other lights. We were lucky to be riding in a limo, so that we could have space to stretch out. Shade was sitting near the wall that separated us from the driver. He had his back towards the driver, facing Aurora and me. All the traveling was making me lightheaded. I felt unbalanced, even though I was sitting down. Then everything turned white.

A man ran through the woods feverishly. He looked back as if something was following him, but nothing was there. His shoulder-length brown hair was drenched from sweat, and it had small branches and leaves tangled in it. He looked familiar, with his muscular build and tan-colored skin. His blue tunic was covered with burn marks as if he had just run through a fire. He stopped for a moment to catch his breath—resting his hands on his knees and sucking in as much air as his lungs would allow. He paused long enough for me to know for sure who he was.

A loud whistling rushed past his ear, and something made a cracking noise as it hit the trunk of a tree. An arrow had missed him by an inch. The man sped off as if he were running a marathon and the starting gun had just sounded. Tree branches slapped him as he passed, and scrapes were accumulating on his face and arms. Finally, he saw an entrance to a cave.

He hurried into the darkness.

He knelt down and waited. In a flurry, a mob of people shouted, and with angry expressions, jetted by the cave. There were nearly thirty of them, equipped with swords, bows and arrows, and torches. They passed by just as quickly as they came. The man got up and walked further into the cave until a faint light ahead caught his attention. The cave shook suddenly. Stalactites fell from the roof of the cave, nearly impaling him. He ran ahead until he entered into an open area. There he saw a bronze dragon. It stood just twenty feet away from him, as if it were waiting for him to enter.

"I do not see why you allow them to chase you like this. You could easily dispose of them if you transformed," said the bronze dragon.

"*I will not kill another human!*" *responded the man.* "*I broke the pledge I made to myself, and I dishonored my family—especially you. I will not let that happen again.*"

The bronze dragon looked away in disgust. Smoke left his nostrils and trailed to the roof of the cave.

"*You must leave now,*" *he demanded, with a hint of rage.*

The man was saddened. As he turned to walk away, he whispered, "*Forgive me, brother.*"

In response, the bronze dragon, full of anger, charged towards the man. The man jumped in the air and transformed into a giant bronze dragon himself, although he was much bigger. The smaller dragon swiped and scratched the other on the right side of his face, leaving blood dripping from three claw marks underneath his right eye. The larger dragon roared in pain, and then roared at his attacker.

"*I will never forgive you,*" *shouted the smaller dragon.*

The larger dragon lifted his head high and stood his ground. He didn't say a word. The smaller dragon did not intimidate him.

"*I will leave you now,*" *said the larger bronze dragon, breathing heavily.* "*I truly am sorry for what I have done.*"

For a moment, it seemed as if the giant dragon was going to say more—but then it transformed back into a human and left the cave.

I snapped out of the flashback as I felt Aurora's head lean against my shoulder. She was asleep. The vehicle was still moving, and it was still dark outside. I figured that not much time had passed, given what Purity had said about flashbacks usually lasting only a few seconds in real time. I was trying to connect the pieces of the flashbacks puzzle together. I figured the larger bronze dragon was my dad. The smaller dragon had to be my uncle Bane. But I didn't understand why my uncle was so angry with him, or why my dad asked for his forgiveness. I decided to drop the issue and get some rest. I had a feeling I was going to need it.

I woke with a start. The car wasn't moving anymore, and it was still dark outside. Shade had curled up into the fetal position on the seat in front of us. He was snoring loudly. I looked over and noticed Aurora hugging my arm. Her head was still on my left shoulder. I tried not to move so that I wouldn't wake her up.

Suddenly, the door flew open.

"We're here," said the driver.

"What time is it?" I asked.

He looked at his watch and said, "4:35 in the morning."

Shade and Aurora woke up. Aurora noticed how she was holding on to me and pushed herself away immediately.

"What's the matter with you?" she said, looking embarrassed.

"What do you mean?"

"Why did you let me fall asleep like that?"

"I fell asleep too, and I didn't notice it until now. Plus, you were the one hugging me so don't be mad at me."

"Don't act like you both didn't like it," Shade teased.

The driver urged us to get out of the limo and stretch our legs. The weather was nice, even if it was 4:30 in the morning. A soft breeze cooled us down. From where we were, the beach was just a short walk away. The driver asked us if we wanted him to drive us to a hotel, but we decided to just stay at the beach and relax there until the sun came up. There were only a few hours left before it rose anyway, so there was no need to spend the money on a room. We got our sleeping bags and I put my sword over my shoulder. We said goodbye to the driver and walked towards the beach.

After crossing a bridge that stretched over a highway, we reached the beach. The view was amazing. The bluish grey moon shimmered over the dark water, and waves crashed gently onto the beach. We took off our shoes and walked on the soft sand to a comfortable spot about twenty feet away from the water. The sand was cool and the atmosphere made me feel relaxed. We dropped our bags and used them as pillows as we lay down.

"Sorry for falling asleep on your shoulder earlier," Aurora apologized.

"Don't worry about it. No big deal."

"I shouldn't have gotten upset with you. It wasn't even your fault. I was just embarrassed."

"Friends are allowed to be upset with each other. I won't hold it against you this time," I said with a grin.

The truth was that it made me feel good having her head on my shoulder. It gave me some butterflies in my stomach, but that was just because I haven't had too many girls, especially pretty ones like Aurora, hold on to me the way that she had. The last time, in fact, was during my homecoming dance in the ninth grade. I had taken Stephanie Parker, and we'd had a great time. Of course, during the slow dance she managed to ease her head onto my shoulder as we swayed to the music. I definitely enjoyed it.

The soft breeze pushed strands of Aurora's hair in front of her face as she stared off into the ocean. Her green eyes lit up in the night sky. I turned away quickly because I didn't want her to think that I was gawking at her. I looked over at Shade, who had his eyes closed and arms crossed as he snoozed. It was an odd scene, two guys and a girl on the beach, relaxing on the sand in the early morning, waiting silently for the sun to come up. As soon as I rested my head on my sleeping bag, I dozed off too.

It seemed like only a few minutes had passed when I felt the hot air hitting my face. Even with my eyes closed, I could tell the sun was up. I lifted my eyelids just a little bit, and was blinded. The sun's warm, slimy rays beat down on my right cheek.

Wait a minute. Slimy? Immediately, I sat up and noticed that a large golden retriever was licking me. It was staring at me and barking. Aurora and Shade woke up as the dog continued.

"SADIE!" a girl shouted from a distance.

The dog kept barking. Then she jumped on me. My face was like her favorite lollipop at that moment, and she didn't stop licking me. The girl ran over and pulled the retriever off me. The girl was pretty, with long, dark-brown hair, olive skin, and blue shimmery eyes that looked like the ocean. She was wearing blue shorts and a pink t-shirt that had *Party Girl* written on it. She wore headphones and her hair was pulled up in a ponytail.

She took off her headphones. "Sorry, my dog's a spaz," she said.

"It's okay," I replied.

"She really seems to like you, which is weird, because she doesn't usually like guys."

"All animals seem to like me a lot," I said, wishing that I hadn't. But I couldn't think of anything more clever than that, after only being awake for a minute or two.

"I guess so. Sorry to bother you guys. I should go now."

She put a leash on Sadie, waved goodbye and continued jogging on the beach.

We decided that we should find a phone book so that we could look up Zana's address. We walked towards some shops in hopes of finding one. I felt awkward carrying my sword with so many people around. Everyone was looking at me as if I was going to attack them. Younger kids pointed at me and asked their moms if they could see my sword. After some time wandering around, Aurora asked a man in an ice cream stand if he had a phone book. To our surprise, he did. He let us use it, but Zana Reed wasn't in it. If Blayne Crow hadn't been so stubborn, he would have gotten us that information. Now we were in Santa Monica and we had no way of finding out where Zana lived.

"Wait!" Aurora said. "Maybe Alpha knows. We should call him?"

Shade pulled out the cell phone Alpha had given us and handed it to Aurora. I had completely spaced that we had the phone in our possession! *We should've just used that, before going around and asking to use the phone book*, I thought, remembering the looks I got as I walked with the sword on my back.

Aurora pressed "send," and the phone rang.

"Hello?" Alpha answered, loud enough for me to hear him.

"Alpha, it's Aurora."

"Oh, Miss Green Eyes, calling back already. I thought it would take longer for you guys to ask for help."

"We just need some information. Do you have the address to Zana's place?"

"Sure… hold on. Okay, here it is. She is in Santa Monica, California. What I would give to go there right now. They have righteous waves there."

"We know. We are already here."

"Nice! Anyway, here is the address. She is at…" Alpha lowered his voice, and I wasn't able to hear him anymore. Then he spoke up again, "Remember that you kids are on a mission, Green Eyes. Try not to get distracted by the beach—even though I totally would."

"We won't."

"Okay, see ya!" Alpha hung up and Aurora ran over to the ice cream man and asked him for directions to the address

Alpha had given her. He directed us back to the beach, and told us to head north and we would find it. We were lucky we didn't have to stray too far from the ocean. As we headed north, we saw some townhomes further up.

"That must be it," Aurora said.

Beautiful, luxurious townhomes equipped with Jacuzzis and balconies sat right on the beach. The setup was amazing, and the homes, which were a few stories high, had big panoramic windows. Suddenly, I heard barking closing in from behind me. When I turned around, a large dog jumped on top of me and knocked me to the ground. It was Sadie.

After I got drenched in dog saliva again, her owner came to my rescue. She explained to me again that this was unusual behavior for Sadie. She didn't understand why the golden retriever liked me so much.

"She's too old to be jumping on people," the girl added.

She introduced herself. Her name was Destiny, and she lived in the townhomes that we were admiring.

We asked her if she knew a woman by the name of Zana Reed, and to our surprise she did. In fact, she was Zana's daughter. We couldn't believe how lucky we were.

"Why are you looking for my mom?" Destiny asked, rolling her eyes in the process. She looked almost bored, as if she had been through this many times before.

We explained our story to her, and how she holds a clue that would help us continue our search.

She obviously wasn't surprised about the whole thing. She simply said, "Yeah, well, I figured you were looking for my mom. Not too many people walk around the beach with a sword on their back. Anyway, the latest recruits usually come around this time of year. It's a waste of time if you ask me… but that's why nobody asks me."

"Unfortunately, my mom isn't here, and she won't be until later on tonight," she continued. "You can come back when mom gets off of work?"

"When would that be?" Aurora asked.

"She should get off around ten, but sometimes they keep her at the hospital until later."

"Your mom works at the hospital?" Shade asked.

"Yeah, she's a doctor."

Destiny explained that water dragons could stay in human form as long as they wanted, but only if they were near a body of water. She told us her mom always loved and protected humans, and that her current work as a doctor was just another way for her to be among them and help them. She spoke highly of her mother, saying that Zana was the most respected doctor in the city and that her patients loved her.

"I usually let Mom deal with the recruits, but would you all like to come inside for a bit?" Destiny invited. It sounded like a great idea to us.

Destiny prepared peanut butter and jelly sandwiches and milk for lunch, and I loved every bite of it. Each bite reminded me of how much my I miss my mom and her crazy peanut butter snacks.

We asked Destiny if she knew why her mom wouldn't give out the clue she had to the others who tried searching for the Dragon Sphere. She just shrugged and said she didn't know. It seemed as if her mind was on something else. I asked her if everything was okay.

"I don't really have people over too often," she explained. "It's usually just me, Sadie and Mom."

I asked her if she wanted us to leave. She shook her head.

"Would you like to have dinner with me?" Destiny asked out of nowhere. "Just you and me?"

I looked around to see if perhaps she was talking to Shade, but her eyes had met mine.

"Me?" I pointed at myself in disbelief. "Of course," I answered quickly and nervously, followed by, "That would be nice."

"Okay, cool! I can make some food for us. We have an amazing view when the sun sets, and it would be nice to have someone else here for a change."

"Is that okay with you all?" she asked, looking at Shade and Aurora.

"We're on a quest. You can't go out on a date," Aurora protested, ignoring Destiny and looking at me harshly.

"Don't worry, we're not going anywhere," Destiny responded. "We are staying at my place." Then she turned to me.

"And besides, you have some time to spare since you're waiting for my mom."

"Landon, we need to plan our next move," Aurora pleaded. "In fact, we should leave now and come back when Zana arrives."

"Landon already agreed to have dinner with me!" Destiny said. "Unless you're his girlfriend? Then I could see why you would be upset. You're not, are you?"

A hue of red rushed to Aurora's cheeks. Was she embarrassed or angry? Maybe it was a little of both. I didn't want to say much, for fear of getting yelled at by either girl, and I folded under pressure. I thought I was good at these situations with girls. The evidence was saying otherwise.

Destiny asked me to return at around 7:00 p.m., with dress clothes, and she directed me to a few stores close by where I could buy some. She also told me to bring flowers, and that she loved lilies. She said that I could get cleaned up at her place and then we would have dinner. Destiny added, before sending us on our way, that depending on how the date went, she might be able to provide me with some information for our quest—information not previously given to any of the prior recruits.

Aurora couldn't believe that I would accept the date, and leave her and Shade alone. Shade looked hurt when she said that. Shade tried to help me out, and asked Aurora to take it easy, and that if Destiny had some information for us then I needed to make it a good date to get it.

Aurora quieted down, but she looked upset. She and I were growing close—but I wondered if she was starting to like me as more than just a friend. I've battled with her, trained with her, and shared long, boring car rides with her, but I didn't feel she was into me. Maybe I was reading too much into it. *Aurora's a very driven girl—and goal oriented—she just wants to get the task at hand accomplished,* I thought.

In every store we went to, Aurora had something negative to say about what I tried on. She got even more upset when I used the credit card Blayne gave us to pay for the clothes and flowers. I felt bad, but not because I was going on the date—it was because I was leaving Shade alone with a very grumpy girl.

I made it back to Zana's place right at seven o'clock. When Destiny opened the door, she looked stunning. Her blue dress matched her radiant eyes and a pearl necklace ringed her slim throat. Her dark, curly hair hung down past her shoulders. I couldn't tell if she was wearing makeup, but it didn't matter—she didn't need it. Her cheeks naturally blushed to a perfect rosy tint. There was an elegance about her when she moved, as if it were impossible for her not to be perfect. At the same time, I sensed no arrogance in her. She seemed as if she just wanted to have fun.

"Very punctual. I like that," Destiny smiled.

After I gave her the flowers, she showed me to the bathroom to get cleaned up. Then she went back into the kitchen to tend to dinner. When I came in, the lilies I had given her were at the center of a table in a clear vase. Two plates and a glass full of fresh-squeezed lemonade were already at our places.

"This is amazing," I told her excitedly, as we sat down at the table.

"I hope you like fish?" she asked nervously.

"I like everything—it all looks great."

I took a bite. She looked at me anxiously, waiting for my response. I was impressed. I smiled at her and took another bite.

Dinner was surprisingly fun. Destiny had a humorous, sarcastic side to her and we wound up having a really good time. She told me that she was home-schooled and that her favorite things were to read and jog on the beach and play with Sadie. She asked me about my mom and how I got involved with this quest. I tried to make it sound nobler than it was by telling her that I was also searching for my dad. She gave me a puzzled look.

"Who is your dad?" She asked. There was a seriousness in her tone that threw me off guard."

"His name is Drayden. I've never met him—"

"Drayden!" She cut me off quickly. "That's why I sensed him." Then she put her hands to her head and muttered under her breath. "Mom is going to freak out."

"Is everything okay?" I asked cautiously.

"Well... I asked you to dinner tonight because you reminded me of someone. I kept sensing him through you, and I was curious about it. Please don't freak out when I tell you this—Drayden is my father, too."

My body went cold. I couldn't believe what I just heard. I thought she was a dragonoid. It never even crossed my mind to consider the alternative... or in this case, the obvious. Dragons have children with other dragons too.

"So you're my sister—well, half-sister—and a full-blooded dragon?"

"I am," Destiny said quietly. The slightly darker hue of red on her cheeks made me believe she was just as embarrassed as I was. She paused a moment while we both soaked this fact in. "I think I need a moment," she finally continued. "I'm going to change, and then, let's talk."

I'm glad she left for a few minutes. I needed time to clear my head. I never thought much of my dad to begin with, but now my view of him went even lower. I felt bad for mom. She continued to admire my dad through all these years. I would think that something like finding out he had another kid my age would make her reconsider how great he was. *Why am I on this mission?* I wondered. I had convinced myself that searching for Dad was the right thing to do. Suddenly, I wasn't so sure.

When Destiny returned, she was carrying some photos with her. She placed them on the table and pointed to an image of Dad in an old black and white. I was now certain that the person in my recent flashback was him.

"You remind me so much of him," Destiny said, with sadness in her voice. "You have his soft, dark eyes and his pointy nose. I haven't seen him in so long. I miss him."

I asked her what she meant. How would she remember him if he disappeared about thirteen years ago?

"Well, Landon," she said. "I'm fifty-three years old. I have had the opportunity to spend a good amount of time with him."

"You're kidding, right?" I said in disbelief. I must have looked dumb with my mouth dropped open and my eyes wide.

"Did you forget that I am not a dragonoid? I'm a full-blooded dragon, and we age slower than you do. I'm still very young for a dragon."

95

I had so many questions to ask her and I didn't know where to start. I decided to find out what information she said she was going to give me during our date. She looked at me.

"I can only give you this," she said. "It is a poem Mom recited to me a few years back."

> *Bred in hatred, the sword will clash*
> *To rise in glory as mountains crash*
> *Then summon up the mighty King*
> *And begin the Great Awakening.*

I remembered what Mom had told me about a Great Awakening. It was something Dad had mentioned to her. Was this the clue he had given Zana? I needed to speak with her. Maybe she would be able to tell me who and what the poem was about.

Before I could ask any more questions, the front door slammed open.

"She needs help!" Shade shrieked as he walked in the house. He was carrying Aurora. Her body rested motionless in his arms, as a stream of dark-red blood dripped down the side of her face.

Chapter Nine
Dr. Reed's Prescription

Destiny quickly helped Shade set Aurora down on the couch in the living room.

"She needs to go to the hospital!" Shade voiced his concern.

"You need to calm your friend down," Destiny said to me as she began to examine Aurora. She slid her fingers through Aurora's hair and noticed a gash just above her left ear. Then she ran to the kitchen, picked up the house phone and began to dial.

"Mom, I need your help. It's an emergency. I'm at the house. Come quick!" She hung up the phone; she had obviously left a message.

"Let's just go to her!" Shade demanded, his body shaking in distress.

"Don't worry, Mom will come soon," Destiny assured. Then she turned to me and said, "Go to the bathroom and look under the sink. Bring me the first-aid kit."

I ran to the bathroom and found the kit, then quickly came back to Destiny and handed it to her. She pulled out the gauze and started wrapping it around Aurora's head. Destiny looked back towards the phone. She looked worried, as if she didn't know what to do and was just trying to buy time.

I knelt down next to Aurora. The blood from her wound was showing through the gauze. I put my hand on her arm. Her body felt cold. I darted to the closest room, pulled a blanket off the bed and covered Aurora with it, hoping that would help warm her up. Destiny sprinted to call her mom again, but still no answer. Aurora's body was trembling. We took that as a good sign, as it was an indication that she was still alive—but for how much longer? We couldn't say for sure.

"We can't just stand here and watch her die!" Shade said in frustration. Then he turned to Destiny. "You don't know if your mom is coming and we need to do something!"

"She's coming," Destiny said, as calmly as she could manage. "I know she is."

I felt helpless as I sat beside Aurora. I put my hand under the blanket and took her hand. Then I did the only thing I figured I could do. I closed my eyes and prayed.

She can't die right now, I begged. I needed her, and I pleaded with the Creator to save her life. I realized just then how much she had helped me in the short amount of time that we had known each other. I would be lost without her. Aurora sighed. I thought I was hurting her because I was squeezing her hand tightly. I loosened my grip.

"Aurora, can you hear me?" I asked, hoping she could find a way to respond. "Stay with us, Aurora! We need you to help us find the Dragon Sphere. That's our purpose, and we haven't completed it yet. You can't leave us."

Aurora's lips had lost their color. They were pale, with a tint of blue. She was still losing too much blood. I wondered whether Zana had even heard her daughter's message. Shade was pacing back and forth behind me, making me even more nervous than I already was.

"Is there any more gauze?" I asked Destiny.

She nodded and handed me a roll of it. I asked her to get me a warm, wet rag. She brought me one quickly. I unwrapped the bloody gauze from Aurora's head and started dabbing at her wound with the wet rag. With every dab of the rag, Aurora winced in pain. I wiped as much blood off her head as I could, and rewrapped it with new gauze. Her blood covered my hands. I handed the wet rag to Destiny. As I stared at the red liquid dripping from my fingers, I had an idea.

I dashed to the bathroom and washed Aurora's blood off my hands.

"No!" Destiny cried. I hurried back and saw her put her head on Aurora's chest. "She's stopped breathing!"

I ran into the kitchen and picked up a knife. I then sped back to Aurora and stood over her. I put my left hand over her lips and cut my palm with the knife. Blood gushed and spilled into Aurora's mouth. If human blood had some healing properties, I was hoping the human blood in me was enough to help her.

A few seconds passed and nothing happened.

Suddenly, Aurora inhaled deeply as life entered her again. Her eyes opened, then quickly closed again. My palm was burning from the incision, but I was relieved that Aurora was breathing again. I remembered what Blayne had said regarding how much blood we could have and that having too much could make us weak and sick. Aurora was already in a delicate state. I didn't want to give her too much. She was breathing again—that's the most we could ask for until Zana arrived—though by then, I was starting to doubt that she would show up.

Only seconds later, a woman wearing blue scrubs rushed through the door. Her blonde hair bounced as she streaked towards us. A seashell necklace hung around her neck. Her eyes were like Destiny's—as blue as the ocean. It was Zana.

"Mom!" Destiny shouted in relief. "We can't stop the bleeding!"

"Is she…?" Zana said looking at Destiny.

"Yes. She's a dragonoid," Destiny replied, knowing what her mom was asking.

"Okay!" Zana exclaimed.

She took off her seashell necklace and grabbed one of the seashells that were dangling from it. She crushed the shell in her hand and started dropping the small pieces into Aurora's mouth.

"How much blood did you give her?" she asked, knowing that we had given her some.

"Just a little bit," I responded.

Zana took a step back from Aurora and stared at her wound. Aurora's wound was healing! Aurora regained the color in her lips and skin, and the gash on her head was disappearing, as if it had never been there.

"Carry her to the room," Zana ordered. "She will still need some rest."

I walked over to Aurora, lifted her up and moved her to Destiny's bedroom. When I walked out of the room, Zana was inspecting me closely.

"Let me see your hand."

I raised my left hand. She grabbed it and told me that she would have to stitch it up.

While she was cleaning and stitching my cut, I asked Zana what she had given Aurora. She told me that she had given her a revival shell. They were capable of healing any wound, as long as the person was alive. Zana expected Aurora to sleep through the rest of the night, so she invited Shade and me to stay the night at her place.

Zana asked what happened to Aurora. We all turned towards Shade looking for answers. He told us that he and Aurora were relaxing and talking on the beach, near a pier with an amusement park theme to it, when they noticed a disturbance in the water. They saw a man rise up from the water. He had long gray hair and a full gray beard. He swam to shore. As he came out of the water, Aurora and Shade saw a long scar on the right side of his body. It ran from the top of his chest to the lower part of his torso. The man looked at them, piercing them with his steely blue eyes. Then he sniffed the air and started yelling at them, calling them "abominations." The man then dove back into the water. Aurora and Shade saw him transform into a blue dragon with a long gray beard. He was at least thirty feet long, had his two forelegs but no hind legs and no wings. His long tail had a fin on its end.

Shade said that the dragon was not afraid to show his true form in front of all the people who were enjoying the arcade games and restaurants at the pier. The crowd flung popcorn and food in the air as they scrambled in terror. Even some who were riding the glowing Ferris wheel jumped from their seats. Aurora darted up the pier as the dragon slithered its way to the top of it. Shade said that he pleaded with Aurora to run. Instead, she confronted the dragon head on.

"Aurora put up a good fight," Shade said, smiling now that he knew Aurora would be okay. He went on to explain that he tried to distract the dragon by setting the pier on fire, but the large beast counterattacked by willing a wave of water to splash on top of him. The dragon's attention was caught just long enough for Aurora to create a powerful whirlwind and send the dragon flying back into the water—but not before the serpent spun around and hit her on the head with his powerful tail, knocking her off the pier and back on to the beach. Shade hurried towards Aurora and saw how badly she was injured, so he quickly picked her up and ran to us for help.

Zana shot a concerned look at Destiny.

"I only know of one serpent that fits that description, and I can only hope that I am wrong." Zana reached for Destiny's hand in search of comfort.

"The fact that he did not come after you verifies that it is," Zana said, her eyes filled with angst. "Proteus is the oldest of us sea dragons and the most violent. He hates dragonoids and will attack them without reason. But Proteus never chases his enemies. We still do not understand why, but that is how he has always been. What worries me is why he came to land *here* to begin with. He rarely does—and when he does, it is because he is up to no good."

"How could he know we were dragonoids, though?" Shade asked.

"Good question. Dragons typically cannot tell the difference between humans and dragonoids at first glance. You said that he sniffed the air when he saw you, so perhaps there was a distinct scent he has become able to identify," Zana mused. "Proteus is an old sea dragon, and a very angry one at that. If any dragon has had a lot of time to learn to identify dragonoid scent it would be him."

"Where do you think he's going?" Destiny asked her mom worriedly.

"I do not know, but he has no regard for rules and, as your friends just saw, he is willing to show his true form in front of humans without thinking of the repercussions that it may have on all of us. This is a dangerous situation. The two of you will rest here tonight. Your friend will be completely recovered by morning. At that time, you must track Proteus. We can no longer ignore the signs. This is just a hunch, but I believe that following Proteus might lead you to the Dragon Sphere."

"How did you know we were searching for the Dragon Sphere?" Shade asked.

"The only time we get dragonoid visitors is for that very reason."

Zana had a softness about her, but not in a weak way. She seemed sweet, kind, and very intelligent. She looked like a woman who knew what to do in all situations, one who could provide sage advice to anyone. I could see why her patients would love her, as Destiny told me they did. I could tell where

Destiny got her flawlessness from, as Zana spoke and moved with such grace.

I asked Zana about the clue Blayne Crow said she had. Although she was hesitant, she was willing to let us have it. She walked to her room, and came back a few minutes later grasping something in her hands. She set it down on the table and I examined it. It was a solid black cylinder-shaped rock about as long as a pencil but as thick as a roll of quarters. One end was flat and the other end had a sharp point. Zana also set down a piece of paper that had the poem Destiny told me written on it.

Zana explained that Drayden had found both items in Arizona, but he didn't specify where. My dad had discovered that a cult was behind the disappearance of the Dragon Sphere, but he could not find out who the leader was. When Drayden captured one of the cult's followers, he picked up the black cylindrical rock and the piece of paper and let the follower go. The follower had begged for him to "bring back the key," as my father left him behind. Zana said that the last time she saw my dad was about twelve years ago when he brought her those items to hold for him. She was the last one to see him before he disappeared. She decided not to show anyone the items, for fear of starting panic among the other dragons.

"With every year that passes and no catastrophes happening," Zana said, "it solidifies my belief that Drayden has been able to stop Aremas from being released, even if Drayden himself did not survive." Zana paused a moment before continuing.

"But now things are different."

Zana explained to us that a few weeks ago she noticed a large chunk of ice that had floated in from the ocean and washed up onto the sand of the beach. It was very early in the morning, and as the sun came up, the ice melted. Lately, too, she has been noticing that the water has become colder – unusually so for this time of year.

"And now Proteus is near the mainland," she said. It was clear that she was worried about what was to come. Zana said she was confident that the black rock had to be a key that the cult was going to use to open the Dragon Sphere. She did not wish to tell us what she thought the poem meant. She just said that we needed to find the sphere and bring it back to them.

"How big is the Dragon Sphere?" Shade asked.

"It is a bit larger than a bowling ball," was her response.

"So how are we supposed to know where to find this Proteus guy? He's probably long gone by now."

"You are going to have to follow the destruction," Zana said sadly. "You should get some rest now. I am certain that, in the morning, you will know where to go."

Shade and I put our sleeping bags on the floor in the living room, then I went to change out of the dress clothes I was wearing. As I walked out of the bathroom, Zana came up to me and hugged me.

"My daughter is right. You remind me so much of him. Please be safe on your journey," she said.

She handed me the piece of paper that the poem was written on, and two shells that looked similar to the ones on her necklace. Then she smiled warmly at me. I nodded and left for bed. I was exhausted. All the worrying over Aurora had taken all the energy out of me. As soon as my body hit the sleeping bag, I was asleep.

When I opened my eyes, I saw Aurora hovering over me. She gazed at me warmly, with a large grin across her face.

"Destiny told me what happened last night," she said.

"Yeah, you gave us quite a scare," I replied.

"You were on a date with your sister," she said, laughing out loud.

I rolled my eyes, then turned onto my stomach.

"I'm sorry for scaring you guys." Aurora's voice was sincere. "I owe you and Shade big time."

Destiny walked in and told us she had prepared breakfast: medium-rare lamb, sunny-side-up eggs and seasoned potatoes. Shade woke up as I was rolling up my sleeping bag. He smiled at Aurora. She mouthed thank you to him. He just nodded his head.

After cleaning up, we sat at the table and ate. Destiny had also given us a little bit of lamb's blood, which helped heal the cut on my left hand even though a scar remained. Destiny turned on the TV, to a news report that showed all the fire hydrants in Phoenix, Arizona, exploding at the same time.

"I guess you know where to start," Destiny said.

"How did he get there so fast?" Shade asked.

Destiny sighed and said, "Sea dragons may not be able to fly, but that doesn't mean that we're not fast. If you all could make it by evening tonight, chances are he will still be there. Proteus is nocturnal, so he is probably going to sleep the rest of the day."

After breakfast, we all said goodbye to Destiny and thanked her for her help. She asked me to come and visit her when we were done with our quest. She handed me a small piece of paper with her phone number, and told me to keep in touch. I told her that I would, and that I looked forward to relaxing on the beach next time. She gave me a hug, and then walked back in carefully so that Sadie wouldn't run out. We weren't really sure how we were going to get to Phoenix, but we had to figure out something fast. Zana told us that it would take us roughly six hours if we drove there, but none of us knew how to drive. More importantly, none of us had a vehicle. We started walking towards the highway and hoped that maybe we could hitch a ride from there.

We walked and walked and walked some more. No one seemed to want to pick us up; I'm sure the sword hanging from my back may have had something to do with it. Finally, a station wagon pulled over and let us in. A guy who looked like he was in his early twenties was in the driver's seat.

"Where to?" he asked.

We told him where we were headed. He said that as long as we paid for gas, he would get us there. His name was Gary. He had messy brown hair and a goatee. He was wearing a muscle shirt and shorts, and he seemed anxious to leave the city behind him. He had just lost his job, and so he was on his way to his parents' place in Fort Worth, Texas. He didn't seem to have many things in the back of the station wagon except for a few bags.

"I didn't have much when I moved to Santa Monica, anyway," he shrugged. He didn't seem to have a care in the world.

We were making really good time with Gary. He was driving at least ten miles over the speed limit most of the way, and we made very few stops. He told us about some of the crazy encounters he'd had at some of the local nightclubs in Santa Monica, and about his friend who would randomly pretend to be an Irishman at the most awkward moments. We laughed a lot on our way to find Proteus. This was a good thing for all of us, and it helped take our minds off things. When we arrived in Phoenix, we promised Gary that we would fill up his tank one last time, and asked him to stop at a gas station. On our way there, a cop came up behind us and flashed his lights.

"Damn," Gary muttered nervously.

He pulled over to the side of the road, looking unusually anxious. Before the cop even made it out of his car, Gary opened the door and ran away. Shade, Aurora, and I looked at each other and knew that we were in trouble.

The cop ran after Gary, and signaled for us to wait in the car.

Shade looked at me and said, "We'd better run. We know we're innocent, but this will delay us in trying to find Proteus."

He was right. I glanced over to Aurora, but she was too nervous to say anything.

"Okay, let's go," I said, and we all jumped out of the car and ran as far away from it as possible.

The desert heat swarmed on us as soon as we got out. I felt as if we'd just been tossed in an oven. We ran a few miles away from where the car was parked, then decided to stop at a Denny's restaurant. Our plan was to wait it out there for a while, and in the meantime, order an early dinner. Every time someone walked in the restaurant, we looked over to make sure it wasn't the police or Gary.

"I knew there was something wrong with that guy," Shade announced. "He was probably a psychopathic murderer leaving the scene of the crime when he picked us up."

Gary didn't look like the psychopathic type, but we were all glad that we didn't stay to find out what he might have been guilty of. I'm sure we didn't look like three normal, innocent teens, with our sleeping bags and my sword. As we ate, we discussed what our course of action would be. We had to wait for it to get dark. If we were lucky, Proteus would do something that would draw attention to himself, and we could locate him quickly. We left the restaurant.

It turned out that walking around Phoenix in the summer was not the best idea. Even though it was evening, and the sun was slowly setting, the heat continued to bear down on us. The atmosphere in Phoenix reminded me of Primus's cave, hot and sticky. We found a park and rested for about an hour. Sure it was in the desert, but there were patches of lush greenery with palm trees sprinkled throughout the large city. From where we stood, I could see the beautiful stretch of the tall metropolitan building lights welcoming us.

We walked around, listening for any disturbances in the city. Everything was silent.

"Maybe it's too hot for Proteus to come out," Aurora mused.

"Maybe he's not even here anymore," Shade replied.

After another hour had passed, we finally heard sirens from behind us. Two police cars flew past and hurried into a small shopping center less than a mile ahead. We decided to check it out. When we arrived, police officers were inspecting the damage in a small magic shop. *MAGIK LAND* was the name of the store. The glass front door was broken, and the windows were shattered. A few shelves full of props and other items were knocked over. The cops looked confused.

"Nothing was taken, not even any money from the cash registers," one of them said.

A car pulled into the shopping center and zipped towards the store. It was a black BMW Roadster with a license plate that read: DRKNES. A man hurried out and made his way toward the police. An officer asked him to step back. The man told him that he was the owner of the store, so the officer let him pass so he could see the damage. We couldn't hear what they were saying, but we did notice the look of anger on the owner's face.

He started kicking the debris on the floor. Then, to our surprise, he yelled, "PROTEUS!"

We had found our next lead.

We waited over by the BMW for the owner of the store to finish speaking with the cops. He glanced over at us a few times, but didn't say anything. Eventually he walked towards us. The man had on a black tank top, black jeans and black boots. He wore a gold chain with a crucifix charm on it. He combed his jet-black hair forward, and stared angrily at us with his unsettling black eyes.

"There's nothing to see here. Scram," said the man.

Aurora and I moved out of the way.

As I was getting ready to ask how he knew about Proteus the man spoke again, "HELLO?… What's the matter with you, kid? Didn't you hear me? I said move."

Shade stood before him, staring at the man as if he recognized him. Aurora leaned over and whispered to me that Shade and the man looked eerily similar.

"Are you Shadow Gambino?" Shade asked nervously.

"Who wants to know?" said the man rudely.

"Dad, it's me. It's Shade."

Chapter Ten
Black Magic Dragon

Shadow Gambino examined Shade more closely. After a few seconds he swooped in and gave him a hug.

"Wow, you're a grown man now," he said. Excitement at seeing his son had replaced any hint of anger.

Shade didn't look as enthusiastic about the reunion.

"Dad, we heard you say something about Proteus. Do you know where he is?"

Shadow looked upset that Shade didn't seem that excited to see him. His eyes turned cold again in response.

"Don't tell me those Elder Dragons have you running around looking for that stupid ball?" he said. Shade nodded his head.

Shadow continued, "Well, I did see him earlier. In fact, he destroyed my store here looking for information I don't have. That old man boils my blood. He's looking for the people that have the Dragon Sphere. He won't find it here, though. There are only remnants of the Sons of Levi here in Arizona."

"Sons of Levi?" said Shade.

"Yeah, some little gang that claimed they had the Dragon Sphere. I know they moved out of this area a while back when an Elder Dragon came through looking for it."

"If you knew about all this, why didn't you do anything to stop them from leaving?" Aurora scolded.

"The Elder Dragons have never helped me, so why would I help them? This is my city. I run this area, so whatever happens in it, I know about it. I've helped them before and that didn't work out in my favor. If the world's coming to an end, then I'm looking out for me."

"Why do you have to be so selfish?" Shade blurted, his balled-up fist showing the frustration he had been holding in for some time. "Mom told me that you were a jerk, but I didn't think that you were this bad. A major threat to all life might be unleashed at any minute, and you do nothing to help avoid it."

"If you want help, I'll help you, son. You could stay at my place if you need somewhere to sleep. If you need food, I could feed you. But I don't have any information on the Dragon Sphere, and even if I did, I wouldn't say anything. I'm not going to get involved in this dragon hunt. If you were smart, you would stop wasting your time searching for Aremas and enjoy your life while you have it."

Shade shook his head in dejection; his smoke-black bangs fell in front of his eyes. It had been ten years since he had last seen his father. It was clear that his father had no sympathy for this cause. Instead, he was discouraging him. Shade was too disappointed to talk further. Shadow showed no emotion.

Shadow glanced at us and said, "I suppose you all are together in the hunt for the Dragon Sphere?" Aurora and I nodded our heads yes—but Shadow shook his.

"Am I the only one who thinks that we dragons ask too much of you all? I know I haven't been a good father to Shade and I know that I wasn't around for him. But that was only because I hoped that he would never have to get involved in these dragon politics. I'd rather be a negligent father than let him get involved with a system that sends children to an early grave."

Shadow still showed no emotion. I thought for a moment about whether Shadow was on to something. Maybe all of us dragonoids would be better off without the politics of our dragon parents.

"I'm sure the two of you have wondered why only one parent was around," he said to Aurora and me, "and not the other. They wait for you to reach a certain age and then tell you you're old enough to give up your life for their cause. I was a part of that system for a long time. I won't lie and say that I wasn't. But I won't be a part of it anymore. That's why I won't get involved in your journey."

Silence fell upon us. What he was saying actually made sense to me. I was living fine without knowing about any of this dragon stuff until uncle Bane sent me to the Infernal Caverns. Since then, I've accepted my fate as a dragonoid—and I even enjoy it—but I think I would have turned out just fine not knowing about my dragon heritage.

Shadow broke our silence and asked us to follow him. He guided us through an alley that led the way to the back of his magic shop. He took his keys out of his pocket, and shuffled them around until he found the right one. We walked into a small office that had a desk and computer in one corner and a large shelf with hundreds of tiny models of dragons in the other. Each model was extremely detailed, with its own array of colors, claws, horns, wings and enraged expressions.

Shadow explained that Proteus was not going to stay in Phoenix for long. He felt sure that the sea dragon was going to continue his search for the Sons of Levi. He also said that if we were to have any chance of getting information from him, we wouldn't be able to do it as dragonoids.

"I don't think there is anything I could say to discourage you all from continuing forward with your mission," said Shadow, "so I will do something for you that no other dragon would have the courage to do. I consider myself to be the best sorcerer of all the dragons, and I will grant you the opportunity to fly the night sky as one of us. If you choose to accept, I have a potion specifically designed to change you into a dragon for one hour. You may find it easier to search for Proteus from above."

I will allow only two of you to use it—and I would like the opportunity to speak with my son." Shadow looked at Shade with the smallest hint of a smile on his face while Aurora and I looked at each other with big eyes. The chance to become a dragon for an hour was right before us.

"We'll do it," we both said in unison.

Shade stayed silent, but I could tell that he wanted to come with us. We needed someone to hold all of our stuff, and this was a perfect opportunity for him to catch up with his dad. Shadow pulled open a drawer from his desk, and took out a small vial with green liquid in it. There were many small potion containers in the drawer, but he seemed to know which one to grab. He poured the contents into two Styrofoam cups.

"Let's go outside," Shadow ordered.

In the small alley behind the magic shop, Shadow gave us two rules. The first and most important was to not be seen by anyone other than Proteus. The second was to not use any of our powers while in dragon form. We had agreed to meet back at the magic shop in one hour. Then I drank the green liquid from the cup. Aurora waited about thirty seconds after me, then she drank as well. We waited in anticipation for the change, but nothing happened. Another minute passed and still no transformation.

"I don't think it's working," I told Shadow as he stared down at my feet.

Black smoke was rising from the ground beneath me. I turned to Aurora and the same thing started happening to her. Shadow and Shade stepped further away from us.

Soon the smoke had completely enclosed me. I couldn't see anything. I started to feel my muscles expand as my body stretched. Yet, it wasn't painful. I could hear my bones snapping, but the only thing I felt was a weak burning sensation in my gut. Then I felt hard scaly skin start to develop, covering the soft tissue that I once had. My vision began to blur, and then an immense burst of light blinded me. When I opened my eyes, an assortment of colors differentiated the objects I was looking at. I realized that I was now seeing things with thermal vision. When the transformation was complete, I stood roughly fifteen feet tall and my tail added at least another seven or eight feet. I was a metallic bronze color, just like my dad and my uncle Bane. I could feel two small nubs on the top of my head, which I assumed were my horns.

Aurora was a sky blue-colored dragon, a few feet shorter than me. Her wings were folded behind her, which made me look back immediately to check if I had mine. We both tried stretching them out. Without any trouble, we were able to command our wings to spread. One of Aurora's wings stretched out so long it slapped me in the face. I saw the look in Shadow's eyes. He was obviously very pleased with the results of his potion. Shade gazed at us in awe.

"Dragons are natural flyers, so you shouldn't have any problems getting off the ground," Shadow said, looking up at us, "but you might have to flap your wings for a couple of minutes just to strengthen them since they've never been used before."

"I didn't know dragons could only see in thermal infrared," Aurora said.

"We can only see in that way for our first fifty years of life. Then we learn to see as humans do. That's how long it takes for our eyes to adapt to human vision. After that, we can switch between the two. You should start strengthening your wings now."

Aurora and I flapped our wings, causing a whirlwind of trash and dust around us. Shadow and Shade moved farther away from us. After a few minutes, I noticed that I was hovering off the ground. I flapped my wings harder and began my ascent towards the sky. I felt such a rush as I flew higher and higher. Aurora wasn't too far behind, shouting in excitement. When, after a while, I stopped ascending and looked down, I could see that Shadow and Shade were tiny red spots below me. When I squinted my eyes, I was able to zoom in on their faces from far away.

"Let's see how fast we can go," Aurora challenged. "I'll race you to the other end of the city."

"You're on!"

I couldn't tell how fast we were flying as we jetted across the night sky. The city lights blurred past us like a video on fast forward. Side by side, Aurora and I cut through the wind with ease and sped towards the outer city limits. I moved closer to her, attempting to scare her so I could gain the lead, but she ducked underneath me and swirled around me as though she had been doing this for years. Aurora pulled ahead, right at the end of our race, and spun around in victory. Flying was such an amazing feeling. My heart pounded with excitement, as Aurora and I laughed heartily at our friendly competition.

"You ready to search for Proteus?" I asked Aurora, wishing we had more time to goof around in our dragon bodies. Aurora nodded her head—and we took off, flying over the city, looking for anything unusual.

We searched furiously, but we couldn't find anything. Then, right before we were about to head back to the magic shop, Aurora spotted some crushed park benches in one of the parks. Then we noticed a great red glow of heat, showing through the branches of an enormous tree. We went down for a closer look.

"That's him," Aurora whispered, as she pointed to the giant sea dragon coiled around the large tree.

"He looks like he's sleeping," I said.

The park was quiet and dark.

"Now would be a good time to attack," Aurora proposed.

I discouraged her by reminding her that Shadow cautioned us not to use any of our powers.

"But he almost killed me," she argued.

Just then, Proteus woke up from his nap and slithered down the tree trunk. He stretched his two front legs, which were the only limbs he had on his entire body. He glanced at us irritably as he uncoiled the rest of his body from the tree.

"What do you want?" Proteus asked harshly.

"We are searching for the great Proteus," I replied.

His deathly stare faded into a confident smile.

"Finally, the young ones are starting to understand what dragons they should admire," he boasted. "Tell me, how did you know I was here in Arizona?"

I looked at Aurora. She readied her claws as if she was preparing to attack. I blurted out the first thing that came to mind, "I followed the destruction."

"Very well then," said Proteus. "How may I help you young dragons?"

He was a very intimidating creature, with his dark, cold gaze and massive body. I explained that we'd heard the Dragon Sphere had been stolen and that we wanted to know what we could do to help release Arcmas. Proteus appeared disturbed by my answer and raised his eyebrows in concern.

"Do not be misguided, young one," he implored. "I do not serve the ancient dragon Aremas. I have taken it upon myself to stop his release, but I fear that it might be too late."

"Why do you say that?" Aurora insisted.

"Can you not feel the change in the air? Have you not noticed the unusual development of ice in the ocean waters? The foolish Dragon Council waits patiently for their inferior half-breeds to bring back the Sphere. For years, they have been unsuccessful. I will not sit back anymore, as Aremas is on the cusp of his release. If you want to gain anything from me, young dragons, remember this—a dragon should never have to hide who he is. We share this planet with humans, but we should not have to hide from them just because they fear us. If they do not know how to share this planet, then we should make *them* hide from *us*. I have no quarrel with the humans and mostly stay out of their way. It is situations like these that make my blood burn in anger with the way the Dragon Council handles them."

Proteus coiled his massive tail in a spiral and rested on it as he scratched his thick, gray beard with his claw. The positive thing was that Proteus was also trying to stop Aremas from being released. The bad thing was that he still hated dragonoids. Aurora and I would be as much his enemies as the cult that stole the Dragon Sphere.

"The dragon named Shadow told us that you were searching for some information that he did not have. What were you looking for?" Aurora asked.

"You will do well to avoid the black dragon. He is a trickster, and only looks out for himself. But yes, I was searching for some information that he has. He knows the current location of the Sons of Levi. He knows because it is his business to know. A few months ago, I had sent one of my students to speak with Shadow regarding the whereabouts of the Dragon Sphere. He never returned. But my student was no fool. He sent me a message explaining Shadow's involvement with the Sons. The black dragon forgot that sea dragons can send messages with a single drop of water. Unless he purposely wanted me to get involved—but I doubt Shadow is that foolish."

Proteus explained that water is the sea dragon's life force. With their ability to control water comes the ability to leave messages in the smallest of drops. If commanded properly, a single drop could travel thousands of miles before the message disappears. All the drop has to do is make it to the body of water that the sea dragon, for whom it is intended, is in. Then that dragon would be able to sense it. It doesn't matter how big the body of water is. Sometimes it could take months or years before a drop finds its final destination. Of course, the messages that take the longest get caught in the natural evaporation and condensation process of the earth. The faster ones travel through streams and rivers to the lakes and oceans. The message sent to Proteus took a couple of months to get to him.

The mighty sea dragon relayed to us that his student overheard Shadow and a man whose back was hunched over talking in the magic shop. They were discussing details of a new underground facility that was holding the Dragon Sphere. The student saw the man with the deformed back hand Shadow a folded sheet of paper. The paper resembled a map.

"The time draws near," the hunchback revealed.

I wasn't sure what to believe anymore. Shadow helped us by giving us the potion to turn us into dragons after saying that he didn't want to aid us on our quest. Proteus was giving us a lot of helpful information, but yet Zana said he was known to be up to no good every time he came onto the mainland.

"We have to go now," Aurora urged.

"Yes, young dragons. I must leave as well, for I have to continue my search for the Sphere. Remember to use caution if you cross paths with the black dragon again. He has fooled many great dragons and has imprisoned them with his deceitfulness."

Proteus closed his eyes as if it pained him to think about it.

"Just a quick question," Aurora broke in. "How has Shadow imprisoned other dragons?"

A crinkle between the great sea dragon's unflinching bluish-grey eyes showed what I thought was a puzzled look, as if he were wondering how we did not know about Shadow's history.

"He tricks them into using his potions that grant them special abilities. After a short while, the potion turns them into a lifeless miniature replica of themselves. I saw his collection of these dragons once. It sickens me to think about it now. Still, I could not find it within me to destroy it, because of hope that one day those dragons may be freed from their prison."

Proteus slowly turned his back to us and slithered away. I turned to Aurora. We both knew that we had to get back to the magic shop quickly. We had to tell Shade what we had discovered, so that he could find a way to help us. We didn't have much time. We flew as fast as we could back to the magic shop and landed in the alley. Our sleeping bags and my sword were placed next to a trash bin, with a folded sheet of paper halfway sticking out under a sleeping bag. It was a letter from Shade.

If you find this, then it's only fair that you know what is about to happen. I know I would want to know if it were about to happen to me. You're not going to turn back into humans. Instead, you are going to turn into tiny statues, just like the ones that he collects. I promise I didn't know about this before you drank the potion. If I had, I would have told you not to drink it. I don't agree with what my dad has done but I need him. He is the only one I have left now. Like the saying goes—If you can't beat him, join him.

Even if this hadn't happened to you guys, I don't think I deserve to be traveling with you guys anyway. I'm like my father. I feel an evil inside me that I can't explain. I can't escape from what I've done. I know why my mom hated my dad. There is nothing good in him and she saw the same evilness in me. That's why I did it. That's why her blood is on my hands and why I ran to the Infernal Caverns after I did it. I'm glad that I made it there. That was the only place I felt relief. I am sorry for how things have turned out.

Shade

Aurora and I couldn't believe what we'd just read. Shade had given up on us. We had lost a friend, failed in our quest and now were about to be turned into board-game pieces. I felt a sense of helplessness take over. Our journey had ended, and there was nothing we could do about it. The black dragon had deceived us, the way he had deceived all the others in his collection. I turned to Aurora and saw a tear travel down her blue-scaled snout. I imagined myself wasting away on a shelf, in a tiny lifeless dragon shell, for the rest of my life. Then it hit me.

"The shells!" I shouted. I suddenly remembered the gift Zana had given us.

I turned to where our things were by the trash cans and tried to unravel the sleeping bags. I had put the shells in there. I didn't know if they would change us back, but it was worth a try. I grabbed at a sleeping bag and tore it open. Nothing. I grabbed at the other one, when I heard Aurora wail in pain. Suddenly, I felt a sharp pain in my own stomach, as if someone had stuck a dagger in it and had ripped it open. I tore the sleeping bag open and the two tiny shells flew to the ground.

"Aurora… eat the shell!" I sputtered. My insides felt as if they had been dipped in acid.

I reached for one of the shells but my fingers were too big. I couldn't pick it up. Aurora gave it a try but had the same problem. My body froze. I couldn't move any of my limbs. Time was up, and the hope that I had from the shells was all gone.

Even though my body had shut down on me and I couldn't move, I was still able to see what was going on. In my peripheral vision, I saw that Aurora was still moving. She bent over and licked the ground, lapping up the shell with her tongue. She turned and saw me frozen in my stance, reaching for the shell. She rolled me onto my side, picked up the other shell on the ground with her tongue, and then spat it into my mouth.

As she moved away from me to give me space, I noticed black smoke rising from her feet. It quickly engulfed her and she was no longer visible. A few seconds later, Aurora was back in human form. But it was too late for me. I wasn't changing.

"C'mon, change back," Aurora pleaded.

Still nothing. My breathing was getting slower. I felt my airway tightening and I couldn't catch my breath. Before I blacked out, the last thing I saw was Aurora's eyes widening.

"You're transforming, Landon. Hold on a little longer."

Lightning crashed in an open field. Heavy rain fell furiously onto the grassy plains. I saw a man walking in the distance. It was my father. He was getting drenched in the rain. His scar with the three claw marks under his right eye was as vivid as when I first glimpsed him.

"Father, show yourself!" my father roared.

A blinding flash lit up the sky and thunder exploded in the background. An enormous fifty-foot dragon stood before my father. His bronze scales were dull and did not shine like my dad's did. Near the tip of his snout was a large black horn. He had no horns on his head, but giant spikes protruded from his back. The dragon's enormous wings were folded in as he lay in the field.

"*My son, you have made your father proud. The Creator has blessed me with the opportunity to watch you grow from hatchling to the mighty dragon you are today,*" said the dragon.

"*But Father, I have shamed the family with my recklessness. How could you say you are proud of me?*"

"*Mistakes are a part of life, son. You have chosen to live a noble life in such a wretched world. You cannot erase the past. At the same time, never let your past actions dictate your future. I have no shame in calling you my son.*" *My dad looked at his father with great sadness.*

"*Do not mourn for me,*" the dragon continued. "*My time on Earth is over. I need for you to take over my seat on the Dragon Council. Your wisdom, courage and heart surpass my own. Years after you are gone, our kind will speak of the great dragon Drayden, son of Ithacus. A father could not ask for a better son.*"

The enormous dragon Ithacus closed his eyes. Sheets of rain still poured down on my father and the old dragon. Dad put his hand on the dragon's snout and whispered something. Then he stepped away and transformed into a dragon. He let out a series of roars that almost seemed to form a song. With another blinding flash, the elder dragon disappeared. I had just witnessed the death of my grandfather, Ithacus.

Instantly the scene changed. A baby played in a living room floor with toys that spread across the room. A man walked in and lifted the baby in the air. The little one laughed hard as the man twirled him around. Then the man put the baby down and left the room. As he left, a coin fell out of his pocket. The baby crawled over to the coin, picked it up and put it in his mouth. Seconds later, the infant began to choke. His face turned beet red as he stopped breathing. The man walked back into the room and quickly noticed the baby squirming and unable to breathe. In a flash he lifted the baby up and patted his back. The coin shot out of the baby's mouth and landed on the floor as the baby gasped for air. He caught his breath then started to cry.

The man held the baby tightly in his arms and said, "Breathe, Landon... breathe."

"Breathe Landon... C'mon, please... breathe..." Aurora begged.

I coughed loudly, then took a deep breath. Aurora let out a sigh of relief. My head was pounding and my vision was blurry. I raised my hand and saw that I was back in human form. Aurora kneeled next to me and grabbed my hand.

"Landon, we're alive. Can you believe it?"

I was so glad to see the excitement on her face, yet, at the same time, I was still trying to take in as much air as possible. After I rested for a few more minutes, Aurora helped me up and I picked up my sword.

"I'm sure Shadow and Shade will come back soon. They'll be expecting to pick up a couple of miniature dragons. What should we do?" Aurora asked.

"Well, Proteus was right about Shadow being sneaky. He's probably right about him knowing where the Dragon Sphere is too. I think we need to make him tell us," I responded.

Aurora agreed. The shells that Zana had given me really made me feel great. I also felt stronger. I knew that a fight was about to happen, and I was sure of one thing—with the black dragon, it would not be a fair one.

Chapter Eleven
Shaken

An hour had passed since Aurora and I had transformed back into humans. We climbed up on the roof and waited there for Shadow and Shade to return to the magic shop. It was a silent hour, except for that moment when I gave Aurora a hard time for spitting Zana's shell in my mouth.

Aurora's face turned red. "I should have just let you turn into a toy," she countered in jest.

I'd never had a friend like Aurora before. Xavier and I were like brothers, but Aurora and I connected on a deeper level. She and I were both dragonoids, so she understood what it was like to be different from humans. She also understood that what the Dragon Council expected of us was much more than what they would expect from any other dragonoid, since our parents were both Elders. We made a good team, and I knew that I could trust her in any situation.

When we heard footsteps coming into the alley, Aurora and I peeked over the edge of the roof. It was Shadow. He was alone and had stopped next to the trash bin where the sleeping bags and my sword were. He examined the shredded bags that still lay on the ground and began to search for his tiny new dragon models. I glanced at Aurora. She was shaking her head as if to tell me that right now wasn't a good time to attack. Shadow stood up quickly and looked around to check his surroundings. As he did, Aurora and I hid quickly so that he wouldn't see us. Soon after, we heard the jingling of Shadow's keys as he unlocked the back door to his shop. Aurora motioned for us to jump down from the roof. We stood up and jumped right in front of the open door. With lightning speed, I

125

thrust my sword into Shadow's side. The Black Dragon roared in pain as green blood oozed out of him.

"You stupid fools! You don't know who you're messing with," Shadow said, wincing in pain.

As I was about to strike again, Aurora fired a gust of wind that picked Shadow up and sent him flying through the office wall.

"Tell us where the Dragon Sphere is and we'll let you live!" Aurora demanded.

"I WON'T TELL YOU ANYTHING!" Shadow boomed. Beads of sweat made their way down his face. He struggled to catch his breath. I knew I had wounded him badly.

Aurora blasted him again with another gust of wind that sent him over the magic shop counter. Shadow lifted himself off the ground and ran out through the broken glass, tearing the yellow police tape that the cops had placed in the front of the store. We pursued him and saw that he had ducked back into the alley again. When we got there, he turned and faced us. A blinding flash of white light lit up the alley as he transformed.

The Black Dragon was about twenty-five feet in length. Razor-sharp spikes poked out all over his body. The two horns protruding from his head pointed forward and ran parallel to his face. I noticed burn holes in his massive wings when he extended them. His long tail swayed behind him, hitting and breaking the concrete walls of the store. Shadow raised his right foreleg and swiped at us with his razor-sharp talons. Aurora and I barely jumped back in time to avoid it. I then sprinted forward and slashed downward with *Apollyon*. That strike left a long gash on Shadow's soft underbelly. The Black Dragon roared in pain. Green fluid dripped from the wound. As soon as it touched the ground, the fluid started eating away at the cement. His blood was acid.

I was about to slash at him again when he turned around and slammed me with his tail, knocking me about thirty feet away. Aurora shot more gusts of wind as she moved backwards, but the dragon just walked forward as if the wind blasts didn't affect him. He took a deep breath, and shot out a stream of fire directly at Aurora. She shot a powerful blast of air at the stream and stopped it before it reached her. At that moment, Aurora remembered the fire charms that Blayne had given us and rushed to tell me about it. I took mine out from my pocket and put it around my neck. Aurora quickly put hers on as well.

Shadow took another deep breath, preparing to let out another blast. Aurora and I charged at him without fear of getting burned as the dragon released his flames. We ran directly into the fire, and came out the other side unscathed. Aurora uppercut Shadow right under his chin, and I followed with a high kick to his head. The force of my kick knocked the dragon's head through the wall of the magic shop. I swung my sword, but he blocked it with his horn. I swung again, harder. The dragon used his horn again to block my attack. My sword sliced right through half of his horn, however, and cut him just above his left eye.

Shadow immediately swung his head towards me, knocking me back. His ferocity erupted to another level—and yet I sensed desperation in him. Aurora didn't let up either as she sprinted forward and kicked him in his jaw, snapping his head back. The dragon spat out the green ooze, which Aurora evaded. The acid quickly disintegrated the cement that was a few inches away from me. I slashed at Shadow again, making him move backwards. He struck at me with his claw, but I rolled out of the way before he could hit me. Aurora stood back a bit and started to concentrate her energy. I had seen this before; she was trying to make a powerful whirlwind.

"Keep him busy," she ordered.

Shadow stood on his hind legs, revealing his bloody underbelly. Then he came down to the ground with a thud and pounded the ground with his fist. A shockwave knocked me onto my back. As he stepped forward, I willed the cement below him to rise and form a sharp point. Shadow stepped on it, let out a howl and immediately jumped back. I got up and ran towards him, then willed the ground below me to rise, elevating me as high as the center of his belly. Once there, I jumped off and slashed down with my sword. I hit his left shoulder, scraping a chunk of flesh off him. When I landed, the dragon spun around and smashed me through one of the stores with his tail. He then retreated in panic. Then I saw Aurora run after him. A powerful whirlwind surrounded her. When she reached Shadow, the whirlwind lifted the huge dragon off the ground. It was strong enough to spin him around, and after a few spins, he crashed into the side of another store. Alarms began to sound.

Shadow started flapping his wings as hard as he could, and managed to eventually escape Aurora's whirlwind. He shot another fire blast at her and engulfed her completely in the flames. When I ran back into the alley, lightning flew from the sky and struck Shadow in mid-air. He fell to the ground as electricity spread across his body. The flames around Aurora had dissipated. I saw her raise her arm, then swing it down, as another lightning bolt shot down and electrocuted the Black Dragon. She raised her arm again, ready to drive another lightning bolt at him.

"Stop!" I appealed, as I ran to her. Her eyes were completely white, and a brilliant energy flowed from her body that made the hair on my arms stand on end. Again I shouted at her to stop, and finally she came to her senses. If she had hit him again, she would have killed him— and we needed information from him.

She was dizzy with exhaustion, and I could tell that she was completely drained of her energy. It was extraordinary seeing her summon lightning bolts. Shadow lay still on the ground, unmoving. Gradually, he opened his eyes.

"Now tell us where the Dragon Sphere is!" I demanded, pointing my black-bladed sword *Apollyon* between his eyes.

"I won't... tell you anything," he scoffed.

I turned to Aurora for a second to check if she was okay. Shadow took the opportunity to retaliate. He spat out a green, acidic liquid right at me. I didn't have time to react as I saw the green liquid coming at me through my peripheral vision. Aurora tackled me out of the way, and we landed on the ground. She rolled off, writhing in pain. The acid had hit her.

At that moment, everything seemed to slow down. I heard the alarms from the stores sounding, police sirens drawing near and Aurora crying in pain. Her suffering summoned up in me a power I didn't know was there. I could feel each pounding palpitation of my heart. My body heated up like a boiler room and my hands trembled uncontrollably. A burning sensation in my chest became more intense with every scream that Aurora let out. I could feel a rush of energy course through my veins as rage took over me. That raging power tugged at me as if trying to pull me apart limb from limb—there was just too much, and I couldn't handle it. But then a burst of power flowed out from me, and I inhaled air as if a tightened noose around my neck had been loosened. My muscles gave way—and I collapsed and lost consciousness.

When I woke up, Aurora was hovering over me. Her tear-filled eyes and terrified look assured me that I hadn't dreamed any of this. I wish I had, though, because when I saw the aftermath, it scared me more than any nightmare I'd ever had.

The alley we battled Shadow in was no longer an alley. The stores were destroyed, and the concrete fence was now merely rubble. Buildings were obliterated and a red glow filled the sky from fires that ran rampant throughout the entire city. Phoenix was shattered. Sirens and screams filled the air from all directions. Cars were completely crushed from the buildings that had fallen over, and some had plunged into large cracks in the earth.

"Landon, we need to get out of here," Aurora said in fear. "Take my hand. Let's go."

She helped me off the ground and we ran away. Aurora didn't have to tell me that she was scared of me. I sensed that she was. As she ran, she never turned back to look at me or speak to me.

When we finally stopped, we were just outside the city limits.

"Are you okay?" I asked Aurora. She nodded her head. "What happened to Shadow?"

Aurora looked like someone had just pulled out her tongue. Even as she opened her mouth no words came through. Suddenly, she rushed at me and wrapped her arms around me. Then she cried. I could feel the rapid succession of her breaths and her trembling body. The tears streaming down her face didn't seem to stem from the pain she was in, but more from sorrow—as if her very soul had been shaken. I didn't say anything. I just placed my arms around her and held her.

I stood on a cliff overlooking the sea. It was a beautiful sight. The moon's white glow reflected gently on the calm, dark water. But that lasted only for a moment. Out in the distance something was stirring. The water bulged as if something big was surfacing. Thundering clouds swiftly rolled in. The rain came just as fast. Webs of lightning spread across the sky. The powerful winds were the first to reach me, then the hammering rain. I could barely open my eyes when I caught the slightest glimpse of something huge, crashing through the sea's surface.

The awesome force of the enormous object created a massive tidal wave that raced towards me. Anything in its path was torn to pieces. I froze in horror.

Then I saw no more.

I woke up as soon as the sunlight hit my eyes. When I stood, I noticed smoke still rising from the city. Phoenix was destroyed. Had I really caused all that damage? Aurora was already awake. She explained what happened the best she could. Through my rage, I had unleashed an earthquake. And although Shadow was badly injured, he had managed to fly away. The energy flowing through me had created a force field that protected Aurora and me from the flying debris as the buildings collapsed all around us.

"Landon," Aurora spoke with a quavering voice, "I am afraid that we may be more dangerous than anyone expected us to be."

My heart sank to my stomach. I was filled with shame. I could only agree with her. We decided that we would go back into the city and try to help out in whatever way we could.

When we reached the inner city we saw that the policemen and firemen were scampering around everywhere, putting out fires and trying to help people trapped under the debris—the rubble from the buildings had scattered in every direction. Others were calling out for lost friends and family members. Aurora and I found a group of people huddled around a single-story building, trying to pull the rocks and other wreckage away from an entrance. We could hear a woman's voice shouting from the other side as we hurried up to help.

"There are five people stuck in there," said one of the women helping to clear the entrance. "We could use whatever help we can get."

Aurora and I started picking up the larger pieces of wreckage, while the others continued to chip away at the smaller rubble. In no time, we managed to move enough out of the way to see the door behind it. I kicked it open, and light rushed in on a woman. With tears in her eyes, she managed a smile and mouthed a "thank you" to me.

Throughout the day we helped others search for loved ones, helped more people who were trapped and extinguished small fires. The power of humanity was on display as we saw strangers help and comfort each other in the disaster. The grim scenes overwhelmed me as I saw mothers crying for their dead children, and children crying for their dead parents.

"It was an accident, Landon," Aurora insisted as she saw my anguish. My mind felt tormented with the guilt of what I'd caused. "You couldn't control it."

The day had quickly gone. Aurora and I followed the herd of people who were migrating further to downtown Phoenix, to take shelter in the sports stadium that had withstood the quake. As we got closer, Aurora picked up a newspaper that was on the ground. *SHAKEN* was the headline. The cover picture showed a crying woman draped in a blanket as the red glow of the previous night burned in the background.

Aurora skimmed the article to see if either a dragon or two suspicious teenagers were mentioned. There was nothing. She did, however, find in a small article that police were searching for three teenagers linked to a bank robbery in Santa Monica, California, who had escaped during a routine traffic stop at the outskirts of the city. The only person captured from that "heist" was Gary Trinnin, who was the guy who had given us the ride here. The morning that we accepted a ride from him, he had robbed a bank and taken $500,000. That was the reason why he didn't have very many things with him. All he needed were the bags in the back of his station wagon—which, we know now, were filled with cash.

Apparently, Gary had told the police that Shade, Aurora and I were involved in robbing the bank with him.

Aurora shook her head in disgust.

"I'm done with hitchhiking," she said. I agreed.

I heard a cell phone ringing. I looked around for a moment before realizing that it was coming from my own pocket. I took it out and answered.

"Hello?"

"Landon! Are you okay? This is Purity."

"Aurora and I are okay, but we don't know where Shade is."

"Is it true?" Purity gave a brutally long pause. "Did you create the earthquake?"

I looked at Aurora, who looked back at me with inquisitive eyes.

"Yes," I responded. "But it was an accident. I didn't do it on purpose."

"I know you didn't, Landon. But Shadow said that you created it during a fight with Proteus. Now the other dragons have put a bounty on you, and the Elder Dragon Council has agreed. Blayne and Shea have overruled Zana, and now any dragon that sees you has the duty to capture you by any means necessary."

"Purity, I didn't get into a fight with Proteus. All of this happened because of Shadow. He's involved with the disappearance of the Dragon Sphere. He tried to kill us!"

Aurora's eyes followed me closely. She read the panic on my face, and heard it in my voice.

"I'm sorry, Landon," Purity replied. "I believe you—but unfortunately it's not me you have to convince. And right now, you are the most wanted dragonoid on the planet. I'll talk to Alpha and see if there's anything we can do to help you. I know you're a good person, and I don't want anything bad to happen to you."

Purity paused again. I could hear her weeping through the phone.

"Be careful, Landon… please." The call ended. How had everything turned so upside down? Now I was the one who was being hunted. I told Aurora what Purity had said, which made her even more panicked.

The way I saw it, I had two choices. One was that I could continue searching for the Dragon Sphere and hope to redeem myself by finding it. The second was that I could go home and see my mom one more time before I ran away for good. I studied Aurora carefully. Her friendship and her kindness towards me during this time were unbelievable. She seemed ready to stand by my side until the end—and that's when I realized what I needed to do. Every moment that Aurora was with me, she was in danger. I had to pick the second option. I would visit my mom first, and then leave Aurora there with her. I had to suffer the consequences of my actions by myself, and I wasn't going to drag Aurora into this anymore. I cared for her too much to do that.

I told Aurora that I wanted to go back to New Mexico to visit my mom one last time before we continued our mission. She didn't seem to mind. The only problem was that our mode of transportation was limited. Buses, trains and planes had been grounded due to the earthquake.

"We'll have to drive ourselves," I said. Aurora gave me a stare that told me she knew we had no other choice. We knew what we had to do, and it wasn't going to make us look any better. We searched for a vehicle that still had its keys in it. Fortunately, it only took us about fifteen minutes to find one. We spotted an old blue pickup truck. The passenger door was unlocked, and Aurora jumped in and unlocked the driver-side door. A turn of the key switched the vehicle on. The extent of my driving experience thus far had consisted of Mom letting me practice around the neighborhood. We had to get out of there, though. So I waited a few seconds, took a deep breath—and then we were on our way.

The brakes were a little too sensitive, or maybe my foot was just too heavy. Every time I tried to slow down, the truck would heave forward as if the body of the truck was about to slide off the wheels. Aurora laughed. Her laughter sounded good to my ears after the intensity of the last twenty-four hours.

"You can try if you think you can do any better," I challenged jokingly. She said that she was too tired to try. Although my body was tired, I didn't feel sleepy as I drove the freeway towards the east. I was determined to make it home by morning. Aurora and I spoke for hours before she finally drifted to sleep.

I couldn't imagine going on without her, but I knew it would be for the best. Hopefully she would be able to go back to Virginia and visit her father. She had spoken a lot about him as we drove, so I knew she missed him badly. She explained that her father was a no-nonsense type of guy with everything, except when it came to her. Even with Shea he was supposedly a very serious guy, although she could tell that her dad really loved her mom. It wasn't anything that he said that showed this affection; it was how he looked at her when he saw her in person or how he talked about her when she wasn't there. My mom was similar. She spoke very highly of my dad before I left for the Infernal Caverns, and she still seemed to be deeply in love with him.

The highway was quiet. Only a few cars and semis were on the road.

When I had just pumped a full tank of gas into the truck, and we were only about two hours away from Albuquerque, the sun was rising. Aurora was still sleeping. I was getting excited about the idea of seeing my mom. I was looking forward to having breakfast with her and finally taking a real shower. I didn't know where I would go after I spent some time with Mom, but I knew that I couldn't stay there long. That would be the first place the Elders would look. Perhaps someone was already there, waiting for me to arrive. I had already seen what kind of power I was capable of unleashing, but if anyone had harassed my mom I was scared to think what would happen.

Although Aurora was with me, I couldn't help but feel lonely. I remembered the faces of the crying mothers who had lost their children in the earthquake. I lost control in the heat of battle, and, as a result, caused massive destruction. I knew that it was not fair to the humans in Phoenix that all this happened. They had nothing to do with our fight with Shadow. I regretted leaving the Infernal Caverns too early. Alpha had taught me so much while I was there, but he still had warned me that there was a lot of work I had to do to control the earthquakes I could unleash. If I had stayed at the caverns, none of this would have happened. And I would be lying if I said that I hadn't come along because Aurora had taken on the mission first. The irony was that now I had to leave her behind for her own safety.

Chapter Twelve
Family Advice

Aurora woke up as soon as I parked in the driveway. We both got out, and I picked up my sword from behind the seat. Then we walked to the door. I knocked a couple of times before Mom opened the door.

"Landon!" She rushed me with open arms. Her welcoming spirit quickly went to work at repairing my broken heart.

I introduced her to Aurora. We walked into the house, and we all sat down in the living room. I told Mom about everything that had happened since I left. It was tough to tell her about Phoenix. Somehow, she already knew.

"But I also knew in my heart that you didn't do it on purpose, Landon," Mom said. "You couldn't have. I didn't raise you to be like that."

I asked her how she knew I had done it.

"Your uncle Bane came to visit me yesterday and told me what happened. I didn't believe him at first. But he seemed so concerned for you. He said that you would probably come home, and if you did, to call him. Maybe I should do that right now."

"No, Mom! Don't do that. The dragons have put a bounty on me—so who knows what he'll do!"

"You don't understand, Landon. Bane did tell me that there's a bounty on you, but he also said that he really wants to help you."

"Why? What's in it for him? All dragons are against me now. I can't trust any of them."

"You would have trusted your father. I know you would have. You are your uncle Bane's nephew—the last of his brother's children. Does he need any more reason to want to help you?"

I looked away, upset because I knew in my heart I needed guidance. What better guidance to receive on hiding from dragons than from a dragon? I nodded my head and asked her if she would call him. Mom offered Aurora some clothes, and Aurora went to clean up in Mom's room. I left to clean up as well.

It felt good to be home again, but I knew that this visit was going to be short-lived. Even with my uncle Bane's help, I had the feeling that I was going to have to leave. After I took a hot shower and got dressed, I followed the smell of pancakes into the kitchen. Mom had made stacks of them for breakfast.

"I made regular, just in case your girlfriend doesn't like peanut butter pancakes," Mom said, with a smile on her face.

"She's not my girlfriend," I responded quickly.

Mom looked at me, smiled and told me to sit down at the table. Aurora walked in a few minutes later, wearing my mom's clothes.

"Nice. Those clothes actually fit you, which means I still have a good figure," Mom said jokingly to Aurora.

"You're a beautiful girl, Aurora. I can see why Landon likes you so much."

I felt my face turn red. Mom stared at me and said, "It's okay, honey. You don't have to get embarrassed. She already knows that you like her. Girls know these things."

I saw Aurora blush as well. Mom motioned for Aurora to take a seat at the table, and asked her whether she wanted peanut butter pancakes or regular. Aurora asked for both.

As we ate, there was a knock on the door. Before I got up to open it, Xavier let himself in.

"Landon, what's up bro?" Xavier greeted me, giving me a bear hug.

Mom had called him over while I was taking a shower. I introduced Xavier to Aurora, and he sat at the table and ate breakfast with us. He told me that his summer had been pretty boring without me there to get him into trouble. I could tell that Mom was happy that her house was filled with laughter again. She had mentioned that it had been getting very lonely without Xavier's and my laughter and talking to fill the house. I was glad to see that Aurora was feeling comfortable enough to get involved in the conversation. She was talking and joking along with us.

Not too long after, there was another knock on the door. I knew it was Bane. Mom got up from the table to let him in. The image of my uncle transforming into a dragon and swallowing me whole popped into my head. To my surprise, he didn't. He waited for me in the living room, but asked my mom if he could speak to me in private. I followed him back outside.

"Uncle…" I acknowledged, not knowing what I'd say after that. Luckily he cut me off.

"I assume, since you are back at home, that you know the seriousness of your situation?"

"Yes. But I didn't mean to do it though." I argued.

"Intentions are rarely considered when something like this happens. I do not judge you, my boy. I only wish to guide you through this tough time."

"I can never make this right again, can I?"

My uncle's stare gave me no hope.

"You need to learn how to control your quakes, my boy," he said. "I want you to go to Denver. I will have my driver take you there. You will meet a man named Kraven. He is my cousin, and he will be expecting you. There you will train to control your power and perhaps, after a while, you may be able to leave the safety of his home. I will do what I can to convince the Elder Dragon Council to drop the bounty. But for now, you will be safe in his home."

"Why are you helping me?" I asked suspiciously.

"Because, whether you like it or not, you are part of my family—and family helps each other in time of need. With that said, I will leave you. I will have my driver come by at two o'clock. I will receive updates from my cousin on your progress. Goodbye, Landon. Good luck."

My uncle turned away and walked towards his limo.

When I came inside I told Mom, Aurora, and Xavier that I was leaving for Denver at two. I felt bad that Xavier had no clue what was going on, but I thought that it was better if he didn't know. Although Xavier was like family, I could tell that he sensed that whatever was going on was beyond him.

"Well, I'd better go finish mowing the lawn," he said, with a bit of nervousness in his voice. "Thanks for the pancakes, Mrs. Brown."

I knew he was lying. We all said goodbye to Xavier. He told me to be careful, and to let him know when I got back. I told him I would.

Once Xavier left, I explained to Mom and Aurora that my uncle Bane would be sending me to visit his cousin, who would help me train some more. I told them he was confident that it was a safe place, and that no one would find me there. I glanced over to Aurora, but she quickly averted her eyes from me. She understood the message that it was just me leaving this time, and she couldn't come with me. The expression on her face was one that I would never forget. Her green eyes glistened, and she looked as though she was holding back tears. Her usually animated face was frozen in place, with a cold unemotional gaze—the color of her lips and her skin not as brilliant as they had been just moments before. Mom noticed it too and moved next to Aurora. She put her arm around her in an attempt to console her. I couldn't tell if Aurora was more disappointed that our journey was ending or that I was leaving her. I felt a knot at the pit of my stomach at the realization that our journey together was coming to an end.

"I knew that this would eventually be your life," Mom said, sad and disappointed. "Maybe if your dad were with us, then there wouldn't be so much pressure on you…"

I considered what Mom said. With what I know about dragons now, however, it would still have been expected of me to be involved in their affairs, even if my father *were* here. I asked Mom if she would help get Aurora back to Virginia so that she could be with her dad. Mom looked at me and nodded her head. Aurora still didn't say a word.

Mom got up from the couch, came over to me, and gave me a kiss on the forehead.

"I'll let you two talk," she informed.

I turned my attention to Aurora.

"I'm so sorry that you can't come with me," I said. She still didn't respond. I walked over to her and sat down beside her.

"Aurora, every dragon, except for my uncle Bane, is looking for me. They want to take me down. I can't risk you coming along and getting hurt for something that I did. I won't let you go into hiding when you don't have to. That's not fair to you."

"I want to show you something," Aurora volunteered. She pulled the collar of her shirt down below her right shoulder.

I saw a horrible burn mark that reached from her right shoulder blade to the ball of her shoulder.

"Do you know where I got it?" she asked. I knew that it had happened when she pushed me out of the way when Shadow spat acid at me. She continued before I could answer her.

"That was at the end of our fight with Shadow," she said. "I jumped in front of the acid so that it wouldn't hit you. I knew the risk of coming on this mission. Did you know that protecting you was all I could think about when I lost control and shot lightning bolts at Shadow? I didn't even know I could do that until then. I was willing to give everything I had to save your life. At first I liked having you around. But now I *need* you around."

I didn't know what to say to her. I knew what she was feeling, because I was feeling it too. When I saw her hurt and writhing in pain in the alley of the Magik Shop, I had lost all control.

"Aurora," I began, searching for the words. "Please understand. I am responsible for killing innocent people. I deserve to be alone. Please promise me that you will go home to your dad and spend time with him."

I took her hands in mine. They were soft to the touch.

"Look into my eyes and promise me that," I pleaded.

Aurora's precious emerald eyes stared deeply into mine.

"Landon, I can't promise you that. I miss my dad, but I'm not ready to go back home just yet. I may try to go back to the caverns and train, if that's what you're going to be doing in Denver, but I can't go back home yet." Aurora seemed firm on her stance of going back home.

"You need to promise me one thing, though," she requested. "Promise me that you will call me when you get to Denver. I need to know that you made it there safely. If it's okay with your mom, I'll wait here until you arrive there so you can call me on her phone."

I promised her that I would, but I was surprised that she was willing to wait with my mom for my call.

After speaking with Aurora, I went to Mom's room and sat down next to her as she was reflecting on one of my baby pictures. She asked me if everything was okay between Aurora and me. I told her that it was. A tear slid down her cheek as she recalled stories about the funny things I used to do when I was a baby. Apparently, I really liked wearing diapers on my head.

Mom's tone changed. She told me that this trip I was taking to Denver felt different than the last one to California.

"For some reason," she said, "I feel as if this is the last time I am going to see you."

I reassured her that it wouldn't be, but that some time had to pass before I could come back. I was a fugitive in the dragon world.

Mom grabbed my hand and examined it. I told her that all the scars on my hand had happened since training with Alpha. She shook her head.

"Not this one," she said, pointing to a tiny scar right in between my pointer and middle finger knuckles. "Do you remember where that one came from?" I shook my head.

She explained. When I was four, we were at the park that was right across the street from our house. A stray dog ran into the area and started barking viciously at everyone there. Mom hurried towards me, and that's when the dog chased her. She couldn't recall what type of dog it was, but she would never forget the snarl on its face and its violent demeanor. The stray snapped at Mom, and even as a four-year-old child I sensed the danger she was in, so I moved between her and the animal and punched it in the face. Mom said that I cried, but not because the dog's tooth had pierced me, but because I was scared for her. The dog's bite dug deep into my skin and left that small scar that Mom was admiring. The stray left us, whimpering in pain, as Mom realized, so early in my life, that I was no ordinary child.

"Ever since you were little, you have been protecting me, Landon," Mom said, wiping the tears from her eyes. "I'm sorry that so much has been put on you at such an early stage in your life. You shouldn't have to deal with all of this—but if there is anyone that can handle it, it's you. I have full confidence in you. What happened in Phoenix is something that you couldn't have controlled. It's awful what happened, Landon, but don't beat yourself up so much for such a bizarre accident. Always remember that I will love you no matter what."

I wish my mom's words were able to comfort me, but in reality they made me feel worse. She said that what happened was an accident, and I agreed with her, but to me it could have been avoided. What did comfort me was that she still loved me, even though I'd messed up so badly. Mom pulled me in and hugged me. She kissed me on my forehead, and told me that everything would turn out okay. Then we walked out of the room.

I spent the rest of the day hanging out with Aurora at the park across the street from my house. It was a nice change of pace. We actually got to relax, and tried not to worry about anything. It was hot outside, but the weather felt perfect compared to Arizona's sticky, heavy heat. We sat in the shade under a tree, our hands close to one another, feeling the soft, cool blades of recently cut grass. I gave Aurora a quick Albuquerque crash course. Easily visible to us was the Sandia mountain range just east of Albuquerque. I explained to her that they were called "Sandia" because that's the Spanish word for watermelon—and in certain lighting the mountains had a pink tint, like the flesh of the watermelon. West from us was "Old Town," which was the original settlement location of Albuquerque, and now home to museums, shops, merchants and a historical church.

Excitedly, I told Aurora about our annual balloon fiesta every October, and wished she could see how awesome it was when hundreds of hot-air balloons from all over the world ascend into the sky at the same time. The balloon glow at night was amazing as well. I shared with her that "red or green" was a serious affair in Albuquerque—because eating chili was a way of life. There was so much I wanted to show her. There was so much that I loved about my city—but time, again, was against me.

Aurora stared at the fire charm Blayne had given us that still hung around her neck. They were useless now. I had taken mine off after I took a shower, but Aurora kept hers on. She said that she liked wearing it. We talked about what we had been through up until this point, and Aurora expressed how worried she was about Shade. Although in my mind he had essentially turned his back on us, Aurora felt Shade was in danger by being around his father. She felt that Shadow would convince Shade to hate everyone and everything good in the world. Aurora said that no matter what Shade's outcome was, she would always think of him as a good guy. If he weren't, he would never have saved her life when she fought Proteus in Santa Monica.

As Aurora spoke, she shifted around on the swings uncomfortably.

"Are you okay?" I asked.

"Ever since the acid burned my back, I've been in a lot of pain. It feels as if the pain in this shoulder blade has spread to the other one."

Aurora pointed to her left shoulder, then to the right. I told her jokingly that she probably just hurt from not sleeping on a comfortable bed for the last month. I joked that maybe Alpha knew a good chiropractor, since he made all of his recruits sleep on the ground. We laughed, but that moment came to an end quickly. My uncle's limo pulled up outside the house. Aurora and I went back over to my place, so that I could say one last goodbye to my mom.

Mom came out of the house, and met me next to the limo. She brought out my sword and handed it to me. The driver stepped out and waited by my door. Mom hugged me as if this was the last time we'd see each other, and told me to be careful. She reminded me to call her when I got to Denver. She knew that Aurora would stay with her until I called. After I hugged her and told her that I loved her, I walked up to Aurora and gave her a hug. She held me tightly, neither one of us wanting to let go. The impatient driver cleared his throat, cueing me that it was time to leave, and he opened my door for me. When Aurora unwrapped her arms from around me, she leaned in and kissed me.

"Be safe, Landon," Aurora concluded with a gentle smile.

I smiled back at her, and the driver closed the door. The scene was very similar to the first time I left, roughly a month ago. The only difference was that Aurora and the blue pickup truck we came in were there. My heart was pounding as we drove off, and I felt as if I was heading into exile. I lay down on the seat and tried to fall asleep, but all I kept thinking about was Aurora. I imagined her grabbing the keys to the truck and chasing after me; then I shrugged the image off as ridiculous. I knew that wouldn't happen. I put my head back, resting on one of the pillows provided, overwhelmed with emotion. After a while, my eyes became heavy and I fell into a deep sleep.

Even with my eyes closed, I could sense the lights flashing by. When I opened them, it was dark outside and we were in a city. As I wiped the sleep from my eyes, the driver rolled down the glass window that separated us and told me that we were in Denver. I couldn't believe I had slept for the entire trip, but I was happy that I had. We were still on the highway, passing by the brightly lit buildings of the city. We drove to the city's outskirts before the driver finally got off the highway. We passed by many subdivisions before we hit a long stretch of bare land, and eventually turned into a driveway that led to a gated mansion with black shutters and very little lighting. The house was not only isolated, but it also looked very uninviting. The closest neighbor must have been two or three miles away. The gate opened for us, and we continued down the driveway.

The driver parked in front of some steps that led to the front door. He got out and opened the door for me. I stretched my legs once I stepped out, slung *Apollyon* over my shoulder and walked to the door. As I reached to knock, the door opened. There stood a man with a thick, bushy, coal-black beard.

"Welcome, Landon. Come in," the man said, with a smooth, confident voice. The deep tone of his words was perfect for reading poetry. His voice didn't seem to match his frail appearance, though. He covered himself with a long black robe to hide his deformity—he was a hunchback. He had short hair that was combed forward, and dark-brown eyes.

"My name is Kraven," the man said. "Bane has told me about your situation. You will be safe here."

I thanked him for letting me stay with him, and he showed me to my room. The house was huge, but oddly, there wasn't any furniture or decorations. A red carpet that stretched throughout the house stood out from the white walls. It all seemed plain and somewhat lonely.

"Does anyone else live here besides you?" I asked. He nodded his head.

"Everyone's asleep. We wake up very early."

Kraven didn't talk much, and his hunchbacked appearance added another element of mystery to him and to the whole place.

I asked him if I could use his phone so that I could call Mom and Aurora, and he directed me towards the kitchen. I picked up the receiver on the wall next to the cabinets, but there was no dial tone.

"The phone doesn't work," I said, handing the phone to Kraven.

"That's strange," he responded. "It was working not too long ago. This is the only phone in the house, so maybe you can try again in the morning. For now, you should get some rest."

Something didn't add up. There was only one phone working in the whole mansion, there wasn't any furniture, and no one else seemed to be around. I decided I would give it until the morning to weigh my options, even though I had that weird feeling that things would only get worse as the night progressed. And I was right!

Chapter Thirteen
Face to Face with a Phoenix

I tossed and turned uncomfortably in bed for a few hours before I decided to get up and tour the mansion. My threat radar was still high, so I took *Apollyon* with me. I was staying in the west wing of the mansion, and the hallway outside my room led to stairs down to the first floor. There were three other doors in the same hallway, but when I tried to gently turn the knobs to open them, I found them all locked. I stepped softly as I sneaked around the sprawling house. A dim light shone on the first floor, so I headed towards it. Quietly, I went down the stairs and stopped at the bottom. I heard a voice. I couldn't make out any words, but I could tell that someone was whispering. The sound was coming from the other side of the wall from where the stairs were. And it was getting louder.

As I heard someone approach the door, I quickly hid underneath the staircase and hoped that it was too dark for anyone to see me. Kraven walked in from the other room, still whispering. He moved into view. He was using a cell phone. He had lied to me! He told me there weren't any other phones in the house. I sat quietly, hoping he would not turn around.

"Does anyone else know he's here?" Kraven whispered into the phone. "Good. What does he know of the Sphere?"

When I heard him say those words, a shiver ran down my spine. It seemed that running away from my quest had only brought me closer to the Dragon Sphere.

"Okay, I'll see to it that he understands his options. If he doesn't agree to help us… well, you know what needs to be done." Kraven stood by the staircase for a few more seconds.

"Yes, sir. We'll see you soon."

Should I emerge from under the stairs or wait it out? I thought. I knew I couldn't rely on patience. I was in Kraven's domain. Who knows what would happen when morning came? The only things I had going for me at the moment were the element of surprise and my sword. I walked out from underneath the staircase and slowly unsheathed *Apollyon*. Kraven's hunched back was only a few feet away from me, so I lifted my sword and poked at it gingerly. Immediately he twirled around, looking as if he'd been blinded by a photographer's flash. He took a step back, but I followed by taking a step closer. I gestured for him to remain quiet and move towards the entrance door. I had him open the door and lead us outside. I felt safer outside than inside the mansion. Not having had the chance to really investigate the place, I wanted to be cautious about any potential traps.

After walking about fifty feet away from the entrance of the manor, I asked him who he was on the phone with. He stayed silent. I pushed my blade closer to his neck.

"It was Bane," he growled, eyeing the sword deviously as if he were calculating a way to get out of his current situation. He asked me to hear him out.

With a firm grip on *Apollyon* I answered, "Talk."

"It may seem to you that you have the upper hand right now, but the overall battle will be won by us," he admonished. He paused for a moment, and the pupils in his eyes lit like fire as he transferred his eyes slowly away from the blade and towards me.

"You don't have to be on the losing side, Landon," he continued. "Your uncle has sent you here to help you. I can show you how to control your powers more effectively. We want you to join us, and help us shape the future."

"What do you know about the Dragon Sphere?" I demanded, with a deadly serious tone.

"That's what I'm trying to explain to you, Landon. The Sphere is hidden, under our protection. The time is coming for us to unleash the ancient king's fury on the world. We can use a dragonoid like you on our side. Think of your mom. Wouldn't you want her to be safe in all of this?"

"Leave her out of this!" I felt the anger boiling inside me. I didn't want a repeat of what happened in Phoenix, so I started taking deep breaths.

"Landon, I could show you how to control those quakes. You don't have to fear what you're capable of. You should never fear yourself. Let everyone else fear you."

"Hold up." A thought crossed my mind that I needed to have answered. "I'm having a hard time figuring out how you stole the Dragon Sphere and didn't get caught. I mean, look at you—not even a disguise could hide you."

"I did not take anything!" he snapped. "It was Bane who went into the Temple of the Elder Dragons and took it. The Elders didn't even know it was missing until a few weeks later. They were so careless in watching over the Sphere. They were the ones who put everything they claimed to protect in jeopardy. But the time for change has come."

"Aremas has been trapped before," I said. "If you release him, he will be trapped again. I don't care if there is a bounty on me. I will side with the Elder Dragons on this one."

"It doesn't matter if they manage to trap him again, Landon," Kraven argued. "Aremas is a threat in himself, this is true. But our reason for releasing him has nothing to do with his taking over the planet. We need him for some specific reasons. We need him to create imbalance in the climate again *and* we need him to begin the Great Awakening. Once these two things have been set in motion, the people of Earth will have a reason to scream. Dragons and humans alike who have not joined us will know terror! They will wish that Aremas were ruling the earth! Instead, his mighty father will wreak havoc on them. He will crush them with little effort!"

"You're delusional! You can't even open up the Dragon Sphere. If you could, you would have already released him."

"Timing is everything, boy. It took us a while to release Aremas, but not because we couldn't. We needed to know how to control him. Now we have managed to do that. Don't you remember your little encounter with him?"

I had no idea what he was talking about. I've never seen Aremas, let alone had an interaction with him. Kraven continued.

"Bane allowed us to test our control of Aremas by releasing him and having him stalk your plane when he sent you to the Infernal Caverns. I heard he gave you quite a scare."

Suddenly I remembered. Aremas was the one who flipped our plane when I was on my way to California. Could what he was saying be true? Could they have tamed such a fearsome dragon? It seemed impossible.

"I can see you trying to work all of this out in your head," Kraven flashed a conniving smile with delight. "What you don't realize is how deep our alliance runs. Every day we gain new recruits who will help us during the Great Awakening. That is the important thing. Even you have been a pawn in this. Your Uncle Bane was very careful in how he dealt with your participation. Giving you the bloodlust berry and making you think that your father had saved it for you was his genius. In reality, the bloodlust berry was payment to Primus for making the device to control Aremas. He was so desperate to rid himself of his flashbacks that he was willing to help us and make you a sword, so that no one would be suspicious of the transaction."

Every word Kraven spoke felt like a hammer beating down on my chest. Any hope I had that I, Aurora, or the Elder

Dragons would be able to stop the Sons of Levi was quickly dissipating. How deep did their connections really run? Was standing up to Kraven really as useless as he made it seem? Then, in the midst of my uncertainty, a sudden burst of strange yet familiar confidence came over me. I couldn't explain what happened or why, but just then I felt my conviction strengthen. I heard a voice in the back of my mind saying, *"You must stand for what you believe in."*

I gazed confidently at Kraven. I felt a gentle breeze tousle my hair.

"With everything you're telling me, I'm one step closer to stopping this whole thing. Soon I will leave here and tell the Elder Dragons that my uncle Bane is responsible for the disappearance of the Dragon Sphere. They will find a way to stop him."

"Landon, you're just not getting it," Kraven said. "Their time is up. The Elder Dragons can't do anything to stop us anymore. And even if you managed to get away, they wouldn't believe you. You are now considered their enemy. But you can join us. We are your family, and we can protect you from anyone trying to make good on the bounty that they put out on you. If it weren't for your uncle, you would have probably been captured already."

"You are not my family! And the Elder Dragons will listen to me! I am the son of Drayden. They will give me another chance!"

I held my sword closer to Kraven's neck. His eyes were dark, and his face was contorted into a wicked grin.

"I personally know the Elder Dragons' limits on forgiveness. They will not listen to you. They do not care for anyone but themselves. I have gone through the same shame. I have had a bounty put on me. I was forced to run for my life with a power I could not understand. Where was their understanding for me? Where was their forgiveness? Our fates have crossed each other, little brother, as both sons of Drayden have been written off as outcasts and murderers."

"Who... are... you?" I asked in disbelief, not really wanting an answer to the question.

"You must have heard of me," Kraven guessed. "I am Brandon Phoenix. I go by Kraven now, since your Elder Dragons have stained my name. I was hunted down like an animal, but I survived. Our uncle Bane was able to hide me and train me. He can help you in the same way. You could be as powerful as I am, and we could lead the Sons of Levi together with our uncle."

"Look at you," I said, filled with a sudden disgust for my half-brother. "How could you think you're powerful? You look like an old man. Is that what I have to look forward to in the next twenty years? You can keep your end-of-the-world plot and our uncle's training. I don't want either one."

Kraven looked irritated. I think that telling him he looked like an old man really hit a nerve. With my sword still up against his neck, I saw him pondering carefully what his next move would be.

"You stubborn little brat!" he hissed. "You won't have the next twenty years to look forward to. Soon you'll be dead!"

With incredible speed, Kraven kicked me in my chest, pushing me back. Then he ripped off his robe and showed his true form.

Two bronze wings stretched out from behind Kraven as he stood up straight, no longer pretending he had a deformity. The wings resembled two long and thin extra arms growing from his back, with long, bony fingers that stretched down to the bottom of each wing. Translucent leathery skin covered them, and his wings flexed at his command. At the tip of each elongated finger was a razor-sharp claw. His appearance was frightening, yet fascinating, at the same time.

"Have you never seen a dragonoid with wings, little brother?" Kraven boomed with confidence, now that he was on full display. His body looked like it was carved out of stone as he displayed his six-pack shirtless torso—no longer resembling a fragile old man. "Maybe you are growing wings yourself as we speak. Perhaps the pain from that growth had caused you to create the earthquake. It is indeed a painful experience, I can tell you. And that pain contributed to my uncontrollable quakes. My wings started to grow at around your age, and they grew fast. That's why it hurt so badly. But the physical pain is nothing compared to the emotional damage. As if it wasn't bad enough that a bounty was put on me in the dragon realm, I had to deal with the human world. They treated me as if I was a monster. I couldn't hide among them; no one would accept me. Can you imagine how that would affect a fifteen-year-old boy? Fortunately for you, you won't have to find out. Your life ends here."

Kraven flapped his wings and hovered over the ground. I gripped *Apollyon* tightly and charged at him. I swung down with my sword, but he darted upwards, avoiding my strike. With his right hand, Kraven shot a fireball that hit me in the chest. The blast burned my skin and knocked me to the ground. Kraven immediately lifted both of his hands, and the gravel below me lifted me to my feet. Then he blasted me with several more shots of fire, hitting me on my shoulders, chest and midsection. Burn holes filled my shirt with each blast as Kraven flew down and hit me with his left shoulder, knocking me to the ground again. For a moment my brain short-circuited, overloaded by processing what just happened. My brother had the ability to control more than one elemental power.

He landed next to me. I swung my sword at his legs, but he easily avoided it. He willed the ground behind me to rise like a fist. I felt the punch to the back of my head. I held my head and got up quickly to avoid another earth-pounding. Kraven swiftly retreated twenty feet away from me. I charged at him and jabbed with *Apollyon* right at his chest, but he was too quick. He easily side-stepped my sword, and punched me in the gut. Then he delivered an uppercut with a fist of fire. The blow knocked me at least ten feet in the air. Kraven was relentless. He flew up, put his hands together and swung down, hammering me back towards the ground. He shot more fire blasts at me, but I managed to avoid them by rolling quickly to the side.

I still held *Apollyon* tightly in my hands. An inch of doubt crept into my mind. Did I even have a chance of defeating him? He was faster than me, stronger than me, more powerful than me *and* he could fly. The only advantage I had was my sword, but it wasn't doing anything for me at the moment. Kraven flew at me again, attempting to knock me down, but I jumped back and willed the ground to rise, creating a gravel wall. Kraven slammed right into it, slowing him down just enough for me to drop-kick him in his chest. As he fell on the ground, I willed the gravel to wrap around his feet and wings. Kraven was trapped for a moment. Perhaps it was all the time I needed. I jumped up, aiming Apollyon at his chest. He broke free from his rocky shackles and rolled over just in time for me to miss. I had stabbed my sword so deep into the earth that it got stuck. Frustrated, Kraven shot a stream of fire at me. I pulled my sword out just in time and jumped out of the way.

Kraven roared in anger. "C'mon, little brother. Show me your hidden power. Bring out the power of Dragos! Fight as the mightiest of our kind. What are you holding back for?"

Before I could even respond, he attacked me again. At his command, the earth below me rose in the form of spikes as I sidestepped, rolled and jumped back from the attack. I also commanded the earth to shoot up to where Kraven was hovering. As he evaded, I willed another column of earth to rise and hit him. The pillar knocked the wind out of him as it hit him in the gut. I lost my focus on him for a moment when I noticed a familiar energy rising. My chest started burning and I panicked, thinking that I was about to cause another earthquake.

As I looked up at Kraven, he was descending to the ground, holding his midsection. I started breathing heavily. I didn't want to lose control again. Kraven touched the ground and began walking towards me with an evil smile on his face.

"Now it's time to really push your power to the limit," he said.

He raised both hands in the air and made the ground shake. I lost my balance, but immediately sank my feet into the earth for support. Large mounds of gravel rose from the ground and formed two monstrous hands. Kraven clenched his fists and the earthy hands followed his command. He motioned the right fist to strike, and it crashed down towards me. My first reaction was to jump out of the way, but I had sunk my feet into the ground to keep me upright. Quickly, I willed a wall of earth in front of me to block the attack. It worked, but his huge earthen hands still managed to crack my wall in half.

I swiftly pulled my feet from the earth and jumped out of the way as the other hand smashed down, a second too late. The left hand swiped at me again and hit me directly, sending me thirty feet in the air. Kraven took to the sky. As he neared me, I slashed at him with my sword in defense. He shot me with a fire blast that hurled me back down to the ground. I managed to land on my feet. How was I supposed to beat him when he knew how to control the earth better than I could, plus he could shoot fire and he could fly? Then I realized what I needed to do. I had to ground him if I had any shot of beating him. It was the only way.

Kraven, still in the sky, willed the ground to shake again. I stood ready for any attacks that he was going to send my way, and waited for an open opportunity to attack him. It was hard to maintain my balance, but I managed to steady myself while keeping my eye on him at the same time. Kraven had amazing control of his quakes as he shook the ground in a nearly forty-foot radius around me. Nothing past that moved. The two mounds that were once his gravel fists collided with each other and began forming something that I couldn't make out. I tried stepping forward but fell right on my face. The quake was just too strong to move in. Kraven changed his focus to the mounds that were forming some sort of object. He quickly flew towards the pile of gravel to pick up the object that he had formed. The quake stopped and I ran toward him.

As I approached, he turned to me. He was holding two small swords grafted out of the gravel. The rocky blades had sharp, jagged edges, bound to a rocky hilt by vines. I couldn't believe my luck. He was giving me the advantage I needed to beat him. I was confident that he couldn't beat me in a sword fight. *Apollyon* was too powerful a weapon for him to fight me with a couple of small swords made of rock. I noticed the vines in the swords tightening around the hilt and sliding down to wrap around his arms. Immediately he threw the sword in his right hand at me. I ducked just in time. Using the vines that were attached to his sword, he was able to pull it back to him after missing me. With the other hand he jabbed his sword downwards at me, but I blocked it with *Apollyon*.

I lunged my sword at him, but he spun to the side and swung his swords around. I rolled away, but not without getting sliced on my right leg.

The cool night air rushed in to my freshly made wound, amplifying the pain. Warm blood dripped down my leg as I pushed myself back to my feet, grimacing. Kraven rushed at me, swinging his swords and launching them at me. I blocked one with *Apollyon*, then dropped to my knees and stretched backwards as the other blade nearly shaved my face right off. Then I jumped to my feet and charged Kraven, aiming *Apollyon* right at his chest. He spun to his right and extended his left wing, slapping my entire body and pushing me to the ground. Kraven launched his two swords down at me. I willed the earth alongside me to shield me just in time. His swords clashed against the gravel and got stuck in the earth. Immediately, I picked myself up off the ground, and with *Apollyon*, cut the vines that were attached to the swords from Kraven's arms.

Without his weapons, Kraven took to the sky again. As he flapped his wings, I lunged towards him and jumped onto his legs. My weight was not enough to keep him on the ground, though. In an instant, we were fifty feet in the air and I was hugging his legs tightly, still holding onto *Apollyon*. Kraven tried shaking me off but I didn't let go. He flipped around, flew in circles and then higher, trying all he could to shake me off. Then he dove towards the ground. He was going to slam me into the ground! Just before I landed, I willed a wall of earth to rise right in front of Kraven. I crashed onto the ground, creating a small crater into the earth. Kraven ran directly into the wall I created and broke through it, sending him scraping against the ground.

My body ached. I was bleeding in several different places on my body, and I no longer had my sword in hand. A thick sheet of dust covered the area. As it settled, Kraven and I both rose to our feet. He held his head and winced in pain. Then both of us fixed our eyes on the black obsidian blade, as it stuck out of the ground between us. Without hesitation, we both rushed at it. My right leg exploded in pain because of the wound, but I knew that I had to get my sword. I would die without it. Kraven reached out for the sword, but I jumped and tackled him away from *Apollyon*. Every coach in any level of football I have ever played would have been proud of the way I tackled Kraven. My form was impeccable, my intensity was immeasurable and my desire was unmatched. I leapt quickly to my feet and gripped the sword in my hands. I felt a sense of confidence come over me, as if everything was going to be okay.

Kraven jumped to his feet and shot a fire blast at me, which I managed to evade. Then, as he turned around in an effort to escape, I jumped on top of him. It felt as if time slowed down and the sounds around us were drowned out. I closed my eyes and let instinct take over as I slashed down with *Apollyon*. When I opened my eyes, I was falling, face first, towards the ground. What had happened? I hit the ground and noticed blood dripping down my sword. Was it mine or his? I quickly looked up towards Kraven.

Kraven was on hands and knees, stunned and breathing heavily. Blood was spurting out of Kraven's left arm, and half of his left wing was missing. The other half of his wing lay beside him. Kraven let out a howl of frustration and pain. The ground shook furiously. I stood up immediately and ran towards the gate in the front of the mansion property. I leapt, trying to make it over the gate, but was blasted right into it by a fireball from Kraven. He darted towards me and punched furiously at me. He relentlessly attacked me and I was only able to block a few of his strikes. Then he lifted me up from my neck with his left arm. I didn't understand how he had so much strength left in his body. With his right arm, he was gathering energy for a fireball. I stared helplessly as the fireball he was creating radiated an enormous amount of energy. I tried to escape, but I was too weak and was blacking out as Kraven choked me. I couldn't even swing *Apollyon*.

"Goodbye, brother," Kraven bellowed angrily in his deep voice, as he grimaced in pain.

His hand tightened around my throat. I saw the hate in my brother's eyes, and then everything quickly faded into blackness. I felt a tremendous amount of heat and energy slam into me like a ton of bricks.

While in that darkness and intensity, I had a vision of a hooded man with fiery red eyes in a black robe, with smoke swirling around him, trying to enter a room but finding it locked. I was inside the room and noticed the door handle jiggling. I kept my mouth closed and tried to calm my furiously beating heart; eventually, the jiggling stopped. Everything went silent. Seconds later, the door exploded as pieces flew across the room and the hooded figure walked in, looking for me. I didn't run away. I couldn't even move. I was ready for him to take me away.

Chapter Fourteen
Legion of Doom

"It seems as if the tides have turned and the humans no longer fear us," my father Drayden spoke to a congregation of roughly fifty people, undoubtedly dragons in human form. Torches lit the room up, displaying golden pillars decorated with sapphires, rubies and amethyst. Also engraved in the pillars was lettering of a language unknown to me. It looked like some sort of temple—a safe place for the dragons to come together and discuss dragon politics.

My father continued, "I still stand firm in my belief that this was no way for humans to live to begin with. But now that they are retaliating against us, it is time for us to make a decision. Can we blame them for their actions? Would we not do the same thing if we were in their position? These Knights prove their valor by standing up to us and protecting the people. They are becoming better equipped and more knowledgeable with each confrontation they have with one of us. Is all-out war with the humans the answer, then? Should we avoid them? What do you say, leaders of the dragon clans?"

The room roared with the voices of the other dragons, trying to make their points. Some shouted for war and others argued for peace. One of the dragons stood up, his piercing steel-blue eyes gazing around the room, and immediately the rest quieted.

"The current order has been in place since the beginning of time," he began. "Not all dragons make humans their enemies, and not all humans desire to kill us. If we continue to meddle with the natural relationship between us and the humans, more problems will arise. We should not have to hide or avoid them

because they fear us. If we do that, then they will most certainly believe that they are the dominant species of Earth."

My father interrupted.

"Proteus, the old order of things is what has gotten us to this point. Relations with the humans have always been and will always be unstable. They will always see us as a threat, and it is a part of human nature to eliminate anything that they feel threatened by. I propose that we never show our true forms to humans again. Let them believe that we have vanished from existence. The advantages of this strategy outweigh the disadvantages. There will be no need for bloodshed. Over time, humans will stop searching for us, and many will believe that we never existed. We will fade from their memories—and we will be left alone."

All of the dragons contemplated my father's words for some time, except for Proteus, who was still disturbed by the idea.

One of the leaders stood up and spoke: "Son of Ithacus, we know that your father's seat in the Dragon Council must be filled, and that his desire was to have you replace him. Many feel that you are still too young to fill this position. You are not yet considered an elder, but your words are wise and you are strong. If what you propose is going to work, we will need you to lead us in this effort in convincing the Dragon Council that it is the correct move to pursue. How will we know whether you are ready to take up such responsibilities? Can anyone here think of a way for Drayden to prove his worth to us all?"

My father remained standing proudly. I could tell that he was ready to prove himself as a worthy successor to my grandfather's seat in the Dragon Council. The crowd fell silent. Either they were thinking of some task that my dad could do to prove himself, or they did not want to challenge him.

After waiting for someone else to challenge my father, and not getting any results, Proteus objected: "I do not agree with having Drayden take his father's seat." He turned to my father.

"I am not questioning whether you are capable of handling the responsibilities," he said, "but the position of Elder should be reserved for someone who is more advanced in age than you are. However, I believe a challenge is necessary for any of us to prove our worth. I believe that I would be a better candidate than Drayden as a member of the Elder Council. I issue a challenge to you, Drayden. The drake Behemoth has been terrorizing villages west of here. No one has taken the initiative to stop him. Behemoth kills dragons and humans alike. He feeds off the destruction and does not care who stands in his way. Whoever stops Behemoth will take his case to the Dragon Council to become one of them, and will have the full support of the dragon clans."

The others deliberated Proteus's suggestion. Eventually, they agreed with the terms of his challenge. Then they turned to my father and waited for his answer. He did not speak, but nodded his head in agreement.

Suddenly the scene changed. I was six years old and playing in the park with Xavier. We were on the swings, trying to see who could swing higher. When we were high enough, we agreed to jump off.

"One," we began counting together,

"Two," we continued as we readied ourselves.

"THREE!" we shouted and leapt out of our swings.

It seemed as if we were in the air forever. I noticed the younger version of myself prepare for impact. My feet swung forward and I was about to land flat on my back. Before I landed, the sand rose in the form of a small slide, and I slid down gently onto the ground. Xavier landed awkwardly on his right foot, and I heard a snap. Xavier cried furiously as I ran across the street to my house and yelled for my mom's help. Mom ran over to check out the damage.

"Is he okay?" I asked worriedly. "Will Xavier be all right? Does he need a doctor?"

"Does he need a doctor?" a voice muttered.

"I think so. He's in terrible shape, but he's still breathing," another voice said.

I opened my eyes and saw two blurry figures hovering over me. When my vision had cleared, I noticed a man and woman staring down at me. They didn't seem to be in very good shape themselves. They were dirty and looked as though they hadn't brushed their hair in months. They didn't smell all that great, either.

"Hey kid, you alive?" the man crowed. His raspy voice sounded as though he'd just finished swallowing a bunch of sharp, broken glass.

"Of course he is, you idiot. He's staring right at us," the woman snapped.

I tried to get up, but I was too weak to move. Every muscle ached.

"Where am I?" I asked.

"You're in our alley," the man said. "Why are you so red? I think you overdid it at the tanning bed."

"Burt, leave him alone," the woman scolded. "I'm sorry about Burt. He's not very good with people. My name is Ernestine. Are you okay? You look like you've had a rough night."

I noticed that I didn't have my sword in hand, so I looked around and asked them if they had seen it.

Burt grinned. "See, Ernie, I told you it was his. Are you a ninja boy?"

I shook my head. He bent down and pulled pieces of cardboard and newspaper away from where he had hidden my sword.

"What is a young man like yourself doing with such a deadly weapon?" Ernestine asked.

"It was a gift. I carry it with me everywhere," I responded.

It was a struggle, but I managed to get off the ground and on to my feet. Burt handed me my sword and asked me if I could show him some moves. I asked him if he had seen my scabbard, but then I remembered that I'd left it at the mansion grounds when I was fighting Kraven.

Every part of my body burned as I stretched my hand out. There wasn't much left of my shirt, which had large burn holes in the front and back. Luckily, my pants weren't in bad shape.

"You're such a good-looking kid," Ernestine said with a kind smile. Then she turned to her companion. "Burt, get one of your shirts from your bag and let him have it!"

Burt looked upset, but didn't argue. He got out a dirty flannel shirt that smelled like old cheese and handed it to me. I hesitated, but I took it anyway.

"So why are you all burnt up, kid? Did you get in a fight with a blowtorch?" Burt chuckled.

"Yeah… something like that," I mumbled. "Hey, do you know where the nearest pay phone is?"

"Yeah, there's one not too far from here. We'll take you," said Ernestine.

All three of us walked out of the alley and they led me to the nearest pay phone. The people walking by us kept their distance from us. I realized that looking homeless and walking around with a sword in hand was not a good look. When we got to the booth, I checked my pockets for change and realized that I didn't have any. Ernestine offered the thirty-five cents and I thanked her. Then I dialed my mom's cell.

"Hello?" Aurora answered, her voice sounded frantic. My heart jumped at the sound of it.

"Aurora! It's me. I need help."

"Landon… I was so worried about you," Aurora said. "Please tell me you're still in Denver, because Xavier and I are just outside the city limits."

"What? Why are you… Oh, never mind."

"Where are you, Landon?"

I had no clue where I was, so I asked Ernestine if she could give directions to Aurora. After she did, she passed the phone back to me and Aurora asked me to wait for them at the phone booth. I agreed and hung up the phone.

While I was waiting, I carefully examined Burt and Ernestine. Burt was a wiry, forty-something man with a large nose and a graying brown beard. His brown, scraggly hair consistently made its way in front of his deeply wrinkled eyes. Ernestine was very thin as well, and had long black hair streaked with gray. Her hazel eyes were comforting and friendly, and looked like they had never seen a day of worry—which I knew must not have been the case.

"Was that your girlfriend?" Ernestine inquired with a warm smile.

I told her that she was a good friend of mine, one that I could really count on.

"Sounds like a good girlfriend to me," Burt chimed in with his harsh voice.

Ernestine asked Burt to try and collect some change. Then she pulled me to the side.

"What's your name, kid?"

"Landon," I replied.

"Well, Landon, I bet you probably see our meeting as pure chance. I, on the other hand, see it as fate. It was as if our meeting was meant to happen this way, and everything in the universe aligned in just the right way for this moment to take place."

"What do you mean?" I asked curiously. She looked around a bit before she continued.

"You know, Burt and I have been living on the streets for about six years now. I have known him for twenty years. We both came to Denver from Oklahoma, and we were pretty successful business owners. He had his bike shop, which was doing really well, and I owned a small diner called Mama's Place. Then suddenly, because of a gambling problem, I lost everything. Burt took me in. A few months later, he had to close down his business. We tried looking for other jobs, but no one would hire us. Everything spiraled downward, and then we were living on the streets. We managed to make it to Denver a few years ago, hoping that one of us might have a shot at a job, but nothing."

I didn't understand why Ernestine was compelled to tell her story to me but I continued to listen anyway.

"Burt and I have lost everything except each other. No matter how bad things have gotten, he has always been there by my side. I guess what I'm trying to tell you is that you should never take for granted the people that will give up everything for you. And you should do everything in your power to give all that you have to them. You must mean quite a bit to this girl who is coming to pick you up—just remember to appreciate that someone cares about you. You can tell her how you saved Burt's life and mine and didn't even know it. I'm sure you two will talk about it for years to come."

"How did I save your life?" I asked, confused.

"Let's just say I haven't totally given up all my gambling ways, and I'd been buying at least one lottery ticket a week for the last six years. After hearing the numbers last night, I found out that I won! This money will be able to help Burt and me get back on our feet. I got too excited, though. Some horrible people found out about my winnings. Four guys made an attempt to steal the lottery ticket. They chased Burt and me into our alley. With knives to us, they had us up against the wall until you came flying in out of the night sky and knocked them all down. Burt picked up your sword and chased them off. Then he hid your sword and we ran. We were just as frightened as those thieves. We came back when the sun rose, and you were still here. The rest is history."

I'd always wondered if it were really possible to have an impact on a stranger's life, even if you only spent a brief moment with them. Ernestine's kindness had already made a huge impact on me. It felt good when she handed me the change for me to make the call at the phone booth. Of course, at that time, I didn't know about her winnings. All I knew was that someone who literally had nothing was willing to give me pretty much everything they had. They showed me a kindness that is rare in this world. I was just glad that I was able to help them out too.

"I still haven't told Burt about what I won. He will be upset that I had been buying lottery tickets this whole time behind his back. I am glad that this time I won, and that it will get us out of this situation."

"Landon, is that you?" Aurora's voice penetrated the morning air.

"I guess it's time for you to go, kid. It was nice meeting you. Take care of yourself."

Ernestine gave me a hug and then went on her way. I ran across the street toward Aurora and Xavier in the blue pickup truck. Aurora got out of the passenger seat and ran towards me and hugged me. I winced as she embraced me. Despite the pain, it still felt good to feel her so close.

"You don't look so good," she said. "You don't smell so good either. Let's go someplace you can rest and get cleaned up. Good thing your mom packed some clothes for you so you can change out of that stinky shirt."

Xavier was happy to see me, and I was glad that he had come. He explained that Aurora went over to his house around one in the morning and asked him to go with her to Colorado. She was worried about me. Aurora told Xavier that she knew something was wrong when I didn't call her. She said that my mom had let her take her cell phone just in case I called. On the way, Aurora had explained everything to Xavier.

"He deserved to know," she said. "Plus, I promised to tell him everything if he went with me to find you."

We pulled up to a drive-through ATM, and Aurora handed the debit card that Blayne Crow had given us to Xavier, to insert it into the machine.

"The password is 1021," she said to him.

Xavier punched the numbers in and Aurora asked him to take out two hundred dollars from the account.

After the withdrawal, Xavier drove to a motel and got a room. We all needed rest since none of us had gotten any real sleep the night before. I took a shower, changed and lay down on one of the beds. I told Aurora and Xavier everything about my encounter with Kraven. I explained how he was really my brother, and that he had been hiding the Dragon Sphere.

After my story, we agreed to head back to Kraven's mansion in search of the Sphere, but only after we got some rest. My eyes were heavy. As soon as my head made contact with the pillow, I was asleep.

It was 2:30 in the afternoon when I woke up. Taking a nap did wonders for me. I didn't feel as weak or sore as I'd felt in the morning. Aurora was watching TV at the foot of the bed.

"Good afternoon," she said, looking back. She picked up a white box with red symbols on it that was on the dresser next to the TV and brought it over to me—Chinese food. "Eat up," she offered.

I was starved. Xavier woke up a few minutes after me, and Aurora handed him some food too. I asked her if she was able to get any sleep, but she said she'd only taken a short nap. After a while, she went out to get some more food, and also to pick up a recovery supplement for me.

Aurora explained that she remembered her mom had told her about various stores throughout the country that would sell supplements specifically designed for dragonoids. Aurora remembered that one of them was in Denver, and she looked up the address in the phone book. There she found the Mile High Miracle Shop. These miracle shops contained hundreds of supplements, but they were also very expensive. Aurora paid one hundred and forty dollars for the pills that were meant to revitalize my health. I swallowed one of the four pills she had with some water, and noticed a difference right away. I could feel my muscles responding to the supplement. I felt stronger and more energized almost immediately.

"We're going to need you at full strength in case we encounter any deadly obstacles along the way," she said, half joking and half serious.

Seeing Aurora again was enough to lift my spirits. I suddenly felt confident that we could finally finish what we started together—finding the Dragon Sphere.

After a while, Xavier, Aurora and I left the motel, and I led them to Kraven's mansion.

"Whoa, what happened?" Aurora and Xavier said in unison, as soon as we reached the property.

The front yard was a landscaper's worst nightmare. The land had been completely annihilated from my fight with Kraven, and the lawn was ripped apart. Gravel was tossed everywhere. We got out of the truck and jumped over the stone wall to the left of the dented electronic gate that I had crashed into. There were no vehicles parked in the driveway, no one standing outside and no sign that anyone was there. I signaled for Xavier and Aurora to follow me around back to search for an inconspicuous way in. We all saw the small cellar door at the same time.

"We might as well start here," Aurora suggested.

I opened the double doors and made my way down the stairs that led to a small, dark room. Xavier and Aurora followed behind me. Aurora took out my mom's cell phone and flashed the bright screen so that we could have a little bit of light to see in the pitch dark. She walked in front of me to lead the way. The dark room looked like a typical wine cellar. Many bottles were neatly placed on a shelf in one side of the room, and a small wooden desk stood on another side. All of a sudden, a dim light in the middle of the ceiling switched on.

"Hey, I found the light switch!" Xavier exclaimed.

We examined the room more closely, and noticed a door behind the wine shelf. I handed *Apollyon* to Aurora. Xavier and I went over to the shelf and carefully moved it away from the wall. Aurora opened the door.

"There's another set of stairs," she said, peering in. "And I can see a blue light at the bottom."

We followed Aurora down the stairs and stepped into a large room. A blue glow lit up the entire area. In the center of the room was the source. A metallic stand with three metal claws gently held the blue spherical object, which was just a little bit bigger than a bowling ball. We had found the Dragon Sphere!

Aurora found the light switch for the sub-cellar and flipped it on, dimming the magnificence of the orb's glow somewhat. The cellar walls were decorated with weapons. Silver and gold axes, wooden spears, steel maces, bronze and steel long swords and short swords as well. There were also two doors against the back wall. The one to my right was labeled **TORMENT** and the other to my left was labeled **CONTROL**.

"Kraven told me that he had a device to control Aremas. The device is probably in the control room," I declared.

"We're going to avoid the other room, right?" Xavier intimated, flashing a half-hearted grin. Xavier always tried to be strong in any situation, but I could sense how out of place he felt being there with us. I remembered what it felt like when my uncle Bane first introduced himself and showed me his true form. It felt as if my eyes were opening for the first time, and it was exciting and confusing. I could only imagine for Xavier that the feeling of being lost in a new world was overloading his mind.

"We're not here for sightseeing. I just want to get rid of that controlling device and get out of here with the Dragon Sphere."

I gripped *Apollyon* tightly as I walked over to the control-room door. I opened it slowly and noticed another set of stairs.

"Man, how far down do these rooms go?" Xavier asked.

We tiptoed our way down into the room. The light was already on. It looked exactly the way I imagined it would. There were empty black office chairs in front of a large desk with three computer monitors on it. Each screen had numerical data that I couldn't possibly decipher; I guessed that one of the computers looked as if it was monitoring vital signs, but I just didn't know. On the wall behind the computer screens were three large flat-screen TVs, all turned off.

"I don't see a device," Aurora said.

"I think the computer is the device," Xavier answered.

Under the desk were the three towers for the computers.

"Even if these aren't the device itself, I'm sure they use these to do the actual controlling. We might as well destroy them," I proposed.

Aurora and Xavier agreed. I knelt over, pointing my sword directly at one of the computer towers. I noticed that there were three holes in a row on each tower. It looked as though something was supposed to be inserted in them. I instinctively opened the drawer next to me and found nine black, cylindrical rocks that looked exactly like the one my dad had found. They must have been the keys that powered the control device from the computer towers.

I aimed *Apollyon* at one of the towers and jabbed right through it. I repeated this with the other two towers, watching electrical spurts shoot from the wires. All we had to do now was get the Dragon Sphere and leave.

We made our way back to the room with the Dragon Sphere when we realized that the light we had switched on before was now turned off. None of us had turned it off when we went into the control room. The Dragon Sphere's blue aura was the only light in the room once again. The hair on the back of my neck stood up.

"*THUMP!*" The noise seemed as though it had come from the torment room.

"*THUMP!*" The noise sounded again, but this time it seemed as if it was coming from the cellar steps above. "*THUMP! THUMP! THUMP!*"

The sound kept getting louder, and it was clearly coming from the torment room *and* the cellar steps. A large man walked in. Over his shoulder was a long steel chain, and attached to the chain was a scythe. He wore humongous black boots, dark jeans and a tightly fitting black shirt that showed off his ridiculously large muscles. His face was frightening. He had no facial features. It was impossible to make out his eyes, nose or mouth. The only other distinctive trait, from the neck up, was that he was bald—but with a blurred-out face like his, you'd hardly notice.

He stood guarding the doorway that led to the outside. The torment room door swung open and another man walked out—completely identical to the first guy. He was dressed the same, was bald and, again, had a blurred-out face. This man, however, had no weapon with him.

"Intruders!" they hissed in a demonic tone that sounded like several deep voices resonating at once.

"I am the guardian of the Sphere," they chorused in unison. "Did you really think something so precious to our cause would be left unprotected?"

"We are going to take the Sphere with us no matter what you do!" Aurora shouted.

"You will try, and you will fail," they said. The man near the torment room walked over to the other guard. I readied my sword for an attack. At that moment, the two faceless guards merged together to form a larger version of themselves.

"Our name is Legion. We are many."

Xavier's jaw dropped.

"It'll be okay," I said, attempting to comfort him.

Xavier tried to speak, but no words came from his mouth. His body froze in terror. This was his first encounter with any of the craziness that Aurora and I had already been exposed to.

"It has been years since we demons have taken over a new body. Yours looks like a good replacement. Allow us to enter, and we will make you stronger than you could ever imagine," boomed the demon Legion.

"Not a chance, freaks!" I responded.

"Then we will have to force you to accept us."

The giant demon grabbed the chain around his neck and held it in front of him, along with his scythe. He charged at us and swung the scythe right at us. I pushed Xavier out of the way, and Aurora and I rolled under the swipe. The scythe stuck to the wall and the demon tried to pull it. I charged behind him and jabbed

Apollyon into his lower back. The demon roared in pain but didn't turn around to face me—he was focused on pulling his scythe out of the wall. As I was about to stab him again, he pulled out the scythe and knocked me back with his right arm. I flew to the other side of the room. Xavier finally snapped out of it and ran towards the Dragon Sphere. Legion launched his scythe right at him, but Xavier ducked in time to avoid being sliced in half. Legion pulled his scythe back and prepared for another attack.

Legion quickly swung his scythe around and threw his weapon at Aurora and me. We both leapt out of the way. Aurora ran towards Legion before he could pull back on his chain. She kicked him in his chest, and uppercut him directly under his chin. She was in the middle of a roundhouse kick when he caught her leg. He picked her up and threw her across the room. I charged him and slashed at him with my sword, but he deflected my attack with his steel chain. I swung again but much harder, slicing right through the chain. I knew that with more force, Apollyon's obsidian blade would be able to cut through it. Xavier got up from the ground and reached for the blue orb in the middle of the room. As he picked it up, Legion ran to the exit to block his way.

Quickly Legion split into two people again. Then those two split into another two and finally, into yet another two. Legion had split into six smaller versions of himself.

"DROP THE ORB!" all six shouted together with demonic hisses and gnarls.

Xavier held the Dragon Sphere tightly and inched towards us. Then the separate demonic entities attacked. Two attacked me, while two went after Xavier, and another two went up against Aurora. The two that came after me kept their distance, as I kept them at bay with my sword. When one of them jumped at me, I stabbed him square in his chest. The other rushed me before I could pull my sword out and tackled me to the ground.

The demon quickly lifted me off the ground and threw me against the wall. He was extremely strong and fast, as he picked me up and tossed me against the wall again. I got up rapidly and tackled him to the ground. Immediately I started punching him in his ugly, blurred face. I pounded and pounded until his body stopped moving. I looked up and noticed the other demon sitting down against the wall, trying to pull my sword out from his chest.

"Magic… sword," he sputtered, as if he was trying to warn the others.

I got up and pulled out my sword. The demon turned to ashes.

The other demon jumped on my back and tightened his hands around my neck, choking me. I turned around and slammed my back against the wall in an attempt to knock him off. My eyes quickly caught a glimpse of Xavier. He was getting pummeled by the two demons that were fighting him. I glanced towards Aurora and saw her kicking a demon in the face. I tried to focus back on taking out my demon so that I could help Xavier. I leapt into the wall one last time, with extreme force, and felt the demon's fingers loosen around my neck. He slid to the ground, and immediately I jabbed my sword into his blurred face. The demon let out a nasty scream, then turned to ashes.

I turned quickly and saw Xavier bleeding from his face, but only one demon was attacking him now. I searched the room and saw that Aurora was still fighting the two that had attacked her. I rushed up behind the demon fighting Xavier and swung my sword, slicing him in half at the waist.

"Will you be okay?" I asked Xavier.

He nodded. His eyes were shut and he looked like he was in really bad shape. I jumped on one of the demons that had attacked Aurora and sliced his head off. Aurora elbowed the other demon in the face and knocked him back. I jumped in the air and came down, digging my sword deep into his chest. Like the others, he transformed to a pile of ash.

"Was that all of them?" Aurora asked.

Just then, Xavier jumped on my back and squeezed his arms around my neck. He had incredible strength. His arms tightened the more I struggled. Aurora ran at us, jumped in the air swinging her foot by my face, and hit Xavier square in his. He flew back and hit the wall. A demon separated from Xavier's body and ran towards the Dragon Sphere that rolled on the floor. I ran after him and cornered him. I swung down with *Apollyon,* but the demon picked up the Dragon Sphere and blocked my attack with it. The blue orb cracked, but my sword couldn't penetrate it. The demon dropped the sphere, pushed me out of the way and ran towards the exit. Instinctively, I threw my sword and got a direct hit, stabbing him in the back of the head. The demon dissolved into ashes.

Aurora and I ran towards Xavier.

My body turned cold at the sight of him. He was badly beaten, with blood dripping down his face, his nose out of place and his eyelids swollen shut. "We're going to get you help," I tried to assure him.

I picked him up over my shoulder and walked up the stairs to the cellar. Aurora picked up the Dragon Sphere and followed me. We passed the cellar and walked up the next set of stairs that led to the mansion's backyard.

Then my jaw dropped. Outside, Kraven and his followers were waiting for us. All of their eyes fixed on the Dragon Sphere in Aurora's hands. Hundreds of dragons and dragonoids, ready to attack. There was no way Aurora and I could fight our way through them. We were trapped—and there was no help in sight.

Chapter Fifteen
Unleashed

Kraven stood before us with an army behind him. None were in dragon form, so it was impossible to determine who was human, dragonoid or dragon. Shadow stepped up to the front of the line and stood next to Kraven. He had a long, red scar just above his left eye, a result of our recent battle. Kraven was showing his battle scars as well. His left wing was bandaged, and missing its other half.

"You just won't die, will you?" Kraven said angrily. "But now what? Who do you have to turn to? You should've joined us while you had the chance. You made your decision, and you will die because of it. It would only be fair, however, if I gave your girlfriend the opportunity to choose whether she wants to live or die. I'm not going to try to convince her. I think someone else would fare better at that than I would."

The crowd separated as someone started walking to the front with Kraven and Shadow. It was Shade! He didn't waste any time trying to convince Aurora to join them.

"Aurora, you're pretty much my only friend. I actually care for you, which says something because I thought I couldn't care for anyone. Will you think about your life and join us? I saved your life before. Let me save you again."

"I can't believe you're asking me to do this," Aurora responded, as if her very words stung her as they left her lips. "I know you can sense the evil in this group. There is no way I would ever join them. Shade, please come to your senses. You're being brainwashed. What's going to happen when their plan goes through? Where will you be in their future? Your dad has never cared about you. Why would he start now? Please, Shade, listen to what I am saying."

Aurora paused a moment to gather her strength for what she said next.

"If I have to die right now then I will. I will not join your group."

Shade looked down at his feet—perhaps in shame. But then, surprisingly, he lashed out on us, attacking us with his words.

"My father is the one who sent for me to go to the Infernal Caverns so that I could train. His letter gave me a place to run to during a time when I needed it most. I had no idea that that trip was going to lead me back to him, but it did. This was his way of showing me who I really am, and giving me an opportunity to be a part of something. He gave me an escape from the nightmare I was in and he doesn't judge me. But you, Landon, on the other hand, your eyes told me everything you thought about me. To you, I was some sort of freak. I see things differently than you do, and I always will, so don't think that you ever helped me by trying to talk your idea of sense into me. Not everyone fits into your perfect world of football and a loving mom. Besides, who's the outsider now? I have an army behind me. What do you have?"

I turned toward Aurora. A part of me wanted her to join Shade and Kraven just so she would be safe. I couldn't imagine her giving up what she believed in, though. That just wasn't her.

Aurora glanced back at me with her beautiful green eyes. Drops slowly made their way down her cheek as she was trying to hold back more tears from coming. She looked down at the Dragon Sphere.

She whispered faintly, "We were so close, Landon. We have the Dragon Sphere in our possession, but this is where it ends."

I laid Xavier down on the ground and held out my hand. Aurora took it.

"I'll tell you what I have, Shade," I announced proudly. "I have Aurora and I have the Dragon Sphere. If you want the Sphere back you're going to have to take it away from us."

"That should be easy enough," Kraven laughed obnoxiously.

"Why don't you fly over here first," I snapped back at Kraven, "Oh wait, I forgot—you can't."

Kraven's face was hot with anger.

"KILL THEM!" he roared.

I let go of Aurora's hand and readied my sword. Then I heard a deafening crack!

Pieces of the blue orb began breaking off. Aurora dropped the Dragon Sphere, and the militia in front of us stopped in their tracks. A bright light shined through the cracks of the sphere. I pulled Aurora closer to me and moved us away from the orb. Then it exploded, unleashing an immense light as a thunderous roar echoed in the sky. A wave of energy pulsed above us and a strong wind nearly knocked us down. When it was all over, there he hovered—Aremas, the ancient dragon.

From snout to tail, Aremas stretched sixty feet long. He had blazing red eyes and two giant horns, with six smaller horns protruding from each of them. Around his neck was a thin silver brace. Without knowing the specifics, I somehow knew that this was the device being used to control him. His scales were a deep, dark purple, but his feet on his two hind legs were black. So were the tip of his barbed tail and the tips of his wings. The massive dragon had no front legs. He was a giant-sized wyvern. I remembered reading a book about wyverns once. It said that they weren't really fire breathers, but that they did have a very poisonous stinger on their tail. Judging by the size of Aremas's stinger, I didn't think any of us would survive the stab wound it would leave behind, much less the poison.

The ancient dragon flapped his gigantic wings, sending people in Kraven's army flying through the air. Then the dragon attacked them. He darted towards them with tremendous speed and picked off two terrified warriors, swallowing them whole. Kraven's army scattered. I saw one soldier from Kraven's army transform into dragon form, attempting to attack Aremas. He was a blue dragon about twenty feet long; he stood no chance. Aremas grabbed him with his talons and tore the blue dragon in half. Aremas boomed with a maniacal cackle. The sky turned bluish-gray. The temperature dropped and snow began to fall.

"Let's get out of here!" Aurora demanded. I could hear the terror in her voice.

I picked up Xavier and followed Aurora. Kraven and his men were too occupied trying to stay alive than to chase after us. We ran towards the iron gate that would lead us outside the mansion grounds. Aurora shot a powerful gust of air, and knocked the gate down. Aremas let out a loud, shrill cry and the snow fell even harder. We kept running and did not look back. I was beginning to wonder whether anyone would be able to stop Aremas. I was horrified by how powerful he was. That was the first moment in my life that I wished my dad were there to protect us.

When I thought about my father, I felt a strong tugging sensation, deep in my gut. It felt as if I had left something terribly important behind. Then I thought, *Why didn't we check the torment room? What if my dad was in there? What if he had been the one who gave me the confidence and energy to stand up to Kraven when I first arrived at the mansion?* For such a long time there was a severed connection between my dad and me, but in that very moment when I wished he were there I felt as if something or someone had pulled from deep within me and reattached a lost spiritual link. I was then confident that he had connected with me, and spoken to me, telling me to *stand up for what I believe*. It was his presence that I felt.

Kraven's army would not allow us to go back and infiltrate their headquarters so easily now, but I knew he had to be in there. I had to come up with something—but first we needed to find help for Xavier. As I followed Aurora through the snow, I asked her where she was going.

"I thought I saw a hospital not too far from us."

Just before we reached it, Aurora and I heard another shrill cry—but this time the horrible sound was right above us. Through the snow we saw Aremas flying away, his claws still clutching each half of the dragon he had torn apart. It was scary how fast he was.

I dropped my sword behind some bushes outside of the hospital, and we rushed in through the emergency room doors pleading for help. I laid Xavier down on the floor and held his head up. A group of nurses rushed over to us, and in no time they took him away.

Everything was a blur after that. I remember calling my mom and letting her know I was okay. I asked her to tell Xavier's parents about his condition. I knew she would have to lie to them about his reasons for being in Denver, and in the hospital, but they still needed to know where he was. Then Aurora and I sat in the waiting room, hoping to get any updates we could from the doctors and nurses tending to Xavier. After several hours we finally received an update. Xavier's jaw was broken, his nose was broken, and both of his eyes were swollen shut. We were able to see him, but watching my friend in this condition was a hard pill for me to swallow. I had dragged him with me when I should have made him stay at the motel. I was starting to hate myself more and more each minute. If there was a Creator out there, He had cursed me. Why was I such a hazard to everything and everyone?

Suddenly, the cell phone vibrated in Aurora's pocket.

"Hello?" she answered, exhaustion in her voice. "Yeah, hold on—let me get him." She covered the receiver on the cell phone and said sarcastically, "It's Purity. She's just dying to talk to you."

I grabbed the phone from her hand and answered.

"Landon... it's Purity," she sounded worried.

"Hey Purity, is everything okay?" I asked, hoping that she would give me some good news.

"Not really. Things are actually really bad right now. I called the phone that Alpha gave you but your mom answered it. She gave me this number to reach you. I hope that's okay?"

"It's fine. What's going on?"

"Landon, Aremas has been set free and he's wasting no time in changing the weather. It's snowing over here at the Caverns, and from what I'm hearing, things are only going to get worse unless someone stops him. That's why I needed to speak with you. You have to stop him."

"What can I do? I won't be able to stop him. I would have no chance against him. I've already seen first hand what he can do."

"You saw him?" Purity said in astonishment.

"Yes. It's a long story, but I know that he is extremely powerful."

"He is, and he will only get stronger as the climate continues to change. Already the Elder Dragons are getting together to make their stand against him. But since Aremas is immortal, they won't be able to kill him. They will have to lock him up in another Sphere, and they are going to need a key to lock it. Landon, you have the key."

I had no idea what Purity was talking about. I didn't have a key with me. Then I remembered the cylindrical black rock that Zana had shown us. That must be the key!

"I don't have a key, Purity, but I think Zana does. I saw it."

"You do have the key, Landon. It's your sword!"

"*Apollyon*?"

"Yes. Primus told Alpha that the sword he created for you he designed specifically with obsidian shards for this very reason. He made you a key to the Dragon Sphere, Landon. I don't know why. All he told Alpha was that he hoped you would redeem him."

I didn't understand what was going on. I was able to crack the Dragon Sphere open with it, but I wasn't sure how it would lock it. Was it possible that Primus could have put any chance of his redemption on my shoulders? If Kraven or my uncle knew that my sword was a key, they would have probably made more of an effort to take it away from me.

"So what should I do?" I asked Purity.

"We need you and your sword. Come back to the caverns, Landon. Alpha will take you to the Elder Dragons and try to persuade them to let you help us. They are going to need it!"

"Okay, I'll do it. I'll do all that I can to help. I'll find a way over there."

"I don't say this to many people, but I trust you, Landon," Purity praised. "Please come quickly!"

"I will try."

After I had hung up, I explained to Aurora what our next move was. Deep down inside, I knew that I wouldn't have much time before I had to travel somewhere again. But I didn't want to leave Xavier all by himself, in pain and drugged up on medication. I wasn't sure if he was able to understand me, but Xavier nodded his head after I explained the situation to him, and why I had to leave. I promised him that I would see him once this was all over. Aurora and I said our goodbye, and then we left.

On our way out of the hospital, I reached into my pocket and pulled out a small piece of paper. I picked up the cell phone and started dialing the number written on it.

"Hello," a girl's voice answered.

"Destiny…? It's me, Landon."

"Landon! Are you okay? I'm so happy you called. I was worried about you."

"I'm safe, but I need to ask you for a huge favor. I'll understand if you say no. I have to go back to the Infernal Caverns to help capture Aremas, but I think I know where Dad is. I was wondering if you might be able to check it out?"

"Of course… I'd do anything to find Dad. I'm here at the condo alone with Sadie anyway, since my mom had to meet up with the other Elder Dragons. I might as well make myself useful. Where is he?"

I gave Destiny all the details and wished her luck. I reminded her that the mansion would probably be swarming with Kraven's minions, but that she had a better chance of going undercover than Aurora and I did. Before we hung up, Destiny told me she knew that what happened in Phoenix was an accident.

"No matter what, I will always side with you, Landon," she said. I was glad to hear that. Her words encouraged me—and boy did I need some encouragement.

It finally came time to leave—time for me to face my peers, Alpha, and the Elder Dragons. As we neared the hospital exit, the television in the lobby flashed *"Breaking News!"* Aurora and I directed our attention to the screen. The reporter spoke solemnly about the disastrous effects of the change in weather within the last few hours. Immediately the news anchor asked his meteorologist to weigh in on the situation. A short, stubby man with glasses stood in front of a map of the United States. He had a puzzled look on his face as he pointed out the significant drop in temperature throughout the entire nation. All of the states in the western part of the country had temperatures that had dipped into the low twenties. In the eastern states, temperatures were also dropping considerably, averaging between thirty and forty degrees.

"Snow, rain and hail have been pounding the western U.S. nonstop for the past few hours, and the storm does not seem like it is going to let up, folks," the meteorologist said, trying his best not to sound panicked. "Things are particularly rough here in Denver. The roads are beginning to get very slippery, so if you have to go out and get supplies, please do it soon before it gets any worse. Be cautious out there."

"I can't believe how fast things are changing," Aurora said as she stared at the TV screen, watching the pictures of Denver being enveloped by snow.

"We have to find a way to get to the Caverns as soon as possible."

It was hard to sound determined. I still couldn't even imagine a scenario where we would be able to defeat Aremas. I tried to shake those thoughts out of my mind, and proceeded to walk out of the hospital.

The cold air outside made my body shiver, and the snow was still coming down hard. I went to pick up *Apollyon* but had to search for it under a pile of snow that had accumulated behind the bush where I hid it. The blade was freezing cold.

We had no plan for how we would get to California, so we decided to just start walking west and hope that something or someone would come along. We thought about running back to Kraven's mansion and getting the blue pickup truck. But both of us knew we had to stay as far away from that place as possible.

"I'll be glad once all of this is over with," I said, trying to sound positive. Aurora forced a smile.

"Are you okay?" I asked.

"I'm fine," she answered. "Just exhausted."

I didn't believe her. I could sense something was wrong.

"Are you cold?"

She shook her head but I could tell that she was. She had her arms folded in near her body as if she was trying to warm herself up. There was something bothering her that she wasn't telling me. What was it?

When we were about three miles away from the hospital, Aurora fell to her knees in pain. Her body quickly went limp, and Aurora fell on her back, crying. I knelt to help her but felt helpless. I had no clue where the source of her pain was.

"What is it?" I begged for her to tell me.

Aurora could not answer. She tried to press her shoulders up against the ground as if she was hoping to get relief from the cold snow. The pain didn't subside until a few minutes later. Then she lay on the ground, huffing and puffing from all the energy she expended trying to get relief. I put my arms gently around her in an effort to comfort her.

Aurora's green eyes were bloodshot from the pain and lack of sleep.

"I'm... sorry," she choked—still weeping. "That was... unbearable."

"You don't have to apologize for being in pain. I just hate seeing you suffer like that. Have you been feeling that way since Shadow burned you with his acid?"

Aurora nodded. "There's been an intense pressure in my shoulder blades since our fight with him, but the pain that I experienced just now was the worst."

I felt my skin crawl. Energy coursed through my body as I thought about how badly I wanted another shot at Shadow.

Aurora sensed my anger rising. She gently reached her hand to my face. "It's okay, Landon. What's done is done, and I'm still alive and here with you. We're a team, remember? I won't let you avenge me—that would be selfish of me. But the world does need for you to be a hero!"

I never considered myself to be a hero—especially after what happened in Phoenix—but her words did comfort me. I knew that she wanted me to focus on helping to stop Aremas, rather than trying to get revenge on Shadow. I offered her my hand as she got up off the ground and wiped the snowflakes off her cheek. We had a long way to go until the caverns, and not a lot of time to get there. My body had seemed to adjust to the temperature outside and I no longer felt cold, even though Aurora and I were still in summer clothes.

We continued walking west, hoping to find someone willing to give us a ride. Not many people were on the roads anymore. I didn't blame them for not trying to drive in this weather. Not only were the roads wet and slippery, but visibility was also horrible with the thick snowfall. The sun was going to set in just a couple of hours, so we needed to figure something out. As we discussed our options, Aurora felt something strange. That's when we heard it—a loud flapping sound coming from behind us. Aurora and I turned around to see an enormous, shadowy creature descending upon us.

Chapter Sixteen
The Sky Queen

My pulse pounded and my body froze in terror as the enormous creature approached us. Aurora didn't move either. The dragon landed a few yards away from us. There was something peculiar about it. Its scales were sky blue. The beast towered over us as it stood on its hind legs. It must have been around forty feet long. The dragon's giant wings folded in, and its tail balanced it as it stood up. The only horn the dragon had on its entire body was the one on its snout—like a rhino. The horn separated its beautiful piercing green eyes, which gazed at us with deadly intent.

Aurora shielded her eyes from the blinding snow. "Mom?"

"Aurora, how could you?" the dragon accused with frustration and sadness.

Then the dragon lifted one of her claws, pointing it at Aurora, and zapped her with electricity. Aurora fell to the ground, unconscious.

"Why did you do that?" I yelled, gripping *Apollyon* firmly in my hand.

"Do not speak, child," the dragon scolded. "I should eliminate you where you stand. Instead, the council will decide your fate. You are a traitor to both dragons and humans for releasing the ancient dragon. Your punishment will be severe."

"No, please listen. We were on our way to…"

I wasn't able to finish my sentence because she zapped me with electricity too, and everything went black.

When I opened my eyes, everything was fuzzy. All I could tell was that I was in a dimly lit room, and my body felt as if it were made out of Jell-O. My fingers tingled so badly it felt as though they were plugged into a wall outlet. I noticed that I was chained to the wall, with both hands cuffed above my head. I pulled on the chains but I was too weak to break them. Something felt different about this room—but I guessed being chained in a room would make you feel that way.

A fire burning at the center of my holding cell reminded me of Travis the fire back at the Infernal Caverns. It lit up the room just enough to make out a few more details. There were six other chains hanging from the cavern walls. All of the others were empty, except for one. At the far end, a man in a dingy, tattered white dress shirt and ripped black slacks was being restrained. A scraggly beard covered his face, and his thick curly hair was knotted and wild. The man did not move. Again, I tried again to break free from my chains.

I tried creating a quake to shake the chains loose, but I wasn't able to summon any of my power. Panic struck me as I continued trying to will the earth to rise or the ground to shake—or just to use my strength to break the chains. Nothing happened. My heart pumped rapidly, sweat beads formed on my forehead and the walls felt like they were closing in.

"Save your energy, kid," a voice echoed off the wall. I stared at the only other person in the room, but his head was still down as if he was asleep. Then I saw his lips move.

"Stop struggling and save your energy. The fire in the middle is magical. It blocks us from using any power in this room by draining our energy. Energy can still be used in here, but it has to be enough to overpower the fire's magic."

"Why am I being chained in here like some kind of criminal?" I questioned, frustration in my voice.

"In their eyes, you *are* a criminal," the man responded. "You must have done something that they really didn't like, because only the worst get locked in here."

"Where's *here*?" I asked.

"The Temple of the Elder Dragon Council. Or, more specifically, Yosemite National Park, California."

I had been to Yosemite National Park before with Mom, and I had never seen any temples hidden in its long, majestic valleys. The man must have been crazy—or perhaps he was joking with me. I decided to play dumb and see what else he would tell me.

"How long have you been here?"

"Too long," the man said, with a grin on his face. "I've been locked up for sixty-three years. What a way to live, huh? Imprisoned for all time. Although, don't think I can't sense the panic that's going on up there. It's just like the good ole' days! You know, I used to be quite the panic starter myself. I've even had movies made about me for it, although none of them got the story right."

"Who are you?"

"The name's Tyrus. I'm the dragon of chaos. There's never been a deadlier dragon than me. Once I break free from this prison, I'll go back to destroying the world. Trust me."

It was hard to take anything Tyrus said seriously. To be honest, he looked kind of pathetic, all chained up and talking with his eyes closed, trying to make himself sound like some major threat to the world. I wonder if he knew what kind of threat was *really* out there? I instantly thought about Aurora. I hoped she was okay, and that the council would see that this was all a big misunderstanding.

"I am the mighty Drake," Tyrus continued. "No one is stronger than me and I will crush those who stand against me. When I assume my true form the world will know that I'm not that wretched lizard from the movies. I am real. I AM VERY REAL." His voice rose to a shout.

195

I had no idea what he was going on about. Then again, I figured, if I'd been stuck in chains for sixty-three years, I would have gone mad too.

"You'd better hope I don't break out of here! Once I do, you will be the first one I destroy, Sky Queen!" Tyrus ranted.

Just as I was about to ask Tyrus what he meant, I heard footsteps. A man in a blue uniform entered our cell. His dark skin reflected the fire's light as he scanned the room. On the pocket of his shirt was a patch with *Park Security* written on it. The guard completely ignored me and stood over Tyrus.

"Are you being friendly to your new guest, Tyrus-zilla?" the man asked facetiously. "I'm not going to play any movies for you today, since the Elders don't want your friend entertained. I would promise to put the movie on for you tomorrow but it looks like the end of the world out there. We'll just have to see how things play out."

The man walked over to me and asked, "Did you know you're locked up with a celebrity, kid?" The man laughed, thinking he was an outstanding comedian, then he walked away.

What a jerk, I thought to myself. I looked over to Tyrus and noticed tears coming down his cheeks.

"I hate him!" he shouted with all his might, moving his body forward as he screamed. Then he relaxed again and began snickering. "I am Tyrus. No one is stronger," he muttered to himself.

I was seriously starting to freak out. I didn't just *think* he was crazy anymore, I *knew* it! Why would they punish him like this? I wondered what he had done to get locked up for so long.

"Hey kid? Were you brought by the Sky Queen?" Tyrus asked me.

"Yes."

"Good, that means that she is here. I just need to escape—then I'll get my revenge." Tyrus's eyebrows moved up and together in an odd arch. "She'll regret the day she tricked me."

"How did she trick you?"

"She tricked me good, kid, let me tell you. She knew that she couldn't beat me in a fight, so she had to cheat to win. I had just stepped onto land from the shores of Tokyo, and she was there waiting for me. I used to love attacking the humans in Tokyo. They respected and feared me. Shea told me that another creature was attacking American soil and that I should go over there quickly to defeat it, so that the people would see me as the Great King Monster. So I transformed to human form and let her take me to the States. When we got here, she threw me in the dungeon and I haven't been able to transform since."

"Wait, the guard said you were a celebrity and you said that they made movies about you. You're not 'Godzilla' from those films, are you?"

Tyrus snarled and kicked his feet like an angry little kid.

"They just based the creature on me, not the films. I always stood unopposed as the champion of Tokyo. It was my city to destroy, and no one ever stood in my way until the Sky Queen came."

"Why did you transform into a human for Shea to take you back to America?"

"I told you, kid. I'm a Drake."

"What is that?"

"Are you kidding me? You don't know what a Drake is? We are the rarest of dragons. We dominated the dragon ranks a couple of millennia ago. We are very few in number now, however. Just because we don't have wings doesn't mean we are weak. We are the largest of all the dragons. You younger dragons need to learn your history better."

At first I felt sorry for Tyrus. After he told me why he was imprisoned, I understood why they would have a hard time releasing someone like him. He wasn't stable to begin with, and it really seemed that he felt his best attribute was destroying cities, especially Tokyo. I couldn't help but think that he should be treated better, though. From what I gathered from the guard, he puts on the *Godzilla* movies as a way to mock Tyrus. That just didn't seem right to me.

"What can you tell me about Shea?" I asked Tyrus.

Tyrus, still with his eyes closed, turned his face in my direction.

"The Sky Queen is an arrogant, no-nonsense, old dragon. She is in charge of the Elder Dragon Council, at least she has been since Drayden disappeared. I hear the guards talking, though. There is dissent among her subordinates. Her unwillingness to follow the rules of the pact made centuries ago has them questioning whether she should still be in the council."

"What pact?"

"Geez, kid. Did they just let you sleep through dragon history? Centuries ago, the majority of our kind, led by a dragon named Drayden, convinced the Elder Council to issue a rule stating that dragons would never reveal themselves to humans again. Since most dragons have the ability to transform into humans for up to four hours a day, they were required to transform daily. The Sky Queen rarely transforms, though, mostly when she needs to be at a place where there are a lot of people. But she is just reluctant to do it—most of her time she spends flying the skies. As technology gets more advanced in the human world, however, she is going to get caught. I would love it if she got blasted out of the sky."

"Well, if the majority of the dragons made the pact, then why didn't you follow it?" I asked, thinking I was quite clever in doing so.

"First of all, a younger dragon like me doesn't get concerned with how a law was passed when it was created. We only concern ourselves with following it or not. Everything has a purpose in life—and I decided that my purpose was to create chaos. That is why I am the Dragon of Chaos. And as such, there is only one rule to follow and that is that there are no rules. You can't be a dragon of chaos and not do anything chaotic."

"You look really old. How old are you?"

"I haven't been able to make myself look nice for sixty-three years. So, yes, that does have an effect on my appearance. I'm only two hundred and fifteen years old."

I had forgotten that dragons age differently than humans; two-hundred and fifteen was still very young in the dragon realm. Another thing I still had a hard time understanding was the dragon's notion of "purpose." A few weeks back, Primus had told me that everything had a purpose... *a role to fulfill.* And now Tyrus was telling me that he wanted his purpose to be as a bringer of chaos. I was starting to accept the idea of a supreme Creator that watches over us, but the concept of purpose baffled me. I mean, what if I decided to join Kraven and my uncle Bane to help them create a new kingdom—or whatever it is that they're trying to build. Could that have been my purpose all along? The idea didn't seem right to me, but I figured Tyrus was probably not the right person to talk to about it.

"Hey kid, what is your name?" Tyrus inquired.

"Landon."

"Well, Landon, could you do me a favor? When the time comes for you to go up in front of the Elder Dragons, can you tell them something for me?"

"Uhh... yeah, I guess."

"Okay, good. Tell them the Dragon of Chaos will come for them soon!"

Then Tyrus laughed the most horrible laugh, that sounded more like an elephant getting run over by a steam roller. I looked away and tried to ignore him but I couldn't. His menacing guffaw triggered my worst memories, as they all started playing over and over in my head. There was nothing I could do to drown out the noise except maybe hit my head against the wall. I was very tempted to do so.

The same guard that came in earlier rushed in, and to my surprise Aurora was behind him. Aurora ran towards me and pushed a small, orange piece of foam into each of my ears. I noticed that she and the guard had them on as well. The guard walked over to me and unlocked my restraints. Aurora helped me off the ground and gave me a hug. The guard immediately separated us and pushed me up against the wall. He put my hands behind my back and cuffed me again. Then he grabbed my arm and led me out of the room.

Outside in the hall, there was a flight of steps carved out of natural rock. Aurora walked up first and then I followed, with the guard pushing behind me. The candles on the cavern walls seemed to have the same effect as the fire in the middle of the room where I was chained. I still couldn't use any of my powers. We entered an enormous room, with many columns of stone holding up the rocky ceiling. A stone temple stood between the gigantic columns in the middle of the room.

Smaller columns held up a triangular-shaped roof. Lush green vines wrapped around the columns, and golden steps with inscriptions carved in them that I could not read were placed all around the temple. In the center of the temple was something that shone so brightly that I couldn't tell what it was. As we walked closer, my eyes adjusted to the gleaming object—an altar made entirely of diamonds. Around the altar were four poles made of precious stones, each holding a fire that blazed on top. They reminded me of the Tiki torches that Mom put in our backyard, except these looked way more expensive.

The guard stopped a few feet in front of the temple steps. We waited a few moments when a large metal door opened. Three dragons entered in single file.

"Don't say a word until you are asked to," the guard warned me, as the dragons neared the temple.

The Sky Queen Shea walked into the temple first and sat down to my far right. The second dragon I recognized because of his deep dark red scales, his eyes and his long whiskers that hung down the sides of his snout. It was Blayne Crow. The last dragon that walked up, I didn't recognize. In fact, the dragon didn't walk up—it slithered. This serpent dragon had darker blue tinted scales, like a royal blue, and it was about twenty-five feet long, but it had no wings or hind legs. It did have two forelegs. The dragon's captivating blue eyes were instantly comforting to me. Then I got it—the big, blue dragon was a sea serpent, a water dragon. It was Zana Reed. Zana was the first dragon I noticed that had ears. They were pointy, elf-like ears. She had fins at the end of her tail, I guessed to help propel her through water when she swam. I think they call those flukes; at least that's what I remember from science class. And although she did not have any horns like most dragons do, she was still just as imposing as the others.

The three Elder Dragons rested inside the temple and the guard prompted us to move forward. The closer I walked toward the diamond altar, the more I noticed a familiar black object resting on top of it. It was *Apollyon!*

"Don't even think about it," the guard said to me as we passed my sword.

We stopped a few yards away from the dragons as they towered over us and gazed at us with their intense eyes. Shea ordered the guard to remove my handcuffs and then to leave us. My wrists were sore from the cuffs and I rubbed them, attempting to relieve the pain.

"You are standing before us, Landon Brown, accused of severe offenses," Shea said. "It is in our best interest as the Elder Dragons to remove such offenders from our ranks in order to keep the balance between humans and dragons safe. And you, Landon, have terribly disrupted that balance."

I wanted to lash out and say that it wasn't entirely my fault that Aremas got released. If they had guarded the Sphere better, we wouldn't even be in this situation. They had no idea what I had been through to do a job that they needed help on. Sure, I had made mistakes, and big ones at that, but my intentions were to maintain the balance, not disrupt it. Of course, I didn't say any of that to them. I kept silent.

"Our purpose," Shea continued, "is to help dragonoids like you and Aurora fit properly into dragon and human society. We understand that at times our young have agendas of their own, but to maintain the balance we need the majority to comprehend their roles. And you, young Landon, have overstepped your role."

"I just need a chance to explain,"

"Quiet!" Shea silenced me. "You will maintain the integrity of this temple. When you are asked to, you may speak. But you have not been asked yet. Elder Blayne will now speak."

All of our attentions turned to Blayne Crow. His fiery red eyes glowed brighter in the light of the torches.

"Landon Brown, son of Drayden, you are being accused of the following offenses: destruction of the city of Phoenix, Arizona, harming and killing many of the city's inhabitants, and releasing the ancient dragon Aremas from his prison. How do you plead?"

That question cut me like a knife. I was guilty, but I knew that they weren't going to give me a chance to explain myself. They were just interested in pinning everything on me. Why wasn't Shadow standing trial, or Kraven, or my uncle Bane? The Elders didn't care about them. They wanted to see someone get blamed for all of this, and I was the convenient choice. Was it even worth my giving them an explanation? They made it seem as though they already had made up their minds that I was guilty.

I held my head high and stared at all three dragons. Then I said what anyone would have said in my position: "Not guilty."

"Stop wasting our time, Landon," Shea said in frustration. "This is not a game."

"Perhaps if we gave him a chance to explain, we might understand his answer," Zana interjected.

Shea looked like she was going to eat me! Silence fell upon us. Aurora had a very uneasy look on her face, as if she wanted to say something but did not want to disrespect her mom. Zana's warm eyes met with mine, and suddenly I felt comfortable enough to say something that I probably shouldn't have.

"There's an evil dragon outside changing the entire world into his icy kingdom, yet you stare at me as if I'm the one destroying the world. You asked for our help to find something that you were supposed to protect. I shouldn't have joined this quest, because all I really wanted to do was find my dad. He was the only one who took initiative to correct his mistake rather than try to blame a kid for helping. And don't get me started on the type of individuals you're getting your information from! Shadow tells you that I destroyed a city and you believe him without asking about his involvement in it. Or what about my unc—" but I couldn't finish my sentence. I felt this sharp tingling pain run down my body. Shea had zapped me again with electricity.

Before I faded out, I heard Aurora yell, "Why did you do that? That's not fair! You didn't let him finish."

My vision was fuzzy, and a horrible nauseousness overcame me. Then I blacked out—again.

Chapter Seventeen
The Replacement

The scene was chilling. A small village had been laid to waste. A red glow radiated as fire lit up the evening sky. Everything was on fire: huts, horses, humans. A gigantic beast nearly one hundred feet tall—and much more frightening than Aremas—towered over the village. I could see the creature's veins pulsing through his incredibly muscular body. He was a dragon, from the drake family—when his enormous tail whipped the earth, the ground shook. The light from the moon and the fire reflected off the dragon's copper scales. His snout was so large it seemed as though he could swallow a school bus whole.

Then the dragon spoke. "How dare you pick a fight with me, then run away? You are cowards!"

As he roared in frustration, I noticed that his teeth were not pointed like the other dragons I had seen. In fact, they looked much more like human teeth, only super-sized!

Another dragon came out of nowhere and torpedoed himself onto the humongous beast's chest. Then another dragon jumped onto the scene and whipped himself around the legs of the massive drake. The copper dragon fell to the ground and crushed the entire village underneath him. If anyone was still there, I knew that they had no chance of surviving.

I realized that my dad and Proteus were the dragons that had taken down the enormous creature. They must have understood that they needed to work together in order to stop him—and even so, their chances looked grim. My father, in bronze dragon form, lifted his right foreleg and willed the ground below the creature to open. The earth split open and swallowed the giant dragon up into its deep, cavernous folds.

Proteus slithered out of the way as fast as he could, and almost fell in as well. My father's power was amazing to me as I watched. But it was not enough.

The enormous copper dragon clawed his way out of the gash in the earth. There was no telling how deep the hole ran, but the copper dragon was determined not to find out. My father and Proteus looked exhausted, as if they had been fighting for hours.

"I AM INDESTRUCTIBLE!" the copper dragon boomed. "My rise from the pits of the earth should not surprise you. I was summoned to rid the world of the humans, and yet you fight to protect them. Why? I will destroy anyone who stands in my way, including our kind."

"You were summoned under false pretenses!" my father revealed. "Whoever summoned you tricked you into believing that dragons were waging war against the humans. There is no truth in that. Now return to your slumber, Behemoth. The world does not need your destruction."

The colossal dragon swiped at my father; he evaded the attack.

"How dare you speak to me that way! I will return once my mission is complete."

Proteus sneaked behind the dragon Behemoth and spun around, whipping his powerful tail and hitting the back of the copper dragon's ankle. The giant beast stumbled back but did not fall. Then my father raced towards him, and struck him in the face with his own tail. Behemoth winced in pain but gathered himself quickly. He made a slashing motion downward with his left foreleg and willed vines with razor-sharp thorns to rise from the earth. Proteus was surrounded by giant green vines, but he evaded each one as they crashed down in an attempt to ensnarl him.

Then Proteus roared. One of the vines whipped him on the right side of his soft underbelly, leaving a long, bloody gash. Proteus was clearly in pain, but he still moved quickly to avoid any more attacks.

My father rushed to Proteus's aid but Behemoth swung his massive tail and sent Proteus flying. I knew there was no way Proteus would be getting back up from that attack. Sure enough, Proteus lay still on the ground where he had landed, unconscious. The fight was now just between my father and the mighty dragon Behemoth. But Behemoth paid no attention to my father—his black pupils were fixed on the helpless body of Proteus. My father quickly realized that Behemoth would not stop attacking until he obliterated him. Roughly half the size of the enormous dragon, my dad used all his might to force Behemoth back—but he was unsuccessful. He swung his tail, clawed, bit and charged the giant monster, but the drake shrugged off his attacks as if my dad were some annoying mosquito. Then, out of desperation, my father pushed the limits of his power in a move so incredible and deadly that I could see the fear even in his eyes.

My father's ability to split the ground open and create a hole in the earth had nothing on this. The grounds of the village shifted slowly. The earth became like liquid, and started to swirl around the giant Behemoth. The land was moving like a colossal whirlpool. Everything in the swirling earth was crushed in its mighty force. It was quite a scene—imagine seeing a plot of land the size of ten football fields swirling around in a vortex. Behemoth was being pulled down into the earth, much like quicksand, and since he had no wings he couldn't fly out. I turned back to look at my dad and saw how weak he looked. The energy to summon such a powerful force was taking its toll, and it didn't look as though he was going to be able to hold it much longer. The copper dragon was now buried up to his waist in the earth, and my father only needed to hold his energy for a few seconds longer.

But it was too much. My father's eyes rolled back, and his body fell from the sky and plummeted to the earth. The plot of land itself stopped swirling immediately, trapping the copper dragon Behemoth all the way up to his shoulders. My father's body fell one hundred yards away from where the giant dragon was. Then there was an explosion of earth. Behemoth pulled his left arm out of the ground and was trying to do the same with his right. He was going to escape, and my father and Proteus would be completely defenseless.

Just when I thought I could not witness any more, out of the forest approached a tiny figure. It raced towards my father and Behemoth. It was a young man, and he was running at a blazing fast speed. When he approached my dad, the man lifted my father's head and checked to see if he was okay. My father woke up and his eyes widened when he saw him.

"Dra... gos!" My father choked. The young man rested my dad's head on the ground again and shifted his focus to the dragon Behemoth, who was still struggling to pull his right arm out from the earth. Then the man sprinted towards Behemoth. The creature swatted at him, but the man evaded with ease. He charged directly towards the dragon's chest. Just before colliding with the dragon's soft underbelly, the man burst into flames. His fiery body tore through the dragon's chest and, just as quickly, burned through the other side of the Behemoth's body.

The roar of pain was deafening. Green ooze splattered out from his chest and back. Then the man shot a stream of fire from his right hand, whipped it around Behemoth's neck and grabbed the other end of his fiery lasso with his left hand. Then he pulled with all his might. The fire singed the dragon's neck as it was pulled tightly across Behemoth's throat.

"Who... are you... warrior?" Behemoth gasped.

The man pulled his fire rope tighter, and said, *"I am Dragos, son of Halos the mighty. Return from where you came, great dragon, or you will live an eternity in pieces."*

The man spoke with so much confidence in his voice that I had to get a closer look. He didn't look much older than me, maybe seventeen or eighteen. He had long, unruly, dirty-blonde hair, and his intense eyes were an odd color. I had never seen anyone with eyes like his before. The iris around his black pupils was a scintillating gold, and they glowed from the reflected moonlight. I couldn't believe that he was making Behemoth consider leaving of his own accord. He shouldn't have had the strength to do any of the things he was doing.

"I will... return to the earth... Dragos. I am... a dragon of my word. I promise to... leave as soon as you... release me," Behemoth begged desperately.

Dragos didn't even hesitate or question. He released the fire rope he had summoned from Behemoth's throat and glared at the monster with his head held high. Smoke billowed off the great dragon's neck. Behemoth roared in disgust because of what had just happened and used the remainder of his might to pull his other arm out of the ground. Then he pushed the rest of his body out of the earth. He could have easily attacked Dragos, but he didn't.

"Never have I seen a warrior like you," Behemoth confessed. *"I will keep my promise and return to my slumber. But the next time I rise, I will search the world for you and kill you! I will promise you that."*

Unfazed, Dragos responded, *"If you rise again in my lifetime, I will gladly fight you. But if you do rise and I have long passed, those who descend from me will stop you in my honor."*

Behemoth turned away angrily and left. Dragos ran towards my father and helped him off the ground. It was weird seeing a six-foot tall man helping a forty-foot dragon to his feet.

My father looked proudly at him and said, "Son of Halos, once again you have shown that you are a true champion of Earth. Dragons and humans around the world will thank you for this."

"They must not know of my interfering, Drayden," Dragos advised. "My father sent me because he heard of Behemoth's rise, and he also heard of the challenge between you and Proteus to stop him. You must claim that it was you who defeated Behemoth, to ensure that you will enter the Elder Dragon Council and lead the dragons without opposition. This may not seem honorable to you, my friend, but this is my father's wish. He asks that you use your reason rather than your pride. He can only trust you now, especially now that your father is gone. Ithacus was his close friend, and he believes you will be an even greater leader than he was."

My father looked sad but seemed to understand what Dragos was saying.

"I do not keep secrets, my friend, but I understand the sensitivity of this matter and I will comply with your father's wishes. I just hope that I won't disappoint him."

My father smiled, and Dragos smiled as well, but it quickly faded as he sensed something.

"Proteus is waking," Dragos observed. "I must leave. Take care, Drayden, and lead the dragons well."

"Thank you, Dragos."

My father quickly flew toward Proteus and helped him up. Proteus was stunned by the way the terrain looked.

"You d-defeated Behemoth?" A look of disbelief came over Proteus. With a painful expression on his face, my father

nodded his head. Proteus continued, "Then the Elder Dragon Council has its new replacement."

"Did you hear me, kid?" A familiar voice said. Hello…? I asked if you'd heard about the new replacement for the Elder Dragon Council?"

I could barely lift my eyelids, but once I did, I noticed that I was back in the dungeon and locked up. Tyrus looked at me angrily but I ignored it. I wasn't even fully conscious yet, but I was already disappointed that I was stuck with him again.

"Tanin told me that the new Elder Dragon should be arriving soon. Then he will decide your fate. How lucky are you? You'd better hope he's not like the Sky Queen!"

"What are you talking about?" I asked. "And who is Tanin?"

"Tanin is the guard."

"I thought you hated him."

"I do. But he always keeps me updated with what's going on. Just because I hate him doesn't mean he can't be my friend."

I decided not to ask Tyrus for an explanation. I knew he was crazy, so I didn't want to give him any reason for him to start laughing that awful laugh again.

"Do you know who the new Elder Dragon is going to be?" I asked curiously.

"Yes I do. Well, I don't personally know him, but I've heard of him. It seems as if the Council is playing it safe and going with Drayden's younger brother Bane."

A sense of grief came over me like never before. I was stunned. Out of all the dragons to choose from, they decided to go with the one that actually stole the Dragon Sphere.

Tyrus continued. "Tanin said that the Elder Dragons are expecting him to arrive anytime now so that they could make him an official member. Then the exciting stuff happens.

211

Immediately after becoming an Elder, he will have the power to create or change a dragon law. Some Elders in the past have even pardoned prisoners. Maybe he'll do that for us?"

I stayed silent, thinking of all these factors and what they meant for me and everyone else. It wasn't rocket science. Every conclusion I came to was leading to the inevitable takeover of the Elder Council by the Sons of Levi, although I didn't understand how they were going to pull that off, now that they weren't controlling Aremas. He was the wild card in all of this. Someone needed to stop him. Even if my uncle and his crew were able to stop Aremas, which I'm sure they weren't expecting to, my life was still in Bane's hands. There was no way he would let me live to explain my side of the story. What I had to say wouldn't matter anyway. Bane would be considered a hero for stopping Aremas—if he were to survive the confrontation, that is.

I had so many thoughts rushing into my head that my brain actually hurt. I hated being trapped! I was jittery and anxious. I wanted to get out of my shackles so badly, but I was too weak to do anything. And Tyrus didn't make things any better. He was talking to himself with his eyes closed again, trying to conserve his energy so he could make his great escape. I didn't really concentrate on what he was saying but I did get the gist of it. He was salivating at the idea of being set free and terrorizing cities again. I couldn't completely throw the idea out that Tyrus would be pardoned. My uncle Bane could choose to do just that, and let Tyrus join him in taking over the world.

"I need to get out of here!" my voice echoed down the darkened cavernous wall.

"Yelling won't break those chains, kid," Tyrus chimed in. "You'd better get comfortable because you're not going anywhere for a very long time, unless you think you're going to get pardoned. I doubt that will happen, though. You're a nobody. There's no chance that Bane would have even heard of you. If anyone has a shot of getting released, it's me."

Tyrus was wrong about one thing: Bane definitely knew who I was, as much as I wished that he didn't.

"What happens if Bane doesn't release you?" I asked Tyrus.

"Then I stay here."

"I know that, but you seem to be putting all of your hope into the idea that he's going to release you."

"All I have is hope that he will. Before today, I concentrated my efforts in trying to escape. Now the idea of someone setting me free has overpowered that. Do you know how hard it is to be the Dragon of Chaos and be in my position? Do you know what it feels like to be completely powerless?"

"Why do you feel you have to fill that role? You can be much more than that. Maybe even one day you will be looked at as a hero?"

I could tell that Tyrus was taking in what I was saying, so I kept going.

"You can't honestly think that the Elders would release you when you have the same mindset that brought you in here, to destroy everything?"

"My father was a Dragon of Chaos," Tyrus said defensively, "as was his father, all the way back to the beginning of time. It is in my blood to carry on a legacy of chaos. You younglings wouldn't understand. Nowadays, young dragons only care about themselves. They know nothing about loyalty and purpose."

"And look where your loyalty and purpose have left you?" I declared, knowing that this would sting.

Tyrus glared at me viciously. If there hadn't been chains holding him back, I believe he would have killed me. I had learned from recent encounters that dragons are not happy when they are argued with, especially when you point out something that they don't want to hear. Tyrus's face turned red with rage—or embarrassment, I couldn't tell. What was odd, though, was that a few seconds after he looked as if he was going to explode, he relaxed his body. Then he fell asleep. At least, I believed that he fell asleep, because he didn't say anything and his eyes were shut. I didn't know what to make of his behavior, so I decided to just leave him alone.

A few hours passed before I heard shuffling outside the holding cell. My first thought was that it was the guard, Tanin, but then the shuffling sounded like it was coming from more than one person. I hoped that it was Aurora coming in to free me, but the likelihood of that was slim to none. I imagined Uncle Bane coming in to see us, and to deliver the news personally that I would be imprisoned for life. I was so anxious, and I couldn't understand why. I had observed that Tyrus got anxious too, anytime there was some sign of life coming down to the dungeon. Apparently that behavior had rubbed off on me.

The door creaked opened and several familiar faces stepped in. I couldn't believe my eyes; my heart skipped a beat in disbelief.

Then I heard the words that got my blood flowing again.

"Hey brah, did you miss me?"

Chapter Eighteen
Climate Control

I thought I was dreaming. In front of me were Alpha, James Braddock and Derek Foster. James walked toward me and unlocked the shackles on my wrists with a key that he had in his hand. Then he helped me to my feet.

"How did you guys find me?" I asked, still puzzled at their presence.

"It was really by chance," Alpha admitted. "I brought the gang to offer their assistance to the Elder Dragons, but I guess they've already taken off to fight Aremas. They are going to have their hands full with that dude. Anyway, we saw your sword sitting on that righteous diamond altar the Elder Dragons have, and figured you were still here. My first guess was that you managed to find your way to the dungeon."

Alpha's demeanor hadn't changed much. Even with the destruction of the world upon us, he was still nonchalant about everything.

"Let's get out of here," Derek Foster said, "I feel weak in this room."

Alpha gestured for us to walk out, then he noticed me staring at Tyrus, who was still sleeping.

"Don't worry about him, brah," Alpha said, urging me to continue. "This hero fell a long time ago."

"What do you mean by 'hero?'" I asked.

"No time to explain, brah," Alpha responded. "Let's go."

We walked out of the room and up the rocky stairs. I let out a huge sigh of relief when I saw Aurora standing next to Purity and Amy Jane Watkins near the temple. Down by their feet was the security guard, Tanin, wrapped in thick vines.

"Courtesy of James Braddock," Amy Jane Watkins said, pointing at the struggling security guard.

"What if he transforms?" I whispered to Alpha.

"Don't worry, brah. He would've transformed by now if he could. James has become a lot stronger since you left. His vine wrap is amazing. It drains your energy while you're bound. Pretty sweet, huh?"

I don't know why, but a feeling of inferiority came over me. James looked much stronger than the last time I saw him, and that was just less than a week ago.

"Landon!" Purity rushed over to me. "I'm so glad we found you. I was trying to have everyone wait for you at the caverns, but now I'm glad they dragged me along."

I noticed Aurora roll her eyes as Purity wrapped her arms around me.

"We're in luck," Alpha butted into our awkward moment. "The Elder Dragons have made contact with Aremas. The fight has begun! They are in Texas. That's the lucky part. Travis can teleport us near the fight. Y'all ready to go to Dallas?"

"How can you be sure they're fighting in Dallas?" I wondered.

"Brah, I'm the Son of War. If there's a big battle going on, I know about it. Plus, I didn't say they were fighting in Dallas. That's just the closest place Travis can teleport us to. Hurry up and get your sword so we can leave."

I picked *Apollyon* off the diamond altar, and the rest of the group gathered around me in the temple surrounding it.

"Travis, brah, we need you to take us to the Dragon Palace in Dallas," Alpha said, as if he were about to burst out in song.

It took only a second for us to be in Texas. I did not like the feeling of teleporting, though; it felt like the dizziness you get when you stand up too fast from sitting. I could barely focus on the strange creatures and informational pieces we passed as we hurried out of the building we had just teleported into. When we walked outside, I was able to make out a sign next to a frozen metallic creature. The sign read: **Natural History Museum**. Sure enough, we had just walked out of the Dallas Natural History Museum. I thought the museum was an odd place to use as a dragon palace, especially since Dallas had a lot more to offer with its many skyscrapers.

The city looked beautiful in the gray sky, with snow pummeling the streets. The roads and freeways were nearly empty; only a few cars braved the elements. As we walked, we saw one car hit an icy patch and slide three hundred and sixty degrees around before it caught traction again and continued. We continued to follow Alpha down the street. Alpha stopped in front of a glass window, then swung his fist and blasted the glass to pieces. Before any of us could react, he reached for a fur coat that had fallen off a mannequin and handed it to Purity. Purity quickly put it on and thanked Alpha. It was easy to forget that Purity was human, since she was raised by Alpha and knew so much about our world. Simple things like her body not adjusting to the cold the way ours could reminded me that she was not one of us.

Alpha continued. Nearly ten minutes had passed when we eventually came across a grocery store parking lot. There were only a few vehicles parked there. We followed Alpha towards a big blue SUV, and then I realized what Alpha was about to do. I had a feeling he wasn't planning on having us walk to the fight. Sure enough, he zapped the keyhole, unlocked the doors and told everyone to get in. We all gathered into the SUV, and Alpha turned the vehicle on by zapping the ignition. We were on our way, while at the same time somebody else—namely, the owner of the car—was going to be stranded. It seemed like I was the only one who was worried about this, though.

Perhaps everyone else was more concerned about the fight that we were about to jump into.

"Okay, dudes," Alpha called for our attention, "We should catch the fight along the Trinity River. It will still be about an hour before we get to their location, so try to relax and enjoy the music."

Alpha turned up the volume and blasted the entire SUV with heavy-metal music. It was actually very comforting to watch Alpha enjoy himself and air-guitar to his favorite tunes. It would have been a little more comforting, though, if he weren't going so fast on the snow-covered roads while steering with his knees.

Aurora sat next to me in the middle row of the vehicle. The music was so loud that she had to lean over and speak directly into my ear.

"Landon, I don't know if I can fight. The pressure on my back is so bad, I don't think I can move."

"You should definitely stay out of this one then," I urged. "You have been through a lot already. You deserve to sit this one out."

In reality, I was encouraging her to stay out of the fight because I didn't want her to get hurt. I knew Aurora was a capable fighter, but I didn't know what I'd do if something were to happen to her.

"But this is the big fight. If we don't win this one, it's over for us. I'm frustrated with myself because I don't think I can help. I feel like a coward."

Aurora looked down shamefully. I gently placed my hand under hers and held it. I don't know how it happened, but I felt her emotions. I could sense how bad she felt about not being able to fight. I felt her disappointment and her anger. I felt the pain she was suffering and understood why she couldn't fight. The burning sensation had spread throughout the upper half of her back, and her muscles were overworked from the throbbing. The pain was so intense that I pulled my hand away to not feel it anymore.

Aurora knew why I let go. She could sense me too. She must have felt the anxiety I had. She had to have noticed the worry and doubt that had overcome my thoughts—the intense guilt that consumed me over my actions in Phoenix, the sadness I felt for my best friend Xavier, the diminishing hope that my father was still alive and my heavy heart for having to leave Mom alone and possibly never seeing her again.

But the most important thing that I was sure she must have sensed was the joy in my heart that I was with her. I saw it in her smile when I let go of her hand. She had to have felt the way my heart raced when I stared into her beautiful emerald eyes, and the way my muscles tensed with excitement when I was in her presence. As teenagers, we were put in pretty crappy situations, but it also brought us together. I knew that without her going through this with me, I'd have been lost. I would have given up.

We stayed quiet, listening to the loud '80s heavy-metal music. I placed my hand over Aurora's and kept it there. I didn't sense any of her emotions this time. However, I was getting butterflies in the pit of my stomach. I realized that the feeling wasn't a giddy one but one of nausea. I knew what that meant. The blackouts had been hitting more frequently. Why did this keep happening to me? I knew there was nothing I could do to avoid it so I closed my eyes and let the flashback run.

"What do you want?" asked a disgruntled man. "Did you come to torment me?"

The setting was familiar. I was in a large open area in a cave lit by torches. My father came out of the shadows in human form. The disgruntled man in the room was practicing with a sword. I recognized the man immediately with his jet-black hair and dark brown eyes. It was my uncle Bane. His muscular build matched that of my father, and on his right shoulder was a tattoo that I couldn't make out.

"Please, brother, give me a chance to explain. I was never given that opportunity," my father begged. I could sense my dad's spirit—broken and tormented!

"So now that you are a member of the Elder Council you feel I should give you a chance to exonerate the murder you committed? I do not think I will do that. I will let you live with your guilt until you die," Bane vowed.

The tension in the room rose to an extreme level. Bane continued thrusting his sword, each time with more power, pretending that my father was not there at all.

"I wronged you. I know I did. That will stay with me until I die. But you need to know that my sin against you was not from malicious intent. I am responsible for your son's death, and it lingers in my thoughts constantly. The guilt of killing my nephew is unbearable, but I did not know who he was, brother. I promise you. He attacked me and I defended myself. He had no knowledge of his bloodlines. He thought of us as abominations."

The painful expression on my uncle Bane's face as he continued to slash with his sword showed that everything my father was telling him only reminded him of his loss. I could also sense my father's sincerity as he grieved over the loss of his nephew. The proud Knight from my first flashback, who sought to destroy dragons, had in him the very blood of the creatures he wanted to abolish. The seal on his shield represented the dragon clan he belonged to. It was the same one that was spread across my uncle Bane's right shoulder:

Tears ran down Bane's cheeks.

"I did not want for him to become a part of the dragon realm," he broke down. "He proved himself worthy in the eyes of the humans. They loved him and saw him as a champion. His entire world was with them. He did not belong in ours. But, still, I loved him with all that I had. I spent all the time I could spend with him, given my restrictions. But now he is gone, and I will never be able to explain to him how special he was. I allowed him to become weak by forbidding him to know who he really was. One's strength lies in one's understanding of who one is. I stole that from him—and so did you."

My father stood before Bane as if he were waiting for him to deliver a verdict. My uncle examined my dad with watery eyes and declared, "Drayden, I cannot forgive you, but I will not abandon you. I know Father's will was to have you lead us, and now you are in the position to do so. Lead us well, brother."

Bane pointed into the darkness of the cave, gesturing for my father to leave. My dad understood and turned from my uncle. Then he left.

The scene changed and I was sitting inside an old car that my mom used to have. It was stopped and was getting pounded by snow. Mom and I sat in the back seat. I was six years old. We were freezing and she tried to warm us up with a blanket, but it wasn't working. Our car had broken down on our way to visit my grandmother in Philadelphia. Mom kept saying that she knew it was a bad idea to drive so far East in the wintertime. Then she looked me in the eyes.

"Landon, I want you to try and remember your daddy right now," she asked of me. "Remember the stories I told you about him and how much he loves you. Can you do that for me?"

I nodded my head and tried to concentrate on him. I saw how cold Mom was as she silently prayed to herself, hoping that this would all be over soon. When you're a child, you never focus on the vulnerabilities of the grownups around you. But through the perspective of this flashback I was able to, and it hurt me to see my mother so scared.

"Okay, Landon. Now I want you to think about being in a warm place and playing with Daddy, okay?"

I saw myself close my eyes and try really hard to pretend I was off with my father somewhere warm. Then I noticed the car starting to warm up. Mom must have known that we were able to adjust our body temperature. My mother, a regular human being, had secretly taught me how to combat the cold the way a dragon would.

I saw the relief in her eyes. Pretty soon it got so hot in the car that we had to take off our jackets and sweaters.

Mom turned to me and said, "See, baby, just because you can't see your daddy doesn't mean that he's not with you. He's protecting you and me from the cold right now, and he will always be there to protect us in the future."

The smile on my face as a little boy was enough to remind me why Mom didn't want to just drop my dad from my life. She knew the impact it had on me by just mentioning him. I realized that this scene, like many others when I was a child, is what helped me push through my childhood without Dad. Even though he wasn't physically there, Mom always made it clear that his spirit was protecting me. And I did feel protected!

I snapped back to reality. The loud heavy-metal music pounded in my ears. I still had my hand placed over Aurora's hand as she stared out the window. It seemed as if I had been out for a while, but just like all my flashbacks, this one only took up a few seconds in real time. I cleared my mind and relaxed my body. Then I drifted to sleep.

I woke up forty-five minutes later to an awful sound. It was like a mixture of screeching and an alley cat's meow. My first reaction was to look behind me, and I saw James, Amy and Derek laughing their heads off at something. I turned to the front and found the problem: Alpha trying to sing. I couldn't help but chuckle as he belted out, "Here I am… rock you like a hurricane." The funny thing about Alpha's singing was that he wasn't content with just singing the lyrics; he wanted to sound out all the instruments as well.

"C'mon, half-lings, jump in," Alpha shouted, through the noise of blaring guitars.

Of course, no one stepped up to sing with him. Alpha didn't care either; he just continued on by himself.

After the song was over, Alpha lowered the volume and said, "Okay, so we're actually pretty close to the fight. I want to give you guys some pointers before you go out there. First, Aremas is crazy-fast. Don't think you can outrun him, because you can't. If you find yourself face to face with him you should charge him, and try your best to attack him, because running will leave you defenseless. Second, remember to follow the leader. Landon will guide you on how you can help defeat Aremas. Listen to what he has to say on the battlefield, and trust his instincts."

I didn't understand why Alpha placed me in charge. Clearly, James was more respected and trusted by Amy and Derek than I was. I didn't question Alpha though, because if the Son of War felt that confident that I could lead the group into battle, I didn't want to second-guess him in front of everyone. Still, I had no idea how we were going to be any help in this fight.

Alpha continued on.

"Third, never doubt yourself. In the brief amount of time that I have had to train you, you all have shown more potential and guts than I have seen in years. Listen to each other, fight for each other and stick with each other. If you do that, you will see that you are truly a force to be reckoned with."

The time to fight was near and I was getting more nervous with every passing second. But this time, I was not going to fight alone. I couldn't show that I was scared, because the others now had to depend on me to lead them.

Purity turned to me with her piercing, dark-brown eyes. "I know you can do it," she encouraged me. "We are all counting on you."

I'm pretty sure she meant that for the whole group, but the way she looked at me while she said it made me feel as though she was really counting on me to save the world. There was enough pressure already on my shoulders, and that definitely didn't help ease the load any.

Aurora gave me a warm smile that helped calm my nerves for a moment. She leaned over and whispered in my ear, "I believe in you." Then she kissed my cheek and the crowd erupted. Okay, maybe it wasn't that extravagant, but I sure did hear it from the group in the back and from Alpha.

Alpha referred to me as "Romeo" again, and the gang in the back seat shouted out things like "lover boy" and "rosy cheeks." I couldn't see it, but I know my face was blushing pretty badly.

We all had a good laugh, but that soon came to an end as Alpha pulled over to the side of the road. Then he asked everyone to get out of the vehicle.

The scene was grim.

The snow was still coming down hard, but we could make out the fight as fire and lightning raced through the sky in the distance. Alpha said that we would have to travel by foot from that point, because, for Purity's safety, he couldn't get any closer. I was going to explain to him that Aurora needed to stay behind with him and Purity but Alpha seemed to already know that she was not going to fight. He just asked me to keep my head clear and to trust my instincts. I nodded my head and turned towards the battle. With *Apollyon* firmly in my hand, I started walking forward. James, Amy and Derek were right beside me.

The roaring in the sky kept getting louder as we neared the battle. The snow melted on contact with my skin and dripped down my face. My heart pounded harder with every step I took.

When we were about half a mile away from the fight, I told everyone to stay together—then we charged. We all ran as fast as we could. As soon as we arrived, our confidence took a major blow. Blayne Crow crashed into the ground less than a hundred feet away from us. The forty-foot red dragon did not move. His whiskers at the end of each side of his snout were twitching, but that was it. The other dragons were still fighting above us, so I pointed towards what looked like a gigantic ice slide.

"That's how we get to Aremas," I said.

The enormous frozen structure poked out of the ground at a forty-five-degree angle. It stemmed from the nearby river, which was now completely frozen. I assumed that Zana had shot a water blast towards Aremas, but he was able to freeze it before it reached him. There were three other similar structures sticking out as well.

"What do we do now?" Amy asked. "The ice is too slippery for us to walk on. We'd just slide back down."

"We need to get to the fight somehow. We're no use down here," said Derek.

I could see that everyone was racking their brain for a solution. Then I had an idea.

"We need them to bring the fight down here to us," I blurted. "If we can get their attention, they could get close enough for us to be a factor in this fight. We need to destroy these large ice structures. There are four of them, so each of us can get behind one. Then we can break them all at the same time."

Everyone agreed, and we quickly ran into position to destroy the ice. Then I yelled as loud as I could.

I slashed furiously with my sword and cut huge chunks of ice off. The ice structure was twenty feet wide and about seven or eight feet thick, though. I willed the earth below to rise and slam into the structure repeatedly. The ice cracked, then it snapped from the base.

I noticed James wind his arm up and punch the ice with his bare hand, shattering the entire area and making the ice formation collapse. Derek heated his up with fire and melted the base, causing the ice to collapse as well. Amy seemed to be struggling to get hers to break, but then I noticed that she was using the liquid water inside the icy formation to crack the structure. She unleashed a powerful rush of water to obliterate the entire thing. Shards of ice flew in all directions—and a few chunks even pegged me.

A loud roar filled the sky. I saw the enormous dragon Aremas plummeting towards the earth, and the other dragons diving down with him. Zana was wrapped around Aremas's neck, and my uncle Bane and Shea each clamped down on one of his wings with their teeth. Then Aremas slammed into the ground, and the other dragons landed on top of him. Snow and debris flew everywhere. When everything settled, we saw that the dragons were all badly injured, except Aremas. He didn't even look as if he had been scratched, even after the fall. He was still down, though, and that gave me enough time to come up with a plan.

I gathered the group and gave specific tasks for everyone to do. I told Derek to melt as much ice as he could from the river.

I asked James to use his vine wrap to bind Aremas's snout. The final part of my plan relied heavily on Amy's mastery of water manipulation. I had no clue how well she could control her powers, but I asked her to use the water from the river to create an enormous liquid sphere.

"I think I can pull that off," she said confidently and with a smile. "How big do you want it?"

"Large enough to fit a sixty-foot dragon!"

Her smile quickly faded. But before I gave her a chance to say anything, I told everyone to move to their positions. I followed James up to Aremas's snout and saw him summon thick vines that slithered out of the earth and through the accumulated snow. The vines began wrapping around the gigantic snout and binding it tight. I asked James to make them long enough that someone could hold onto them from the top of Aremas's head. He gave me a look that I assumed meant, *Are you crazy?*

I looked ahead at Aremas and told James, "It might be a long shot, but I'm going to try to force Aremas into the water sphere that Amy is creating. You need to wake the other dragons. When we are in the sphere, I need you to tell Shea to shoot it with a lightning bolt. Even if I'm in there with him."

"I can't do that," James said.

"Do it. He's waking up. Go now!"

I jumped on top of Aremas's snout and picked up the thick vines that ran to the top of his head. I saw Aremas's red eyes fix on me as I passed by them. Then I stood in between Aremas's giant horns, studying the other six sharp protrusions that jutted out from each one. With the sword and vine in my right hand, I decided to do something that was probably not the smartest thing. I slapped the flat of my blade down on the crown of the dragon's head... and he felt it.

227

Aremas grunted in pain and sped off at an amazing speed. There was no way that I was going to let go, though. The snow slapped against my face hard as Aremas jetted through the sky. When he leveled out, I managed to straddle the upper part of his neck. I tried pulling back with my right arm with all my might and was able to change our direction slightly to the right. It took so much out of me to do it, though. Then I did the next best thing—I stabbed him in the side of the neck. But this time Aremas didn't change directions—he stopped completely. I lifted my arm to stab him again. Just as I was about to do it, someone else attacked him.

My uncle Bane had slammed into Aremas's gut. The impact almost made me lose my sword. Bane shot a stream of fire right at Aremas's face but Aremas dodged it. The ancient dragon spun around and flung his tail, which hit my uncle on his head. That's when I made my move. I dug my sword into the side of his neck again. Frosty air left his nostrils. I felt his body tremble and his tail swung like crazy. He was getting desperate.

Bane again rammed into Aremas's soft underbelly with his horns. Aremas's cry was muddled by the vines around his snout. Blood flowed as my uncle Bane pulled away.

"I know I can't kill Aremas, but I can kill you, boy!" My uncle Bane yelled out.

He swiftly charged at Aremas's neck, opened his mouth wide, and bit down near the area I was holding on to. I let out a sigh of relief as he sank his teeth a few feet away from me. Then I realized that he wasn't trying to bite me.

Uncle Bane dove towards the ground, dragging Aremas along, while I held onto the vines for dear life. On our way down I saw the gigantic water sphere that Amy was creating. The ground was closing in on us fast. With all my strength, I lifted my sword and drove it as hard as I could into the back of

Aremas's neck. Aremas twisted in pain, which loosened Bane's grip, then Aremas sped away right before hitting the ground. My uncle was not as lucky as he slammed hard against the earth, creating an impact crater. Before Aremas could move too high into the sky, I pulled back as hard as I could with my left arm, veering him off to the left and directing him straight for the water sphere. Then I braced myself for impact as we collided with a wall of water.

I let go of the vines and held on with all my might to my sword. I shot through the sphere like a torpedo and was sent flying through the other side. The cold air stung my face as soon as I passed through the freezing water. I was too weak to will the ground to soften my blow as I was about to land. But before I hit the ground, I was caught in mid-air. As I hung upside down, I saw a lightning bolt shoot down from the clouds and electrocute the water sphere. Sparks flew everywhere as the entire sphere lit up in a blinding flash. I focused just below it and noticed Amy Jane Watkins and Zana Reed concentrating on keeping the water sphere stable. Next to them were Blayne Crow and Shea, still knocked out from the fight. Next to Shea, though, was Aurora, who had tendrils of electricity shooting off her body.

My heart almost jumped out of my chest in excitement, as it seemed we were about to win, but quickly I remembered something very important: if Blayne, Shea and Zana were still down on the ground, who had caught me? I swung my head up and saw a soft, white underbelly. And then I noticed the tail swinging back and forth, and the shimmering bronze glinting in the light.

Chapter Nineteen
Showdown

I was gently placed onto the ground after hanging upside down for what seemed like forever—only it was probably more like a few seconds. When I looked up, a familiar forty-foot bronze dragon towered over me. I easily recognized this dragon with his two large horns that curved forward like a bull, the bony spikes that came out of his spine from the top of the neck to his tail and the six foot-long spikes that protruded out from there. This dragon was my dad. He looked exactly the way I had seen him in my flashbacks, except that he wasn't as shiny and was much thinner.

A white flash blinded me as my father transformed from dragon to human. His human form reflected his dragon form. He was thinner, and looked much more tired, than any time in the flashbacks I'd had of him.

His presence made everything feel right. Finally, everything was going to be okay.

The familiar features of the three claw marks under his right eye that my uncle Bane had given him, and the white patch of hair in the right corner of his chin, brought me chills. This was the first time that I had seen my father in person since I was a baby.

There was so much to ask him. Instead, I just let instinct take over. I rushed to him. As I wrapped my arms around him, my insecurities about not having a father all those years completely vanished. It was as if they had never existed. I always played it off as if it didn't matter that he wasn't around; it was just an act, though, a way that I could cope with his absence. Finally, he was here—he was hugging me, and showing me that he wasn't just an image in my head anymore.

"Landon," my father said, "I am glad to meet you, my son." I could feel the overflowing love that poured out from his greeting—there was relief that shrouded him as he gripped me.

"Dad, I'm so happy you're here. What happened to you?" I barely managed to get the words out, as the eruption of my emotions stopped me from asking every other question running through my mind.

My father sighed. "I was trapped, Landon," he said. "I was held prisoner for nearly ten years, locked away in a dungeon. My brother Bane and his followers attacked me and captured me. They only kept me alive for one reason: I was their source of credibility."

"What do you mean?"

"Bane and his minions used me as a recruiting tool to build his army. He would show me to his prospective recruits, and glorify his plan to end the reign of the Elder Dragons. It was a scare tactic that worked quite well for my brother. By imprisoning me, he was able to coerce many that a new order would be ushered in soon, and that the time to choose sides was upon them. Very few chose not to join, and those that did not, did not live to warn anyone about his cult. The Sons of Levi are in a state of panic now, thanks to you. You have breached their headquarters and ruined their plans."

"But Aremas was released anyway, and still managed to cause a lot of damage."

As soon as I said that, I remembered that the others were still dealing with the monstrous wyvern. I turned around and saw the gigantic water sphere Amy had made—it was still holding Aremas, but now there was another dragon helping to hold it together. I had never seen that dragon before, but I had a feeling I knew who it was.

Just before I was about to ask my dad about the dragon, he answered as if reading my mind.

"Yes, Landon, that is your sister Destiny. She was able to free me because of you. She is strong and courageous as well."

Destiny was small compared to the other dragons. She was about ten feet long and, just like her mother and all other water dragons, she had no hind legs or wings. Her scales were a very dark blue tint and she had a couple of nubs on the crown of her head, which I knew would be horns one day. Her big blue eyes were fixed on the hovering globe of water just above her.

Aremas's body floated in the water sphere. We all knew he couldn't be killed, but the fact that he wasn't moving was a good sign for us.

"Let us join the others," said my father.

Immediately he jumped twenty feet in the air, released a blinding white flash and transformed back into a dragon. He picked me up and tossed me onto his back, then we flew to the others. I noticed Aurora as we were approaching. She looked tired and weak, but she was able to manage a smile.

I smiled back.

Suddenly my body jerked. I was tossed another fifty feet into the air. Bane had just blindsided us. He and my dad crashed into the ground, creating a snowy explosion. I was falling at a tremendous speed, but suddenly, Shea picked me out of the air. She brought me down slowly next to Aurora. Amy, my sister Destiny and Zana were still busy keeping the water sphere stable. Everyone else's eyes were fixed on my dad and Uncle Bane.

They had gotten to their feet and were staring each other down in typical western- showdown fashion.

"We need to help him," I expressed my concern. "He is still very weak."

"Quiet, young one," Shea answered. "Do you not see that Bane is weak as well? Our fight with Aremas has weakened all of us. Also, look beyond your father and uncle.

Reinforcements have arrived, but I have a feeling that they are not here to help us."

I took another look. Beyond my father and my uncle stood our enemies—the Sons of Levi. Shadow was in black dragon form, Kraven stood next to him, and next to Kraven stood Shade Gambino. Some of their other soldiers had come along with them and looked ready for battle.

"We need to fight. We just can't let them attack my dad. They'll kill him."

"They will not step in," Shea said sternly. "This battle is between your father and Bane. We will not interfere unless his forces do, and they will not interfere unless we do. It is best that we wait for them to make a move. We have three on our side still holding the water sphere with Aremas in it. We cannot jeopardize his release. Besides, your father has always been the superior warrior between the two."

The snow wasn't coming down as hard anymore. It seemed as if Aremas being trapped in the sphere was breaking his control over the climate. The two bronze dragons continued to size each other up. My father was at least fifteen feet longer than my uncle Bane, but he was fighting after being trapped in a dungeon for ten years. The tension was high and everybody was on edge as we witnessed the clash between the two.

My father made the first move and rushed at Bane. He let out a stream of fire, but Bane blocked it by willing a wall of earth to rise in front of him. My father didn't back off. He rammed the wall, broke it down and crashed into my uncle. The two rolled violently on the snow-covered ground. Tails whipped in every direction, claws ripped flesh and razor-sharp teeth punctured scales. Then the ground started to shake.

"Somebody wake that indolent red dragon up!" Shea ordered.

I had forgotten that Blayne Crow was still passed out. James and Derek sped towards him and began banging on his snout.

Shea turned to me and said, "It is your turn to show your strength, Landon. We have to release Aremas from the water sphere and place him on the ground. Aremas needs to be encased in a sphere made of earth."

Shea flew off. She landed next to Zana and started giving her instructions. Aurora hurried over to me and asked me what was going on. Before I could answer, the ground again shook violently and knocked us down. The fight between my father and my uncle Bane was altering the land. Bane's horns were inches away from my dad's chest, as my dad used all his might to stop them from piercing him. I turned back and saw a wall of water slam into the ground. The water sphere had collapsed, and Aremas awoke.

Aremas's massive tail swung around and slammed Zana and Shea into the ground. Blayne, who had woken up as well, shot a fiery blast that burned the ancient dragon's back. Aremas quickly turned around and tackled Blayne, pressing down on him with his foot and pinning him to the ground. Aremas's barbed tail rose up behind him, showing off his poisonous stinger. Just as his tail struck down, the giant wyvern was blindsided and tackled. His stinger landed inches away from Blayne's neck. Then my eyes widened in disbelief as I saw the gray-bearded sea dragon Proteus lift his head.

Proteus wrapped himself around Aremas's chest and squeezed as hard as he could. Aremas thundered in pain. Blayne Crow rose to his feet and released an enormous blast of fire into the air. Then he began moving his forelegs like an orchestra conductor, as if he was drawing something in mid-air. He was manipulating the blast of fire he had just shot into the air, transforming it into a giant, fiery spear. Then he took aim and shot it at Aremas. The ancient dragon, not paying attention due to fighting off Proteus, was hit right on target as the fiery spear pierced his gut and protruded out the other side of his body. Blood oozed from the entrance and exit points of the spear and flames surrounded the area.

Aremas bellowed in pain.

Then the ground shook again, which toppled the giant wyvern to the ground. Proteus slithered away just before Aremas could fall on top of him and crush him. Aurora, still weak from the thunderbolt she had unleashed earlier, fell over into my arms. The landscape continued to shift around us as the battle raged on between my father and my uncle Bane. I looked back for a moment and saw my father swing his powerful tail against Bane's chest, knocking him to the ground. Bane was lucky that my dad's spikes didn't pierce him. My dad willed the earth beneath Bane to rise and knock him skyward. Then he released a fiery blast that burned Bane's entire body. My uncle was in pain, but he flapped his wings and sped through the sky to extinguish the flames that had engulfed him. Then my father took to the sky.

"NOW, LANDON!" I heard Shea scream.

Aurora stepped back from my arms as I called all the energy I had in my body to rise. I brought forth power so deep in my body that I felt pain in the pit of my stomach. I willed the earth below Aremas to fold onto itself. Then large chunks of land broke off and pounded the earth around Aremas. The power coursing through my veins was taking its toll on me, though. My vision started to blur, everything went silent and my body started to tremble. The pain in the pit of my stomach got worse with each passing second. Then, without a moment's notice, everything went blank.

"My son... you are so special," I heard my father's voice *echo from inside some room.*

I peeked inside and saw a crib and a playpen. I recognized myself as a baby, maybe close to a year and a half, playing on the floor of the playpen. My father was sitting on a chair next to it, watching me toss my stuffed animals around.

He continued speaking as I played. "Innocent, sweet child. The Creator has blessed me with you. Yet, I have to leave you and your mother behind again to search for something that has been taken from us. This is one of the downfalls of being a leader. I will do all I can to make a speedy return. As is the custom however, dear child, there are a few things I need to say to you just in case I do not make it back. Only the Creator knows when our time is up. I never go on a quest with the idea that all will be safe. That is the first thing I want you to understand, Landon. Be confident in who you are, and in your skill, but never underestimate any situation."

My father reached out his hand, and my infant self instinctively moved to touch it. A warm smile lit up his face as he continued. "In the event that something does happen to me, I obviously will not be there to teach you many things about yourself. Even if this happens, you will still come to learn that you are the son of a dragon. We dragons have the ability to transform into humans, but most of us are only limited to being human for four hours in a twenty-four-hour period. Rest easy, my son. You do not have to worry about turning into an actual dragon—only special circumstances allow a dragonoid to become a full-fledged dragon. I would not wish that on you, Landon. We dragons have pledged to hide our true nature from humans. You will find as you get older that your human form holds magnificent powers in its own right."

A small beeping noise sounded from a clock on top of one of the drawers in the room. My father's warm smile faded and his voice sounded hurried.

"I do not have much time now, Landon. I must leave, but first there are three more things I want to explain to you. The first deals with the reason why I'm explaining all of this to you right now, as if you were able to understand. Flashbacks. All dragons deal with them, and most dragonoids do as well. The flashbacks we experience are slightly different than what you will come to learn human flashbacks to be, however. Dragon flashbacks are much like human flashbacks in which we recollect moments in our past that have taken place, except that in dragon flashbacks we are immersed in those recollections. It is like reliving a moment but watching that moment from another's perspective, and not being able to change the outcome. We also experience the environment in the exact same way that it first occurred when we are in this dreamlike state. My hope is that this will be one of your first flashbacks, and you will see that even if I am not around, I did everything possible to help you understand who you are.

Secondly, it is important for you to understand the intricacies of the earth. Why earth? As a bronze dragon, I have the power to control the ground around me—and you will too someday. Do not take this gift for granted. There is much to learn about the art of influencing the earth. Not utilizing your powers properly may have disastrous results. If I am not around to teach you how to control your power, you must seek out Alpha, the Son of War. Your mother already knows that you will need to see him when you are fifteen years of age. Remember, Landon, manipulating the earth can be very dangerous, but learning to control your power will allow you to do a lot of good as well. Always keep this in mind and use your gift wisely.

Lastly, remember that I love you, and I wish nothing more than to see you grow into a man. The thought of that alone will help me on the quest I am about to embark on. I will do all I can to come back to you and your mother. For now, I leave you this message, in hopes that you will receive it when you come of age. I am proud to be your father and I love you. Always remember that."

My dad rose to his feet, lifted me up and kissed my forehead. Then he placed me back in the playpen and walked out of the room.

"Landon!" Aurora screamed, "You have to control his tail."

I snapped out of my flashback and noticed that Aremas's tail was swinging wildly. The rest of his body was being crushed under the earthen sphere that I was forming. As I willed another chunk of earth to rise, the sky above us turned red. My father and uncle Bane each released enormous streams of fire that collided with each other. The heat was so intense that all the snow below them melted. Both bronze dragons looked majestic as they flapped their wings mightily in the air, and lit up the sky with their powerful breaths of fire.

"Drayden! Move away!" Shea shouted a warning to my father.

I saw what she was trying to warn my dad about. Aremas's tail was just below him and Bane. With all the energy I had left, I willed the chunk of earth I had just collected to slam against the enormous sphere. With blazing speed, Aremas's tail struck and stabbed my dad in his underbelly and just as swiftly, struck my uncle Bane. Then the chunk of earth slammed against his tail and into the sphere.

Anger filled my heart, and the only thought that I had was to crush Aremas. I compacted the earth sphere with all my power. Blayne Crow shot a stream of fire that engulfed the sphere. Immediately after that, Zana and Proteus willed water to wash over it. Then Shea struck it with a bolt of lightning. An immense intensity of light came over the sphere. When it faded, what was left was an enormous crystallized ball. There was a small hole in the sphere, however. Everyone noticed it immediately.

"Use your sword, Landon!" James, Amy and Derek ordered simultaneously.

I picked my sword up off the ground and ran towards the sphere. Then I jumped in the air and shoved *Apollyon* into the hole. The sword fit perfectly. A layer of obsidian enveloped the sphere and sealed Aremas in for good. I pulled *Apollyon* out safely and jumped off. I quickly ran over to my father, who was now lying on the ground, and also noticed my uncle Bane was also lying unconscious near his followers.

I knelt down next to my dad. Struggling to breathe, he whispered the most haunting words I have ever heard.

"Landon, I'm dying."

Chapter Twenty
Death of the Great Dragon

Imagine being trapped alone on an island for years. Then, one day, a plane flies by and, for the first time in a long time, you feel a sense of hope. The presence of the plane transforms your sadness into unfathomable joy. But then the plane keeps flying by. It does not turn around to pick you up, and it never brings anyone else to help you. That feeling of abandonment was exactly what I felt as my father lay on the ground, dying. It was as if I was seeing the plane leave—and I knew it was never coming back.

Zana pushed her way through the crowd that was now huddled around my father. She examined his wound closely, but I could see the worry in her eyes.

"Mom, please help him," Destiny cried. She was now transformed into a human and tears streamed down her face.

Zana didn't say anything, which only solidified the feeling I had that she wasn't going to be able to help him.

"Give him a revival shell, like the one you gave me," Aurora offered.

"They do not cleanse the bloodstream, child. Even they are useless now." Zana tried to hold back her tears. "The wyvern's poison is the deadliest in the world. Drayden has only a few minutes to live, if that. Please give him some room. Let him speak to his children."

Zana whispered something to my father, then stepped out of the way. Destiny and I were left alone with him.

"Forgive me," my father managed. "I was blinded with rage—that was my fatal flaw."

"Don't speak like that, Father. You will be okay," Destiny attempted to comfort him.

"My beautiful daughter, I wish that were the case. But my life has come to its end. I have had a good life, and the Creator has blessed me with your presence. Thank you for saving me and releasing me from my torment. Your bravery exceeds anything I have ever done, and I am so proud to have you as my daughter. I love you, Destiny."

My sister could not contain her tears. I felt so selfish for thinking that I was alone in all of this. I had never considered what she was feeling. I never thought that this might hurt her even more, because she'd actually been able to spend time with our dad. I had my father's memories but I didn't get the chance to really make any memories with him. Destiny did.

"My son," Dad looked at me, "you were the only reason I did not give my spirit up. Every day that passed presented the difficult challenge of choosing to give up all hope or keeping it alive. My desire to see you was my strongest ally in the fight against death. Having you here before me was worth all the struggles—even if this moment together is so brief. Now I can leave this world happy that I saw you one last time. Please tell your mother that I love her with all the love that I have, and that I am sorry I never returned for her. She is a special woman who deserved so much more than the heartache I gave her."

Tears welled up in my eyes. All the emotions that I had ever felt seemed like they were being jumbled up together—happiness, sadness, anger and so much more tugged at me. At the same time, I hated the feelings of betrayal that were brewing inside of me as well. As my father lay dying, I still felt betrayed by him for leaving Mom and me behind. This time, the feeling came with the finality that only death can bring. As these feelings began to consume me, my father said something that caught me by surprise. Had he read my mind?

"Death is not the end, Landon," he said in a low and strained voice. "Physically, I will not be around. But as I enter the afterlife, you will continue to live and carry on the precious blood of the bronze dragons which I am proud to be one of. I will always be a part of you, my son. I know that I will see you again one day. I love you, son."

"Dad... wait! Please don't leave us yet. Please hold on," I pleaded desperately with my father.

He smiled warmly and spoke his last words. "Tell Brandon I forgive him."

Then my father drew his last breath. Destiny held my hand and pulled me back as my father's body glowed. A white light flashed, and my father's body was gone. My legs gave way and I fell to my knees. The pain of his loss was worse than any physical pain I had ever felt. Then Destiny dropped to her knees and put her arms around me. Aurora did the same, and held us both tightly. James, Amy and Derek followed Aurora and knelt next to us, putting their arms around us as well.

A few moments later, we heard a scream. It was my uncle Bane, howling in pain.

"Look, they're betraying one of their own," exclaimed James.

The rest of us looked over and saw Kraven kneeling on top of Bane's chest. His comrades just stared as Kraven pulled a large machete out of my uncle's chest. Then he shoved his hands back into the area he had sliced open.

"We must attack them!" Proteus roared. "He is going for the heart."

Proteus lunged forward, but Blayne Crow pulled him back.

"Let them betray their own," Blayne said. "Aremas is again locked in a Dragon Sphere and we cannot afford to give them a chance at it. They know we have won the battle. They are not going to fight against us today."

Kraven pulled his arms out of my uncle's chest, and out came his heart. Bane's body glowed and vanished in the white light.

Kraven held up my uncle's heart and yelled over to us.

"This is not the end," he exclaimed. "This is just the beginning!"

Kraven and Shade jumped onto Shadow's back, and they flew away. The rest of the Sons of Levi followed their lead.

Proteus was furious. "We just let them escape! We needed to destroy them all, and we just let them go?"

"Proteus, calm yourself," Shea said. "We are done battling for now. We must now focus on getting the Dragon Sphere back to the temple of the Elder Dragons."

Proteus quieted down and turned his attention to me. He was frustrated, yet sad. "Your father was a great dragon. I am sorry for your loss."

Then he turned and slithered away without saying anything to anyone else.

"Awkward! What's his deal? We just lost Landon's dad," Amy offered.

Zana smiled at her warmly. "He is an old and angry dragon, young one. His battle tactics are much different than our own. If it were up to him, we would have fought Shadow and the others right now—and if there were more involved with them, he would want us to seek them out and destroy them all. We Elder Dragons do not believe that is as effective as winning the small battles in order to win the war. But do not get me wrong; I feel much safer knowing that he is fighting on our side."

"Where is he going now?" Derek Foster asked.

"He is probably going home to prepare his students for battle," Shea answered. "We all get the sense that this will not be the last time we see the Sons of Levi—especially since one of their half-lings stole Bane's heart. It seems as if he wishes to become the alpha dragon now. He and Shadow will surely try to perform *Elexium*."

"What is that, Mom?" Aurora asked with a look of concern.

"*Elexium* is a dark, ancient practice of transforming a human or half-ling into a dragon. In order to perform it, one must consume a dragon's heart. The transformation is a long and dangerous process. Many believe the reason for the length of the process has something to do with the metamorphosis of human blood into dragon blood. But we simply do not know. The only dragon that may have an idea is impossible to find."

Zana and Blayne looked at Shea as if she were saying too much. There was still so much of the dragon world that we dragonoids were clueless about. I understood their desire to keep things secret from humans. But if they were going to effectively train us dragonoids and allow us to help them, they couldn't keep us in the dark about their world. We belonged to it just as much as they did—even if we are half-blooded dragons, we are still dragons.

Aurora asked her mom who the dragon that was impossible to find was. She answered with one word. "Dragos."

Where had I heard that name before? I remembered that during my fight with Kraven, he had mentioned that name. Also during one of my flashbacks, my dad was helped out by a dragonoid named Dragos who defeated the enormous dragon Behemoth.

Impulsively I added, "Dragos, the son of Halos. Is that who you are talking about?"

Shea and the other elders looked shocked that I knew that information.

"Yes Landon, that is correct," Zana said, still confused about how I knew. "The son of the Golden Dragon Halos is the one we speak of. But his legend is no longer told after he consumed his father's heart and he himself became the new

Golden Dragon. He was the most powerful dragonoid ever to have existed, but his greed for more power took him over when he decided to steal his father's heart. But enough of this talk! Let us head to the temple and properly mourn the loss of our hero."

For the rest of the evening, I couldn't concentrate on anything. I was exhausted, and no one asked me to help with moving the Dragon Sphere. I had left the Sphere the size of a military tank, but I do remember Zana comforting me and telling me that I did well in compacting it as much as possible. She said that the last time Aremas was put into his holding cell, it took five bronze dragons working together to make it that small. I don't even remember how they managed to get it back to the temple of the Elder Dragons this time. I do remember all of us meeting up with Alpha and Purity, and then getting a lift from Blayne Crow back to the Temple.

I remember entering Yosemite Valley and looking over the beautiful landscape as we made our way back. Even in the dark, I was able to make out the enormous cliffs covered in snow. Snow covered the beautiful meadows and countless trees, reminding me of a Christmas postcard picture. I remember entering through a secret passageway that opened up in one of the cliffs where the temple of the Elder Dragons was located.

The Elders did have me stand trial in what they said was the most informal setting they had been a part of, but they were determined to close the matter that loomed over me about my actions in Phoenix. They determined that Shadow and the Sons of Levi's involvement were the contributing cause to the devastation of the city. They found me guilty of negligence and ordered me to have extensive training with Alpha, every summer and winter break, until the completion of my schooling. I thought I could live with that judgment.

That same night, a ceremony was held in honor of my father. News had traveled fast of my father's passing, and many came to pay their respects. The room quickly filled with dragons of all different sizes, colors and shapes. Yellow dragons, green dragons, even pink ones had come to mourn his death. The Elder Dragons placed Destiny and me at the foot of the temple, and sent over every new arrival to meet us. I felt honored as each dragon approached us and gave us their condolences. Many could not hold back their tears, which only made things harder on my sister and me. But I was very grateful for everyone's sincerity. I could tell that they really loved our father.

When everyone was done paying their respects, Shea, Blayne and Zana led the others in a series of roars. The echo, throughout the cavern, of the mournful choruses of roaring dragons was hauntingly beautiful. The ceremonial demonstration paid homage by transforming the many dragon voices into one powerful song to exalt a great hero.

Through the triumphant roars, Destiny hugged me and said, "Our father was a great dragon. I have a feeling you will be just as great."

Her words meant the world to me. The only thing I could do for my sister in return was to hold her tightly in my arms.

The days following our father's death were especially hard. Going back to Albuquerque and explaining things to Mom was the toughest thing I'd ever had to do. Mom felt so guilty for listening to Uncle Bane and thinking that he was actually trying to help us. It was hard for me to see Mom cry. She was a strong woman, and it hurt me to see her so vulnerable. It felt good to be home again, though. We spent hours together, reminiscing about Dad. She made me peanut butter pancakes in the morning and steak and potatoes for dinner. Mr. Rodriguez called us every day from the hospital in Denver to keep us updated on Xavier's condition. Although he'd been severely beaten, the doctors were confident that he would make a full recovery. I badly wanted to see him, but the airlines were still closed from all the snow.

Aurora called me every night from the Infernal Caverns. Alpha gave her special permission to use the phone, as long as she stayed and trained with him until school started. I didn't blame her for staying. In fact, I debated going back for a little while too. School in Albuquerque didn't start for another two weeks—plenty of time for me to get some good training in and also to see my friends. The one thing that held me back was the thought of leaving Mom alone again. She already knew that I wanted to train more and learn as much about my dragon heritage as I could. She also knew that I wanted to see Aurora again.

Four days after the fight with Aremas, I received something in the mail from Yosemite National Park. It was a big box but it was very light. It almost felt as if nothing was in it. A card was attached to it:

Thank you for everything you have done.
We send this gift as a token of our appreciation.
Sincerely, Zana, Blayne and Shea

I took the box into my room and opened it. I was shocked to find what was inside. Magic fire! The Elder Dragons sent me my own version of Travis the Fire, except with this one, the flames were blue. I didn't even think twice. I turned the box over and let the flame sit in the middle of my room. It wasn't radiating any heat or burning the carpet. I put my hand in the flames and it didn't burn me either. Mom walked into the room and saw my hand in the fire and nearly had a heart attack. It took me a few minutes to calm her down and convince her not to toss water at it. When Mom is in panic mode, she seems to tune out anything I say. I explained to her all the cool things that these magical flames could do, but the best thing about them was that I could teleport directly to the Infernal Caverns.

I hoped my mom would get used to the magic fire being in my room a little better than the time she bought me a hamster. When I was younger, she brought a hamster home for me because I had begged for one for a long time. It didn't take long for her to forget that I liked to let my little friend roll around my floor in his exercise ball while I was gone. One terrified kick from mom and the hamster was no more. I didn't think anything like that would happen with my blue fire, but it was hard not to think that it couldn't.

After dinner, I told Mom that I thought it was best that I go back and continue my training at the Caverns until school started. She had already expected it, and encouraged me.

"Don't worry about me, Landon. You need to master all of your gifts. I know it's important to you. Just promise me one thing. Promise me that you will give it all you've got."

I smiled and nodded my head. It had been a while since Mom had told me that. Ever since I'd started football, Mom discouraged me from giving it all I had. This request always confused me, but now I knew why. I was definitely going to give it my all this time around, however.

I decided to leave that night so I would be able to start training the next morning. I went to my room, said goodbye to Mom and asked Travis Junior—that's what I ended up calling him, creative, right?—to teleport me to the Infernal Caverns. Immediately the scene changed to the inside of the cavern. Travis was burning bright, and Alpha was giving a lesson to the group.

I felt very queasy from the teleportation.

"Landon!" Aurora shouted excitedly. She ran up to me and hugged me.

Alpha turned around to greet me. "Hey, brah! How did you…? Whoa, don't tell me the old dragons gave you some magic fire?"

Before I could respond, Alpha continued. "That's a great honor. They're very selective on who gets that stuff. I'm going to have to show you how to use it so you can take full advantage of its powers."

"Thanks, I'd like that."

After greeting the others, I sat down and listened to Alpha continue his lesson on spirits.

"So, where did I leave off?" he said. "Oh yeah, neutral spirits! Neutral spirits don't take sides in the eternal battle of good and evil. We were created to perform specific jobs, and that is all. Some of those jobs may seem like they belong to a certain side, but that is simply not the case. An example of what I am talking about would be the situation with my father and my uncles. My uncle Death, for example, was created to collect the souls from Earth and transport them to receive their judgment in the end of days. Let me tell you, he gets a bad rep because of it, but if you ever got a chance to meet him, you'd find that he's actually a pretty funny guy. My dad, on the other hand, is not so funny and takes his job a little more seriously than the others. That's why he created me. I came about because of his desire to see more evenly matched wars. I was born when he cut off his left hand and formed me out of it."

"You were created out of your dad's left hand?" Amy said in disgust.

"Sure thing," Alpha said. "Spirits can't really have kids, so if they want help with their tasks, they cut something off and form them to their likeness. Then they call them their 'kids.' It doesn't happen often, but when it does, this is how. I've given you more information than necessary—but the important thing to get out of this lesson is that we neutral spirits have our jobs and we do not take sides."

"That's good to hear," said a familiar voice from the entrance of the cavern. "I was getting worried that you wouldn't accept me again."

My mouth dropped as the figure in the shadows stepped into the light and Shade Gambino appeared.

Chapter Twenty One
The Awakening

An uncomfortable silence came over the room. There was an evilness to Shade that wasn't present the first time he was here at the caverns. I wasn't the only one to notice it. It seemed that everyone else felt very uneasy with his presence as well—except for Alpha, that is.

"Okay, well, I was pretty much done with my lesson," Alpha said, looking over at Shade. "It's time to hit the sack. We have a long day of training tomorrow. Before you go, everyone needs to remember that I am serious about this being a neutral training ground. There are to be no fights unless I allow them. If there is a fight without my permission, then there is going to be a problem."

With that said, we all went straight to bed.

The next morning, we woke to heavy-metal music and the smell of breakfast burritos. Alpha was loosening up as usual by shredding some air-guitar riffs. After breakfast and washing up in the cleansers, Alpha had us jog for an hour. Then he worked with us individually for a short while as Purity taught the rest of us take-down techniques. When it was my turn to work with Alpha, he made me focus on turning hard earth into loose material and turning it hard again. It wasn't easy. His goal was to eventually show me how to make quicksand and sinking holes. He felt this would be a more effective and less destructive way of using the earth to my advantage. He explained that taking large chunks out of the ground is like leaving cookie crumbs behind for anyone who might be tracking me. I agreed that trying to become subtler when using my abilities was a good idea.

After our short session, Alpha sent me to Primus's cave.

"He requested to speak with you," he said, handing me a flashlight.

Off I went to the next cavern over. I found the *DO NOT ENTER* sign and walked over to the second wooden door. I opened it, and there was Primus's cave again. I'd forgotten how hot it was in there. I pushed for my body to adjust to the temperature quickly. I continued past the boxes with the *Blayne Crow Inc.* label on them and found Primus in the next room, putting on his working gloves. When he saw me, he took his gloves off and greeted me.

"The young hero returns!" he said. "I am glad to see that you are safe, Landon. I truly am. But I am afraid that my request to see you is for the purpose of apologizing to you."

I remembered that Kraven told me that Primus had created *Apollyon* in exchange for the bloodlust berry so that he could rid himself of his flashbacks. I wanted to confront him about it right away, but I made a conscious decision to listen to what he had to say first.

"The reason for my apology," Primus continued, "is because I misled you. I purposely created a sword for you because of something that I should not have been involved in. A deal was struck many years ago between your uncle Bane and me—a deal that would have me create a device for him to control the ancient dragon Aremas. In return, he would send me a bloodlust berry."

"So you agreed to put yourself and your needs over the safety of the entire world?" I questioned. "We were all in jeopardy, Primus, including your son. My father's life was taken because of Aremas. Did you think it was worth it?"

"I cannot ask you to understand or care why I did it," Primus said, for the first time choosing not to look directly at me. "And you are right. I did put my own needs over those of the world when the offer was put before me. It was not worth it, but I cannot take that back now. That decision will haunt me for the rest of my life. I agreed because I was tired of the torment and needed relief from the flashbacks. Those haunting flashbacks would force me to watch the scene of her death over and over again, and I just couldn't relive it anymore. It became more than I could bear."

Sympathy came over me. I realized that I would always be haunted by the flashbacks of my incident in Phoenix for the rest of my life. Reliving those moments as if they are happening for the first time and not being able to change the outcome did seem like torture.

"She was a special woman, my wife that is," Primus added, "but I did not love her. I became territorial over her though, because she bore my son. When another dragon wanted to be with her, I snapped. When I found him at her doorstep, we battled in broad daylight. She came out to stop the fight and got crushed in our wake. It was my fault that she abandoned Derek when he was a small child. The guilt is fresh in my mind every day, especially when I see him."

Hearing his words felt as if I was being hit by lightning. I was stunned at his confession. I had no clue what to say to him and, even if I did, I wouldn't have been able to say it anyway. Primus stared at me as if he was waiting for a response, his eyes tearing up. Then, as I scrambled to find something to say to him, an interesting thing happened. I had a human flashback.

Glimpses of my journey returned. Hundreds of mental pictures literally flashed on the screen of my mind—every event from my uncle Bane speaking with Mom to my plane trip to the Infernal Caverns to meet Alpha and the others. I saw Aurora and me fighting against the wind demon Soldier, receiving my sword *Apollyon,* and so on, up until now. There were definitely major highs and lows from my recent journey, but when I compared them, I found that the highs greatly outweighed the lows. Meeting my sister Destiny, getting to spend so much time with Aurora, and finally getting the opportunity to see my dad in person were enough reasons for me to know that I would go through it all again.

With this insight, I looked up at the large, muscular man and said confidently, "Primus, we are all capable of doing bad things. We do them even if we don't intend to. But if we are given another chance, we should make every effort to do the right thing."

Then I walked up to him and offered him my hand. He looked down at it, examined me again, and shook it. No other words needed to be said. I left his cave and went back to my training.

That first day back with Alpha was pretty intense. After lunch, he had us do some more jogging, and then we moved on to strength training and defense drills. There were laughs and groaning, but it felt good to be training again. For a moment we all forgot that Shade was our enemy. It seemed he had forgotten as well. But that was just for a moment. Later that evening, after dinner, we would find out that there was more to his return than his desire to train under Alpha.

All of us felt that Shade came back to train so that he could check up on how we were progressing. We also figured that he was training so that he could fight against us one day. More about his intentions were about to be revealed, however. When Shade was given permission to speak to us after dinner, we noticed that even he felt very uncomfortable with the message he had.

But then he found the courage to speak his words, and began by reciting a poem:

Bred in hatred, the sword will clash
To rise in glory as mountains crash
Then summon up the mighty King
And begin the Great Awakening.

Hearing his poem made my skin tingle. Aurora grabbed my hand and held it tightly.

"The Sons of Levi have declared war," Shade said to a silent room. "I tell you this to give everyone here a fair opportunity to make their own decision as to which side they choose to fight on. This battle will be epic, and every dragon and dragonoid will have to choose. Our numbers are great already and we should not be underestimated. The time for revolution has arrived. Dragons and dragonoids will again rise to the top and no longer hide from humans. We will take our world back by force, destroying all who oppose us. Our plan is in full effect, and the Great Awakening has begun. Aremas was only a pawn in the grand scheme of things. The Sons of Levi only wished to use him to disturb his father's slumber. The change in climate has done just that."

"Even as the Earth's weather shifts back to normal, these results work in our favor due to the excess water from the melting snow and ice. The greatest dragon ever to be created will wake up and rise to claim the Earth as his kingdom. And the Sons of Levi will serve him and fight for him."

Then Shade's message changed from a threat to a plea.

He continued, "I've heard stories about this dragon, and it seems that the world is in for disaster. I've trained with you all and gotten to know you guys. Please join me so that you all—who have really been my only friends—can be spared. Please consider what I'm saying. This is happening, and there is no stopping it. No one will be able to stop the great dragon Leviathan. I bet even Alpha will confirm the fact that he has been awakened."

All eyes turned to Alpha.

"Shade is right," he said. "Leviathan has been awakened. He will need time to regenerate, though, and who knows how long that could take. But when he is at full strength, he will bring down some wicked destruction."

"How bad is this guy Leviathan really, Alpha?" James wondered, as if Alpha might have been using this to his advantage to get us to train harder.

Alpha answered, "Well, brah, that's hard to say. I mean Aremas is a total weakling compared to him, but Leviathan has never had to use his full strength. There's no point in lying to you. Everyone should be worried. The only thing we can take care of now is how prepared you all are in dealing with it. If it makes you feel better, you need to remember that I have family that will be released in the End of Days. I think it's safe to say that Leviathan won't bring the end of the world, although he is very capable of bringing the end of the world as you know it."

For the first time I saw an indication of sadness in Alpha's eyes. His gaze reached Purity, who was sitting next to James, and I could sense that he wished, for her sake, that none of this were happening.

"So what can we do? How do we prepare for his coming?" Aurora asked.

Shade butted in. "You can join us and not have to live in fear."

"Or you can keep training and continue living your life," Alpha answered. "All of the great heroes I've trained had two things in common. These dudes would take care of the things they could control—like making sure they were in the best fighting shape possible—and the second was that they would take advantage of every other moment when they weren't training."

After that, Alpha asked Shade to sit down. Then he came before us and changed the subject.

"Ok, dudes and chicks, prepare yourself—for I am going to tell you about the greatest band to ever set foot on stage—METALLICA!"

For the rest of the night, Alpha amused us with his great air-guitar skills and his very creative story of the great band Metallica's rise to glory.

The days flew by quickly as we trained hard with Alpha. It was tough not to think about everything Shade had said, but Alpha worked us so hard that it was almost impossible to think about anything else but sleep at the end of the day. Since his summer training was ending, he really wanted to make sure that he covered everything that he wanted to teach us. Even though we were allowed to stay with Alpha and continue our training if we wanted, he encouraged us to go back to school and re-learn how to integrate into society with our new knowledge of ourselves and the world around us. Alpha emphasized that this was one of the hardest tests of control, and very necessary for us.

What he said made sense. Controlling our powers didn't only mean that we were capable of summoning them at will, but also being able to conceal them when we wanted.

One evening, Alpha led us outside to enjoy the beautiful night. A cool breeze swept over us as we gazed at the stars. Aurora and I held hands as we laid back, staring into the night sky.

"A few days ago, when Alpha gave me permission to inform the Elder Dragons about Leviathan's rise, I had a chance to speak with my mom," Aurora told me. "She is really worried, Landon. I'm sorry to bring this up, but she thinks that without your dad here to lead us, we may lose many dragons to the Sons of Levi."

"Why does she say that? Just because he isn't here doesn't mean that his principles are gone."

"I know, Landon, but she doesn't think that these things are stronger than the fear that Leviathan brings. I think what we need to do is…"

"Aurora," I cut her off. "Let's not worry about all of this tonight, okay?"

I gazed deeply into her glimmering green eyes and leaned in to kiss her. As our lips touched, my heart pounded fast. I could feel electricity in the air—literally. Aurora's energy was causing electric sparks to fly all around us. At least that let me know that she was enjoying the kiss as well.

These few moments of bliss were short lived, however.

Aurora moved away and screamed. Everyone rushed to her aid as she twisted in pain. Everything moved from magical to terrifying in a matter of seconds. I couldn't bear to watch her in so much agony, and I couldn't understand why this kept happening to her. I moved down to console her as much as I could, and placed my hand on her shoulder blade. And that's when I felt something warm and wet. I looked down at my hand and saw blood dripping from my fingers. Then Aurora let out another horrifying scream.

I turned to Alpha, "What do we do?"

Then I heard Amy say with a shrill in her voice, "She's growing wings!"

Aurora's back was drenched in blood. She kept screaming from the pain, but there was nothing we could do to help her. Alpha took command of the situation and scooped her up in his arms. Then he carried her back inside the cavern. The rest of us stayed outside for a while longer, all worried about Aurora. Purity eventually led us back inside and urged us to get some sleep, which was something I was definitely not able to do.

It felt as if I had slept for only five minutes when Alpha woke everyone up. Immediately, I asked him if Aurora was okay. He assured me that she was, and told me that she had been asking for me. Then he said that once everyone else left for the morning jog, he would bring her out so that she could see me.

When Purity took the others out for the jog, Alpha walked Aurora out. She came out wearing a white robe and looking extremely tired. Then I asked her how she was doing.

"I'm okay for now," she said, trying to force a smile. "It's not fun growing wings, but Alpha said that the hardest part is over."

"That's a good thing, right?"

"I guess," Aurora said, a dejected look on her face.

"Aurora," I offered with all seriousness, "I just want you to know that I don't see you any differently because of this."

"Thanks, Landon. That means a lot to me. But you and I both know that things are going to be different. I can't go back to my school anymore, and I don't even want to think of how my dad is going to react to this."

"I'm sure your dad will understand," I said, trying to sound reassuring. "So… does this mean you're going to stay here?"

Aurora nodded her head.

"Well then, I'll stay with you."

"No, Landon, you can't. If these wings weren't growing, I would be going back home myself. You need to go. Spend time with your Mom and keep an eye on Xavier. I'll be safe here. Anyway, it's not like you can't teleport back here any time you want."

Aurora hugged me. I carefully placed my arms around her.

A few moments later, Alpha walked in. "Okay, Miss Green Eyes, you need to get some rest now and he needs to start jogging."

Aurora smiled and said, "Maybe we'll catch another demon before you leave."

I flashed a smile at her, cracked my knuckles, and answered, "It would be just another day in the office for us." Then I turned around and made my way out of the cavern.

The sun was still low and there was a perfect morning breeze. All the ice and snow from Aremas's storm had melted, and there were no signs that such a major shift in the climate had ever happened. The area was full of color again and the Earth had naturally repaired the damage caused by the ancient dragon Aremas. I could relate to the Earth in that way. The suffering I'd endured over the last couple of weeks was overwhelming, but I had a feeling that, with the people I had supporting me, I could overcome all of it. And if war really was on the horizon, then I felt lucky that I had something worth fighting for.

Although my father was lost and his leadership gone, there was no greater honor than to stand and fight for a cause he believed in.